Broken Man on a Halifax Pier

Broken Man on a Halifax Pier

LESLEY CHOYCE

DUNDURN
TORONTO

Publisher: Scott Fraser | Acquiring editor: Kathryn Lane | Editor: Dominic Farrell
Cover design and illustration: Sophie Paas-Lang
Printer: Webcom, a division of Marquis Book Printing Inc.

Library and Archives Canada Cataloguing in Publication
Title: Broken man on a Halifax pier / Lesley Choyce.
Names: Choyce, Lesley, 1951- author.
Identifiers: Canadiana (print) 20190084995 | Canadiana (ebook) 20190085002 | ISBN 9781459745247
(softcover) | ISBN 9781459745254 (PDF) | ISBN 9781459745261 (EPUB)
Classification: LCC PS8555.H668 B76 2019 | DDC C813/.54—dc23

1 2 3 4 5   23 22 21 20 19

We acknowledge the support of the Canada Council for the Arts and the Ontario Arts Council for our publishing program. We also acknowledge the financial support of the Government of Ontario, through the Ontario Book Publishing Tax Credit and Ontario Creates, and the Government of Canada.

Care has been taken to trace the ownership of copyright material used in this book. The author and the publisher welcome any information enabling them to rectify any references or credits in subsequent editions.

The publisher is not responsible for websites or their content unless they are owned by the publisher.

Printed and bound in Canada.

VISIT US AT

 dundurn.com |  @dundurnpress | dundurnpress | dundurnpress

Dundurn
3 Church Street, Suite 500
Toronto, Ontario, Canada
M5E 1M2

For Linda

Prologue

If I had been able to see into the future, I may not have gone down to the harbour that morning. I may have continued with my sorry, lonely existence — a man without a job, without a purpose, without a real friend.

If I had seen what was coming, I may have walked up to Citadel Hill instead, and sat on that stone wall built in the eighteenth century and peered down at the city, pondering the lives of those still sleeping in their houses and apartments below. Wondering how they had succeeded in being comfortable in their ordinary lives. I would have been jealous of them all. How had they figured out the formula to live, to connect, to find meaning in what they did in their everyday lives? How did they find someone to love, how did they enter into relationships, make commitments?

If I knew the mistakes I was capable of, I could have chosen a different path and spared the world some grief, gone back to my dingy apartment, so well suited to a man whose life had gone into the gutter.

But I knew nothing of the future, understood little of the meaning of my past life up until then, and had not a clue as to how to live gratefully in the present.

And so there I stood at the water's edge, not at all knowing that the story was about to begin.

1

She never really told me why she was there at 6 a.m. on that damp Halifax morning in April. I can't even rightly explain what I was doing there either, standing at the end of a dilapidated pier, staring into the dark waters of the harbour, lost in thought.

I suppose it had something to do with the fact that my life had gone to shit, that I no longer had a job, that I'd lost my life savings and was reduced to living in a "bachelor" apartment in the North End. Yeah, it might have had something to do with that. But I think that a guy like me, fifty-five years from being born, just finds himself eventually at a moment like this, staring into the water. Contemplating.

Even now, I like to think of it as a literary moment. I was a writer, after all. Not like a real writer. Not a Hemingway or Fitzgerald, not one of the greats. Not even one of the lesser greats. A pipsqueak of a writer. After playing at reporter for a number of years, the *Tribune* let me write features about anything I wanted. But, alas, the *Tribune* was no more. How could I know when I set about embarking on my so-called career that newspapers were going to slowly begin to vanish? I was a dodo bird. A dinosaur. Pick any extinct species and I was just that.

But if any of this is going to add up to anything, I should go back to the beginning. The whole convoluted tale will come out in due time. So let's get back to April, the pier, the fog, the lone man standing by the edge of the water where once, long ago, the bodies from the ill-fated and legendary *Titanic* were landed ashore. This was a literary moment, remember. Ill-fated ship, April the cruelest month, my life a modern Shakespearean tragedy, man fallen from great heights (modest heights, really) through his own hubris (a word I had just recently added to my vocabulary). Man alone, alienated in a hostile universe. No, an uncaring universe. A universe that didn't give a Monday-morning shit about him or most probably anything else.

And then she walked up to me.

I didn't notice her at first, didn't hear footsteps or anything. It was like she dropped out of the sleepy grey clouds hovering above. I was deep in reverie — yes, a grandiose, dark, endless, self-pitying reverie. A man feeling bad. Just plain bad. With no particular shred of hope for things to get better. Must have been painted all over my face.

"I get it," she said with no other words of introduction. "Broken man."

At first I thought it was just one of those many voices in my head. But then I looked in the direction from which the voice had come. It was a woman. A good-looking woman at that. All alone. On the pier at 6 a.m. by the misty misbegotten harbour.

"Get what?" I asked.

"Get you. *Broken man on a Halifax pier,*" she said. And her mouth went up on one corner. Not a smile exactly. An indication of a game.

"Oh," I said. "Stan Rogers. 'Barrett's Privateers.'"

"Very good," she said. "Can I take your picture?"

"Sure," I said. "But why would you want to take my picture?"

Instead of answering, she lifted a cellphone out of her purse, walked a step closer to me and clicked.

"Gonna post it on Facebook?" I asked. "You got your caption."

"No. Nothing like that." She walked another step closer, stared down at the water and then directly at me. For a second,

I thought I knew her. Or at least that I had seen her somewhere before. Something about her was familiar.

"It looks cold and uninviting," she said, nodding at the swirling foam in the harbour water below.

"I wasn't going for a swim if that is what you were thinking."

"No stones in your pockets? Did you forget them?"

"I'm not good at planning ahead," I said. "Besides, I'm more of a bridge man. A leaper, if it ever comes to that. Unfortunately, they have the bridge walkways all caged in now. Always someone trying to take the fun out of everything. The bastards."

Now she just stood there, not talking. Then she lifted her phone and took another photo. Closer up. Mug shot.

"You want me to take my clothes off?" I asked.

"It's too cold. All I'd get is a picture of goosebumps."

"True," I said. I suddenly realized I was in the middle of a conversation with a rather attractive and mysterious woman. "Do I know you?" I asked.

"You've seen me. At least I'm guessing you have. If you haven't, I'll be pissed."

I looked her over again. Inspecting. She noticed, did a little slow twirl. Front and back. I didn't have a clue who she was.

"Give up?"

I nodded.

She looked a little miffed. I figured I should say something. "Well, you're not the queen of England, I know that. Too young, too beautiful." I was trying to pull it out of the trash can. She wasn't young — forty something, fifty maybe — and not exactly classically beautiful, but she was truly pretty and absolutely most interesting. And I much preferred looking at her to staring down at the water.

She snapped another photo of me. I think I had a funny look on my face — man just thrown a lifeline, man shifting back from the brink from some abyss, man wandering alone in a wet world just given a blanket over his shoulders.

"What do you call that look? The one you just gave me."

"I call it my happy look," I said.

"You call that happy?"

"Relatively speaking. Happiness is relative, right?"

"Philosophy major?"

"English."

"Ah. April is the cruelest month, right?"

"That's exactly what I was thinking when you came along with Stan Rogers."

"How I wish I was in Sherbrooke now."

"Sherbrooke. Nova Scotia or Quebec? I could never quite figure it out."

I wondered if we'd stand there and trade Stan Rogers lyrics for the rest of the morning. It would have been fine by me. I had nothing better to do. Take her through the Northwest Passage, *tracing one warm line, through a land so wild and savage.*

"What comes next?" she asked.

"In 'Barrett's Privateers'?"

"Idiot. No. Right now."

It had been a while since anyone had flirted with me. I was way out of practice.

"Um," I must have said.

"Um. That's all you got?" she asked with a sharp edge in her voice. "You, an English major. Can't come up with a line from James fucking Joyce or John fucking Milton?"

For a split second I thought she was actually angry with me. I didn't know then that she was an actor, that she'd been in movies. I was beginning to think she was deranged. I was curious to see if there were weapons involved.

The weapon was the phone — lifted, pointed, snapped. "That's a real crowd-pleaser. 'Man Befuddled by Woman' reads the headline."

"Headline, why headline?" I was wondering if she knew who I was.

"Just a phrase. Why does it matter?"

"It doesn't," I said. And I tried smiling. It had been a while. It hurt. I guess it showed.

"Ouch," she said. "That looked painful."

I wanted to explain my lack of happy moments in my recent tenure on the planet but clammed up, shrugged instead.

She must have liked the shrug. "Buy me breakfast?" she asked.

"I'm broke," I said. Paused. "Well, I think I have five bucks and a couple of quarters. But I'm waiting for the banks to open."

"Never heard of ATMs?"

"They don't like me. I don't know what it is. They just don't seem to want to deal with a guy like me."

"A guy like you?"

"Down on his luck."

"Okay, you want to play that card? I'll buy you breakfast."

"Now you're talking," I said.

And so began a new chapter in my life. If I can stretch out the cinematic moment, I would say the sun came out, or it began to pour rain, or there were birds and flowers, quotes from Shakespeare or unison singing of "Fogarty's Cove." But there was none of that.

She touched my arm once. And we walked in silence to the Bluenose Restaurant on Hollis Street. She ordered poached eggs and toast. I ordered scrambled eggs and bacon. And then all the waiters and waitresses and morning-weary breakfast patrons broke into song.

2

I was only joking about the singing. Actually, I played with my toast and she sipped black coffee. It was awkward. Awkward, as in seventh-grade awkward, when you like the girl and the girl likes you, but you just can't get over your shyness and have a simple conversation.

Whatever spell had come over us on the pier had been broken by the intrusive ordinariness of sitting in the Bluenose Restaurant having breakfast.

"Fuck," I said out loud. Accidentally.

She looked up at me. "That's kind of rude."

"No. I didn't mean it like that. It was my inner voice expressing my frustration at not being able to say something nice, something intelligent to you. Something like a protagonist in a really good novel would say to a woman who has just come into his life."

"Is that what I did? Come into your life?"

"Yes. And I want to thank you for that."

"You're thanking me?"

"Hell, yes. See I'm not all that rude. What were you doing on the pier anyway? Why were you there?"

"You'd like some intriguing, complex answer, but now I have to disappoint you. I couldn't sleep. I went for a walk."

"You live nearby?"

"Oh, now you want to get personal. Are you asking me where I live?"

"Should I not do that?"

"Who am I to tell you what you should do or shouldn't do?" I could see she had a thing for the verbal dance. We might go on like this for a long time. Me saying, her throwing it back to me. Hell, what else better did I have to do?

"So?"

"So I live in the Towers."

"Richmond Towers? On the water."

"Thirteenth floor to be exact."

"I thought only rich people lived in the Towers."

She did a little thing with her eyelashes.

"Oh, and you were asking me to buy you breakfast?"

"I thought men were supposed to buy."

"That was last century. Not no more."

"*Not no more*? English major?"

"I lied. I studied English at Dal but graduated with a Psych degree — Abnormal Psych was my thing. Then I went into journalism so I could write about people, using my Coles Notes knowledge of what makes us all tick."

"Ah, journalist. Who do you write for?"

"No one, now. I was with the *Tribune* for twenty years. Then one day, they packed it up and left town. Just like that."

"I'm sorry. I didn't often read newspapers or maybe I would have read some of your articles."

"That's okay. You obviously were not alone. Folks stopped reading papers, so one day I was out of a job. And just for the record, I rather liked that previous century I was talking about. The one that is not no more. The one where men bought pretty women breakfast and then the two of them probably sat cozy-like in the sunshine and read the morning paper."

"Not no more," she echoed. "So what would the name be on — what was it called? — the byline on your articles?"

"Charles. Charles Howard."

"Your friends call you Chuck?"

"What friends? And no, only my brother was allowed to call me Chuck and that was back when we were twelve. So now you know my name. I'm presuming you have one too."

"A reasonable presumption."

"Well, Miss Thirteenth Floor Richmond Towers, give."

"Ramona," she said.

"Ramona? Really. No one names their daughter Ramona."

"My mother did. It was her grandmother's name."

"Well, hell yes. I can see someone's grandmother named Ramona but not …" I trailed off. Another blunder. Silly dumb Chuck. Chuck the Fuck.

"Not someone living in Richmond Towers?"

"Stupid me. Sorry."

"No worries. I even have a last name."

"I promise to keep my opinions to myself. Please?"

"Danforth. Like the street in Toronto."

"Ramona Danforth. Now that does sound like someone living the high life in a rich-ass apartment." I scratched my jaw just then like something Humphrey Bogart would have done in one of his *film noir* movies. "Ramona Danforth. That rings a bell."

"I was hoping it might. I have this delusion that people actually still remember who I am."

"Oh, yeah. You did TV for a while and a couple of movies. Sorry, I don't watch much TV or go to the movies much."

"You are part of a fairly large group of the population. Which is why TV and movies have gone down the tubes — Canadian TV and movies anyway. Guess we're both fully paid up members of the last of a couple of dying breeds."

She let me study her then. I did remember this Ramona woman. A couple of fairly decent TV dramas produced by the CBC in Halifax, then a couple of films shot in Toronto that made the rounds of film festivals. Then a short stint in Hollywood, like every Canadian actor, trying to land a big role. And then what? I didn't know.

"Then you did all right for yourself," was all I could seem to say.

"I had a good run at it, saved my earnings, got some guilt money from a family trust, invested all of it wisely before my so-called career went down the drain."

"Somehow I get the feeling that the plumbing was kinder to you than me."

"Are you really broke, or is that just a line you use to pick up women?"

"No, I really am. Just barely made the rent. I too invested wisely and I had a little nest egg for a rainy day, to mix metaphors. But then, just before the newspaper business folded up and left town, I was infected with philanthropy. I was patting myself on the back, thinking I had it so good and others had it so bad that I should try to help. It did not go well."

"Not everyone can handle being a philanthropist. What happened?"

"Gus, an editor at the paper, had this twenty-three-year-old son, Benjamin. A good kid. I'd known him most of my life. He'd gone through a wild phase but seemed to have settled down. We had a couple of heart-to-heart talks and I was telling him he needed to get out of Nova Scotia, go find some adventure, but also do some good. Something meaningful. Those were my exact words."

"So you were a bit of an idealist."

"I talked the talk, but didn't usually ever walk the walk. The pen is mightier than the sword and all that."

"And?"

"And then another earthquake hit Haiti. Benji came to me and said, 'This is it. I'm going down to help. Gonna raise some money, go down there, help out in any way I can. Just wing it. Do it on my own and find allies along the way.'"

"How much did you give him?"

"Forty thousand. My entire savings. I was a believer."

No questions, just a sad, pained look.

"Guess what? He never made it to Haiti. Came close but no cigar."

"What do you mean?"

"He decided instead to go to the other half of the island — the Dominican Republic. He and a buddy. They went from one resort to another. Forty thousand didn't last all that long. Gus said he was really sorry for his stupid, selfish son; that he'd try to make it up to me. But then the paper was kaput and that was that. I'll accept your pity now."

"I'm sorry, Charles. That was a terrible thing."

"It's okay, Ramona. I guess I deserved it," I said, realizing that we had both just said each other's name like lines from a cheesy script. "I'm a bad judge of character, I guess, novice at human nature."

Another bout of silence put us back into our places. The waiter, an earnest young man, came up and said that he recognized Ramona and knew who she was. Smiling at her, he poured her some more coffee while completely ignoring me. He flattered her with an adoring look and added, "I admire your work."

As he shuffled off, I said, "You have a fan club or what?"

She blushed. "Nothing like that. A few years back, some pimply faced teenage boy found a clip from one of my early films. Some worthless piece of trash I acted in in my first year in Hollywood. It had one bedroom nude scene I foolishly agreed to do. It resurfaced on the internet — just that one scene, not the whole film. I started getting Facebook messages from teenage boys. Just what a woman of fifty needs, right?"

"Fifty? You said fifty."

"It's a number. Half of one hundred. Happens to be my age."

"You can't be fifty."

"They could have made a mistake on my birth certificate but I do believe I am."

"You look too young."

"I'll accept the compliment. Thank you, sir. You know what they say. Fifty is the new forty. But then forty is the new thirty, etc., etc. Where do you place yourself on the whole chronology issue?"

"Five years your senior, schoolgirl. Fifty-five years before the mast. Too old to be young, too young to be old. Forced into an early retirement and pondering each day what will come next."

Breakfast was over. We'd set out the portraits of our lives, the bare bones, mostly fragments, but we'd both been brave or foolish enough to reveal things personal and important. Pessimist that I was, I expected our little bubble to burst. That momentary friendship, that flirtation, that chance encounter, it had a certain inevitable ending.

Or did it?

"I like a man with no money and loads of time on his hands," she offered.

That caught me off guard. "Oh, and why is that?"

"Because I can probably boss him around. C'mon, we're going for a drive."

3

She had the car. Mine was sitting in the parking lot of my building, inspection three months overdue, same with registration and, of course, the insurance had run out. But then she'd already said she liked a man with no money. Some people might call that destiny.

Her Lexus was parked along Lower Water Street. It was black. She unlocked it from half a block away and I saw the lights flash. "Here," she said, tossing me the keys. "You can drive, right?"

"It's been a while," I said. "But I think I remember. You have to stay on the right-hand side of the road, yeah?"

"It's up to you," she said.

Sitting down behind the wheel of that beauty made me take a deep breath. I inhaled the new car smell and it suddenly occurred to me that I might be dreaming. But then my dreams were never good, and especially never that good. Ramona flipped the sun visor down and inspected herself in the mirror. "Just checking to see if that's really me sitting in my car with a strange man I found on a pier."

"Strange. You think I'm strange?"

"Strange and kind of cute."

I could not suppress a smile. Where had this woman come from? "Where to?" I asked as I fired up the engine.

"You choose. Someplace rural."

"How much time do you have?"

"All the time in the world."

Yeah, she really said that.

Well, the someplace rural tweaked. It had been a while since I'd been back there. Back home. At least the fragments that were left of it. Stewart Harbour, way down on the Eastern Shore. The old homestead was gone, but my father's fish shack out on the water was still there, unused, locked up, empty except for all the dusty memories stored inside. It was abandoned but not forgotten.

"I want to take you to this place. It's a kind of pilgrimage. You ever been on a pilgrimage before?"

"Well, yes, I have. I walked two days on the El Camino de Santiago in Spain."

"Was that with Shirley MacLaine?"

"No, it was with my boyfriend."

"So you have gone out with men before?"

"Gone out with them, lived with them, fell in love with some. It always ended the same way."

"And what way was that?"

"I walked away. Even in Spain. That was Alexander. I just couldn't take it anymore. So one morning I woke up in the hostel, grabbed my sleeping bag, and caught the first plane home."

"Ouch."

"He deserved it."

"I'm sure he did. Couldn't have been your fault."

"No. It probably was my fault."

"You marry any of those chaps?"

"Not a one. Not the marrying type, I guess. You?"

I was pulling onto the MacKay Bridge just then. Traffic was light. The sun was coming out. A light north wind was chasing away the clouds. We were headed east. I was happier than I'd been in a long while.

"Me? Married. I came close. But no one would have me. Too messy. Too disorganized. Too caught up in my own ego."

"You didn't tell me you had an ego."

"Well, I used to have one. Not anymore. I don't hold myself in particularly high esteem."

"They say that happens when a man loses his job."

"Well, I guess I'm a textbook case. You like fish?"

"Fish?"

"There might be fish where we're going."

"Ah. The mystery thickens."

She sat back after that and we drove on in silence. Not the uncomfortable kind of silence. The good kind. It felt good to be driving. It felt even better to not be alone. Almost every day the previous month, I had woken up feeling like there was a wall in front of me. A high, thick, ugly wall. Now, instead, there was a door. An open door. And I had already walked through it.

The suburbs of Dartmouth gave way to a burned-out patch of forest along the 107 near Lake Echo. It was an ugly scar on the land from a forest fire that had swept through there a few years ago. But in the middle of the charred trees stood two giant, porcelain-white wind turbines. To me they were like monuments of hope in a wasteland of despair. As we drove on, she still never asked me where we were going.

The big highway gave out near Musquodoboit Harbour and we were back on the old Highway 7. Up ahead I saw cars pulled over on the side of the road, some with their flashers on. A small circle of men and women were standing in the middle of the road and an old guy in a flannel jacket was waving for me to slow down and stop. I pulled the Lexus over to the side. Ramona gave me a look that told me the spell had been broken.

We got out and walked toward the others. In the middle of the road was an injured deer half-kneeling, trying to stand, then falling back down.

"I didn't see it," a man in a business suit was saying. "I would have slammed on my brakes. But it was just there. All of a sudden."

People nodded.

"It wasn't your fault," a largish woman said.

We'd all hit some creature at one point or another. A bird flies into your windshield, a squirrel dives under your tires. You pray you never hit somebody's dog or cat. Or kid. The deer looked pretty bad.

"Three," someone said. "Three broken legs, for sure. Most likely serious internal injuries."

An RCMP car pulled up then. Lights flashing but no siren. A young Mountie, not much more than a teenager it seemed, got out and walked toward us. He looked at the deer, looked at us, then walked back toward his car. He was talking on his radio, asking someone back at headquarters what he should do. I felt bad for the kid. I already knew what they were telling him to do back at the cop shop.

I thought about getting Ramona back in the car and just turning around, driving away, back toward town — anywhere to get us the hell out of there. But there was an inevitability to the scene and we both must have felt a strange responsibility to stay and see it through.

I'd interviewed wildlife rescue people before and even spent some time helping out. I knew what you could do to help and what you couldn't do. I watched the nervous young Mountie unsnap the strap over his revolver and click off the safety.

"Everybody over to this side of the road, please," he said, motioning us away from the deer that tried to stand again, only to fall back on its side, panting heavily.

The Mountie held out his gun, his hand shaking, then wiped his forehead with his other hand.

"It's okay," the old guy in the flannel shirt said. "It's what you gotta do. We all understand."

He was right, of course. There was not a word of protest. Nonetheless, it was a mighty sorry scene.

The seconds stretched out. The large woman put her hand over her eyes. Someone sniffled. The scene stretched out way too long. Then he lowered the gun. He couldn't do it.

Why I walked up to him, I'm not sure. It was more like something my own father would have done, not me. Mr. Responsibility. Do the right thing, even when you hate doing it.

I held out my hand to the young man.

Amazingly, he handed me the gun, probably breaking a dozen or more of the rules and regs he'd been trained to follow. I tried not to look at Ramona.

I took two steps forward, studied the panting injured deer. If you've ever looked directly into the dark, beautiful eyes of a deer, you know what that's like.

"I'm sorry," I said. Then fired two bullets into his head. The sound of the blasts drew gasps from the people watching. But it was the burnt smell of the gunpowder lingering in the air that gave the whole scene a surreal feeling.

Ramona's eyes were wide as she stared at me. The large woman was crying into her husband's shirt. I handed the gun back to the Mountie. He nodded, flicked the safety on it, put it away. "I'll call Department of Natural Resources to come clean up," he said as the old guy in the flannel shirt and another man dragged the carcass to the side of the road.

The Mountie got back in his car and reported back to his people. Others were getting back in their vehicles and starting up.

Ramona was staring at me. I couldn't read the look. Shock. Disbelief. Anger.

Disgust.

I held out her keys. She grabbed them, walked back to her car.

With some difficulty, she made a U-turn and sped off back toward Halifax.

The Mountie drove off as did the others. No one looked at me. Soon enough, they were all gone and I was all alone. I sat down alongside the fallen animal by the side of the road. I stroked the fur on his flank. I could feel the body was still warm.

It looked like I had plenty of time to reflect on my bad decision.

4

I will admit freely to anyone willing to listen that I have a history of making bad decisions when it comes to women. I don't mean that I picked the wrong women, although that did sometimes happen. I mean that I would often, well, almost always, end up saying the wrong thing, doing the wrong thing, or simply screwing up what might otherwise have been a fine relationship. I had started to tell myself I just wasn't cut out for *any* kind of relationship. Nothing long term. No way. Not me. Not in the cards.

But that was a first. Ditched by the side of the road east of Musquodoboit Harbour, having shot an ailing animal. What was it she thought of me as I discharged the Mountie's firearm? Why the fuck did I take it upon myself to do that in front of her, anyway? Why couldn't I just have let the poor animal suffer? Walk away. Drive away. Leave the schoolboy Mountie to figure things out on his own.

Fuck it.

Guns. I always hated guns. My father had guns around the house — a couple of handguns that he liked to sit with and clean while he watched television. One .22 rifle that he walked around with during hunting season, although I can't say I remember him ever coming home with anything he killed. And a shotgun that had belonged to his father that he used to scare teenagers who would drive out to the fish shacks to party on a weekend night.

He was an angry man at times, a kind man at others. But he never shot anybody or anything — other than some tin cans once in a while, a carton of sour milk, and, just once, an old mattress that someone had dumped at the end of the road.

But I'd been around guns, had handled them on those nights when my father cleaned them, as my mother clucked her disdain over her husband allowing his son to play with guns. That's partly why, I suppose, I felt a sense of duty in helping the Mountie get the job done.

But that was enough pondering about my bad decision. I stood up and brushed the dirt off my pants, thinking how appropriate it was that cars just kept driving past me with passengers giving me dirty looks. There I was, a man sitting by a dead deer on the side of the road, and no one slowed down, no one stopped to see if I was okay. Folks just kept driving past. Everyone in their own little bubble of opinion or indifference.

I couldn't quite decide which direction to walk. East toward Stewart Harbour or back toward Halifax.

Right about then, a DNR truck pulled over and two burly men in coveralls got out. It seemed they had been arguing about something. "He should have been thrown out of the game," the bearded one said. "No one should treat Crosby like that. No one."

"The kid deserved it," the other one said. "He needed to be knocked down a notch or two."

"The hell he did," Beard said as he walked toward me, studying me, trying to figure out my relationship to the dead animal. He looked at the deer, then at me, spit something on the ground off to the side of the road and said, "How long ago did he meet his maker?"

I shrugged. "Twenty minutes, maybe."

Beard grunted. "All righty. Venison steak it is, then. Skid, help me load this sucker into the back of the truck."

Skid reluctantly ambled over and the two of them dragged the deer and lifted it into the back of the pickup. They started to get back into the truck. All in a day's work, I reckoned.

I walked over to the truck as Beard was about to start the engine. "You wouldn't be willing to give me a ride?" I asked.

Beard looked at me like I'd just asked if I could sleep with his wife. "We gotta deliver this to Stewiacke."

"Maybe then just a lift back to Musquodoboit Harbour?"

"We got all these tools up here. Not much room." All I saw was a hammer on the seat between the two of them. "But you can ride in the back if you want."

"Sure," I said.

They dropped me off at the intersection by the RCMP headquarters and turned inland toward Stewiacke. I decided I was already on my way back to Halifax and that would be that. Go back to my crappy apartment and go to sleep. Pretend none of this had happened. I realized I didn't have the courage to keep going east, all the way down the Shore to revisit the little fishing shack, all that remained of my past down that way. It would just be too depressing.

I looked around. Across the street, I watched a teenage boy painting a fish and chips restaurant. He wasn't doing a very good job, splashing white paint on the windows and just slopping it on thick and drippy. I started walking past the old train parked and rusting there by the side of the road for tourists. It looked tired and neglected — I could relate to that. No dignity in disuse, I was thinking. I stuck out my thumb, but it turned out I was invisible to the drivers passing me. So, I kept walking. I couldn't get Ramona out of my mind. And I couldn't help thinking how one minute you can be on top of the world and the next minute, you're back in the doghouse.

After a bit, I gave up with the thumb altogether and resigned myself to possibly walking all the way back to Halifax, or maybe at least to the Porters Lake Superstore, where I might be able to catch a bus. But then I realized, of course, I might not even have enough change in my pocket to pay for a bus. If that was the case, I'd have to panhandle. It just kept getting better and better.

That's when an old Honda passed me by and then pulled over onto the shoulder. A young man got out. Without his uniform, it took me a moment to recognize him, but then I realized that he was the young Mountie from the roadside. He waved. I waved back as I approached him.

"I thought that was you," he said. "Want a ride?"

"Yes, please," I said.

I got in and took a deep breath. The back seat was filled with weight-lifting equipment. "I just got off my shift," he said. "Thank God that was over. Hey, thanks for helping me back there. I really appreciate it."

"No problem," I said. "Thanks for stopping."

"Weren't you with a woman?"

"Was."

"Oh." He decided not to ask anything further about her. He looked over at me for a quick second and then back at the windshield. "Hey, you won't tell anyone what happened back there?"

"Not a soul," I said.

"Thanks. It was just those eyes. The deer was looking straight at me. I couldn't do it."

"I understand."

"Made me think maybe I'd chosen the wrong line of work."

"Yours is a tough job. You must see all kinds of shit."

"Sometimes. Mostly family troubles. Husbands and wives arguing. Kids vandalizing things. Drunk drivers, of course. Lots of drunk drivers."

"Guess you don't usually have to shoot many of them." Maybe that came out a little too sarcastic.

"Oh, I could shoot a criminal if I had to. Stop him dead in his tracks. That would be different."

Again I was struck by how young this guy was. But then all kinds of people in authority seemed young to me these days. "How old are you? Twenty-two?"

"Twenty-six," he said. "But I look young for my age."

"I did once too," I said. "That'll change. Where you from?"

Like many Nova Scotians, I often asked people where they were from. We want to be able to label people based on who their family is or where they grew up.

"Liscomb," he said. That wasn't far from Stewart Harbour.

"Yeah, I'm from down that way myself."

"I'm Tom, by the way. What's your name?"

"Charles. Charles Howard."

He scratched his youthful jaw and scrunched up his forehead. "You related to Desmond Howard?"

"That would be my father," I said.

"Really, the guy that tore down his own house?"

"That's him."

"What ever became of him, if you don't mind my asking?"

"He died," I said.

"Oh. Sorry."

"It's been a while."

"They say you never really get over the death of a parent."

"You don't. I've lost both."

"Sorry again."

There wasn't much traffic as we were headed down a long open hill. Coming our way was a car. A black car. At first I thought it was an illusion, my feeble mind playing tricks, but as it got closer, I was pretty sure it was a black Lexus. I knew there could be more than one black Lexus on the road but you didn't see a lot of them. Tom looked over at me as I leaned forward and peered out the front window. "Holy fuck," I must have said out loud.

"What is it?"

I turned my head as the car shot past us. It was her. Ramona was driving back.

"Tom," I suddenly shouted. "We gotta turn around."

Tom looked rattled. He was realizing he had picked up a crazy man, a crazy man he had once loaned his revolver to. "Just turn around, please!" I blurted out.

Tom hit the brakes, pulled into a driveway, backed out and in a second we were back headed east. "Why are we doing this?" he asked.

"The woman," I said. "That was her. I think she was coming back for me."

"And that's good, right?" he asked, now sounding more like a little boy than ever.

"That's damn good," I said. "Damn good."

Tom smiled then. A weird, crooked, what-the-fuck-is-going-on kind of smile, as he tromped on the gas.

The Lexus was stopped on the side of the road where the deer had been shot. Ramona was standing there looking at the bloodstain on the pavement. Tom pulled up behind. I opened the door.

"You want me to wait?" he asked.

"No," I said. "Thanks, brother. Thanks."

He held out his hand for me to shake. "Good luck," he said, smiling. And he pressed a business card into my other hand. "Let me know if I can ever return the favour."

I took his card and shoved it in my pants pocket.

I think he would have liked to stick around for the rest of the story, but, instead, he dutifully began to turn his car around again and head west.

Ramona studied me as I walked toward her. I didn't have a clue what I should say. So I didn't say anything at all. As I got closer, she reached out and touched my face and kept her hand there, warm and soft on my cheekbone. I must have closed my eyes, afraid to move. When I opened them, I discovered she was about to kiss me. There was nothing for me to do but let it happen.

5

I have to admit it wasn't exactly like a lover's kiss, more like that of a mother after her little boy had fallen off his bike and scraped his knee. But it was a kiss, nonetheless.

"I'm sorry I drove off," Ramona said.

"I'm glad you came back."

"Why? Why did you take the gun and shoot?"

"I don't know. It's what my father would have wanted me to do. Put the poor thing out of its pain."

"Did you always do what you thought your father wanted you to do?"

"Hardly ever. But look, I'm truly sorry I scared you like that."

"Promise not to touch any more firearms for the rest of the day?"

"Yeah, I promise."

"Good. Shall we resume the pilgrimage?"

"Please."

She handed me the keys again. We were back on track. At least I was hoping so. We drove along in silence for several miles, passing an abandoned bowling alley, a closed Chinese restaurant, a junkyard, and mile after mile of spindly spruce forest. It wasn't exactly the scenic route.

"Funny, I've lived in Nova Scotia most of my life but I've never been down this way."

"That's the Eastern Shore, for ya. Not much reason for most folks to trek down here. But wait until we get to the Harbour. I think you'll like it. It's another world."

"I like the sound of that."

"Hey," I said, feeling suddenly a tad more bold, trying to regain some of the confidence I imagined that I'd once possessed. "How come you kissed me back there?"

"You looked like you needed kissing. Besides, I didn't know what to say to you just then."

"Actions speak louder than words. It was a good choice. You do a lot of kissing as an actress?"

"Some. It's harder than you think to fake a good kiss."

"I never really thought about it. But I guess you're right. Kiss anybody famous?"

"Tom Hanks."

"Bullshit. Really?"

"I had a small part. It was one scene in a bar. I'm not particularly proud of it."

"Still, not everyone can say they kissed Tom Hanks. Did you spend any time with him?"

"No, Tom Hanks wasn't one of my boyfriends. I'm not sure he even knew who I was. Just another dumb girl with a small role in a film."

"Okay, so what about the real men in your life? How many serious relationships have you had?" I was pushing things, I knew, but I was curious.

She looked away from me just then, out the window of the car at the scrubby forest. "Diving into the deep end of the pool, are you?"

"How deep is it?"

"Well, let's just say, I've had a lot of lovers. Not sure exactly how to divvy them up into serious and not-so-serious."

"Give it a try."

I thought she wasn't going to answer but then I saw her counting on her fingers. I almost laughed out loud.

"Nine," she finally said. "Maybe ten."

"That's a lot of men."

"They weren't all men."

I guess my own sudden silence freaked her out a bit.

"Well, only one wasn't. I was in L.A. I had just broken up with a creep. Selina was my friend at first and then she wanted to get serious. I said, why not?"

"And how did that go?"

"It wasn't the best and it wasn't the worst. We were almost like college roommates, but we were, um, intimate."

"I can understand why women are more fun to be around than men. Men have such limited interests and all they do is drink beer and watch sports on TV."

"Do you do that?"

"Never. I was just trying to say something in defence of you trying out alternate relationships."

"Alternate relationships? That's a nice polite phrase. You want to know what was the best thing about having a girl for a girl-friend?"

"Should I be afraid to ask?"

She slapped my arm in a playful way. "Shopping, silly. We had great fun shopping."

"And I thought men were shallow."

"I broke it off with Selina when I found out she was fooling around with another woman, an accountant from Laguna Beach."

"So that leaves you with eight or nine others to tell me about."

"I'm not even sure I remember all their names. I know that sounds awful."

"Maybe just give me the Coles Notes version as best you can."

"Well, for starters, I was always the one to break the relationships off. Sometimes I started them; sometimes it was the other way around. But I always ended them."

"I'm sure there was always a reason. Like with Selina, for example. You can't stay with someone bonking an accountant from Laguna Beach."

"Bonking?"

"Or whatever. But why do you think it's you who always ends things?"

"The truth is, I think I've come to the conclusion that I'm not capable of a long-term relationship. In my own defence, I'd like to say it's more like serial monogamy."

"That sounds like something you eat at breakfast."

"Fuck off."

We were driving through Sheet Harbour now. I was pretty sure we needed coffee so I pulled into a Tim Hortons. "I'll get us something to drink," I said.

"Isn't it a little early?"

"I meant coffee."

"Oh. Sure. Latte light with soy milk."

"You fuck off now. This is Tims. Double double or what?"

"Black. Just black."

"Coming up."

She seemed to be content to sit in the car while I got the coffee because she pulled down the visor and studied her beautiful face in the mirror, traced a finger across her lips, the lips that had kissed me. Walking into Tim Hortons, I felt buoyant, I felt grand, I felt better than I'd felt in a dog's age. The feeling was so alien that it was almost like an out-of-body experience.

When I went to pay for the coffees, I was suddenly reminded that I was broke. I pulled out the change I had and, strangely enough, I had enough to pay for the two coffees. What was left of my cash, and there wasn't much more than a couple of dimes and nickels, I left as a tip.

People in the place were watching me as I laughed out loud at my poverty and walked my coffees out the door. They kept looking as I got into the expensive car and sat down beside Ramona. I think it was at that moment that I finally returned to my own body, realized this was real, and not a dream or a movie. I was sitting beside a beautiful woman in a black car outside the Tim Hortons in Sheet Harbour without a penny to my name. And I felt like the happiest man alive.

6

We sipped our coffee and drove on. "You realize I just spent my last cent on you. My last red cent as they used to say. I could barely cover the tab."

"I forgot. You're broke. But it couldn't have been your last cent. We don't have pennies anymore here in Canada, remember?"

"Well, my last nickel."

"But you're smiling."

"You noticed."

"What was that line from the opening of the Henry Miller novel?"

"Henry Miller? The sex fiend? I could quote you Hemingway maybe but not Miller."

"He said, 'I have no money, no resources, no hopes. I am the happiest man alive.'"

"My sentiment exactly, but this is not Paris. It's the Eastern Shore Tim Hortons version of it. And I do have a glimmer of hope."

Ramona graced me with a smile. And a great smile it was. "So I'm still trying to figure you out. Trying to put the pieces of the puzzle together. You grew up on the Eastern Shore, far from civilization, is that correct?"

"Well, we had some form of civilization. But only one channel on TV."

"What about the gun thing? You looked like you knew what you were doing."

"I grew up around guns. My father had them, but he didn't like to shoot anything but tin cans and beer bottles. He taught me how to shoot when I was about twelve. I killed more Moosehead beer bottles and Campbell's tomato soup cans than any boy alive. But, don't worry, I'm not packing."

"That's good to know."

I turned off the main road and onto the bumpy little road leading to Stewart Harbour. "It's been a long while since I've been here. A really long time."

"Why so long?"

"No reason really to come back. Parents both gone. Brother living in Fort McMurray."

"Where exactly are we going? Your old home still there?"

"No, not the house. That's a story I need to tell you, but not now. My father's old fish shack is still there near the wharf. At least I hope it's still there. He was a fisherman. The real McCoy. Up before dawn, out on a rough sea, living a rough life. And loving it. Well, mostly."

The pavement gave out and I slowed the Lexus. "Car like this isn't much good on a road with so many potholes."

"I'll trade it in on a Land Rover as soon as we get back to civilization. Anywhere around here a woman can take a pee? I think the coffee wants out."

"I can see you must have been a good actress. You got a lot of good lines." I stopped the car. "See that bush over there? It looks like it needs watering."

"Shut up," she said playfully, but got out and went to pee behind a bush like it was no big deal. When she got back in the car she corrected me. "We don't really use the term actress anymore. We're all just actors. But I'm not even that now. I'm retired, remember?"

"Retired at fifty?"

"Yes. I had no intention of playing old crazy women. That's what happens. One day you're cast as the romantic lead or the sexy but ditzy dumb blond, and then, before you know it, you're old and wrinkled and cast as a senile old woman on her deathbed."

"You don't look wrinkled or senile to me."

"Thanks for the compliment."

We were coming to the end of the road now. The real end of the road. Nothing but rocks and ocean beyond there. Beside us was the familiar line of little cottage-like buildings, mostly weather-beaten, some empty. I stopped in front of the one third from last. "This is it. Pilgrimage destination."

Some shingles were missing from the roof and the wooden shakes on the walls were grey, worn, and mossy in places. The window frames hadn't been painted in decades and the windows themselves were streaked with salt. But the building itself was unmolested by vandals. Out of respect for my father, I reckoned.

We got out and I went looking for a key. Not under the mat, not under a likely stone by the door. But when I lifted the lid of the rusty mailbox nailed to the wall, there it was. With a modest amount of wrestling, it opened the padlock on the door. The door swung inward and a tidal wave of memory swept over me. The good and the bad.

"After you," I said.

"Are there spiders?"

"Definitely."

"Then after you."

I took a deep breath and stepped forward into my past. Like a lot of rural kids, I had abandoned my roots, preferred not to think about how primitive a childhood it had been. As my eyes now adjusted to the dim light, I could see that everything was much like it had been when I was a kid forty years ago. The old sink with the hand pump. The bare bulb hanging down from the ceiling. An old, ratty chesterfield, plush red, with springs popping through; the tiny one-bed bedroom with a big picture window looking out over the harbour. And my father's old knee-high rubber boots still standing in the corner.

Ramona was quiet now, studying me, I guess. She probably saw that I was gobsmacked, the nervous energy from all that caffeine slipping out of me.

"I like what you've done with the place," she quipped. We'd quickly become quite adept at delivering our clever little lines on cue. But I'd suddenly lost myself. I wasn't sure why I was there. And why had I brought Ramona there?

"You okay?" she asked.

"Give me a minute," I said. "Sorry. I wasn't expecting to feel this way."

"I understand."

"Good, 'cause I don't think I understand. It's like I'm eighteen again, the last time I walked out of this place, said goodbye to my father and then never saw him again. I went away to school, to Dal. I wanted to be a writer. I wanted to leave all this behind and become part of the world out there. I wanted to make my mark, somehow." And then I swallowed hard.

Ramona stood silently and waited for me to finish.

"But now that I'm back here, it makes me feel like my life didn't really add up to much. Like I was just going through the motions. I don't think I should have stayed here. It's not that. But I feel like I never really committed to anything. Just rolled along. I think I blew it."

Ramona looked at me and I recognized the pity in her eyes. Okay, so I'd lost my job, got swindled out of my money by a teenager, was living all alone in a crappy apartment in the North End, and I was broke. But it was more than that. Much more. And for the first time I truly realized just how badly I'd really fucked up.

I walked into the small bedroom and sat down on the edge of the bed. The sheets, the blankets were still on it from that morning when my father had left this place and left the world forever. I looked out at the water through that big window. Someone had given him the window. At four foot by six foot, it was totally out of place for an old fisherman's crash pad. But he'd installed it and would often lie there and look out over the water, watch the gulls, the waves, the tide go in and out. And those were the times he was most at peace. Or so I thought.

I sucked in my breath, realizing that, unlike my father, there were never any moments in my life when I truly felt at peace. I had written my stories for the paper and I kept trying to write my fucking novel, something more meaningful, something that went beyond the day-to-day events and people I was writing about. But I could never complete it. I made friends, lost friends, fell into relationships with women and then just sort of gave up and abandoned them when I got distracted. And ended up alone.

Ramona had given me some space and was waltzing around in the main room, humming a tune I didn't recognize. But I quickly realized my little reverie was going on a bit too long. She poked her head into the bedroom and saw the hangdog look on me. "Maybe this was a mistake," she said.

We'd had that bizarre little roller coaster of a morning. She'd walked out of the fog into my life like in a dream. And I was about to blow it yet again. I thought I better say something. "Ernest Hemingway once said, 'Never mistake motion for action.' I suddenly just got this feeling that all my life I was just going through the motions."

"Hemingway was a bit of a macho turd and a fascist, if you ask me. And probably misogynistic to boot."

"Hey, you're talking about one of my heroes."

"Sorry. I admit he wrote a few good books. But then he killed himself, right?"

"He wanted a clean ending. He didn't want to just fade."

"A shotgun was involved, right? Nothing much clean about that."

"Fuck Hemingway, then. But I got one more quote from the old dead bastard. 'Never go on trips with anyone you do not love.'"

"Tell that to Francis Macomber."

It only took a second to sink in. The short story. "The Short Happy Life of Francis Macomber."

"Hah," I said. I had dozens of Hemingway quotes stuck in my head. But that was the only one with the word *love* in it. I hadn't intended it to mean much of anything. But now that I'd said it, a switch threw in my mind. I decided to return to the here and now.

"The way things have gone for me recently, I may end up having to live here. You mind helping me tidy things up a bit?"

Ramona smiled again, pulled her long hair back and tied it into a ponytail with a rubber band. "Not at all. I'd love to. I love a good challenge. And this looks like it's just you and me up against four decades of dust."

The hair thing changed her. No longer the movie star, no longer the attractive exotic woman on the pier. More ordinary but still lovely. "Well's out back," I said. "I'll go fetch us a pail of water."

"Sure thing, Jack."

"Jack?"

"Jack and Jill. And you used the word *fetch*."

7

And so our day became one of domesticity. Rural coastal domesticity, if you wanted to be accurate. Me and a woman who once kissed Tom Hanks. Go figure. But she dove right into it. Maybe actors could do that. Switch roles. Switch lives. Maybe that's why she had so many relationships. Switch on, switch off. I too had gone through a life of serial monogamy, but I recall a degree of suffering, well, agony to be honest, at the end of each and every relationship. In that regard, I think we were different.

We mopped and dusted and wiped for over an hour. There were dead bugs, dead mice, one dead rat. Ramona had found the offensive carcass. Actually, it was just the bones; the creature must have been dead for decades.

"There seems to be a lot of dead animals in our relationship," she said matter-of-factly. Yeah, she used that word. *Relationship*.

I decided not to flip it back to her in any clever way. Instead, I said, "I'll try to turn that around."

As we continued to clean, I was in a bit of a muddle. I really didn't have a clue as to how the day would play out. Why had she been willing to come with me? Why had she run off and then come back? What was she expecting and what was I supposed to do? We'd had breakfast, gone for a drive, she watched me kill a deer, then drove off, came back, then coffee, now we were here. Scrubbing floors and tossing dead mice out the door.

"Okay," she said, lifting a shredded, ragged curtain from a window. It had been made from an old feed bag. As she held it up, it simply disintegrated in her hands. She seemed fascinated by this. "So, I still need a few more pieces of the puzzle. Your puzzle. You're fifty-five. You think your life sucks. You left home when you were young and apparently never looked back. Wanted to be an Ernest Hemingway reporter type. But no war, right?"

"No war. Never left the province. Wrote about provincial politics, entertainment, car accidents, floods ... oh, and stories about odd folks."

"How odd?"

"Man with the largest collection of beer cans in the country, woman who wrote a book about clothesline etiquette, another who taught her dog to play piano. That sort of thing."

"Sounds like a grand life to me. Get to meet all kinds of people."

"All kinds."

"I need more. You asked me about relationships, so now I ask you. What about the women? Or were they maybe not all women?" She was still studying the curtain that was falling apart in her hands.

"Yes, they were all women."

"How many?"

"I never counted."

"Not fair. I had to come up with a number."

I shrugged, studied the dirty water in my bucket. "How do you know where to draw the line as to which ones could be called serious and which ones involved just hanging out, fooling around?"

"Oh, come on. You can do better than that. I drew the line. I knew. I gave you a number."

"I'd have to think about it before I could answer."

"Thinking is like cheating. Okay, no number. Just begin at the beginning."

No way was I going to spend my day working through the tale of my romantic affairs. But I had to give her something.

"High school," I said. "Beth Ann LaPierre. We'd been boyfriend and girlfriend when we were younger, then moved on. Then fell back together in our last year of high school."

"Now we're getting somewhere. Story, please."

"I think she was the real thing. I'd had so-called girlfriends before, but she was the one. I could tell that she was really in love with me."

"How could you tell?"

"The look she gave me whenever we were together."

"It's great, isn't it? That look, I mean."

"I don't think I've seen it since. Once girls are out of high school, I don't think they use that look anymore. Makes them too vulnerable or something."

"But did you have that look for Beth Ann?"

"It wasn't quite the same."

"Schmuck. Typical male."

"No. I liked her a lot. Maybe I loved her because she loved me."

"That can work. It's not the worst basis for a romance."

"But …"

"Here it comes."

"But I had to get out of here. I had this plan."

"Your Hemingway dream?"

"Something like that. Serious newspaper reporter writing about big international stories. Maybe publish a novel or two."

"Oh, I didn't know about the novels."

I didn't want to go there.

"I shouldn't have left. Or I should have taken her with me. I was eighteen. She was seventeen. I went off to university and my life had freedom written all over it."

"So you ran?"

"No. I walked."

"Still, you left someone who was in love with you."

"Well, I sure wasn't ready to settle down."

"But she was?"

Now I felt trapped. "Hey, I was eighteen. I wasn't ready for all that."

"What happened to Beth Ann? You broke her heart and then what?"

"We wrote letters to each other for a while. Real letters. She kept asking me when I was coming back to see her. I said I would. Soon. But I didn't. I'm not a hundred percent sure why. Then she stopped writing. Life went on."

Ramona gave me a hard look. "Maybe I shouldn't have asked. Where is she now?"

"I think she's still here. We don't stay in touch. But I know she married a guy I went to high school with. Joe Myatt. A fisherman like his father, like my father."

"Happily ever after?"

"I think so. Maybe." Now I felt guilty. About Beth Ann and how I had acted. I hadn't thought about her in a long while. And I wasn't about to continue on with the story about my other relationships, I knew that. I'd said enough. Fortunately, there was a knock on the door.

A head appeared in the doorway. An old guy. Really old. Reddish puffy face, black ball cap, ZZ Top salt-and-pepper beard. "I don't believe it," he said, looking straight at me, ignoring Ramona.

The years flooded back. "Rolf?"

"Chisel?"

"God, no one has called me that in a hell of a long time."

Rolf now gave Ramona the once-over. "You finally found the right one, did ya?"

"Not exactly like that. But this is Ramona. Ramona, Rolf. Old friend of the family. Rolf owns the shack next door."

"Old is right. I wake up most mornings and have to pinch myself to see if I'm still alive. Even then I can't tell for sure until the coffee kicks in."

Old Rolf looked plenty alive to me. Damn, it was good to see the old buzzard. "How's Evelyn?" I asked.

Rolf dipped his head and tapped his chest. "She passed. It was a while back."

"I'm so sorry."

"The way it goes. I'd probably be dead too, but the doctor says I have one hell of a stubborn heart. Had pneumonia three times. They say it's the old man's friend, a blessing. Can't say I found it that kind. More than happy when it decided to pick on someone else. So, what in the name of hell brings you back?"

"Hard to explain. You might say I'm semi-retired."

"You seem kind of young for that."

"I don't feel so young."

"Pretty fancy car out there. Must have done okay for yourself."

Down there people often judged you by what you were driving. Most folks drove old trucks.

I nodded at Ramona. "Not mine. Hers."

Rolf winked at Ramona. He'd always been a winker. "Come down to see how the other half lives?" he asked, his eyes twinkling.

"I love it here," she said. "Any real estate available?"

"Hell, yeah. A lot of folks have picked up and moved out. Not as much fishing anymore and not much to keep young people here."

Ramona nodded. I could tell she liked Rolf immensely. Everybody always liked Rolf and his spirit. He had been my father's best friend. They both had boats back in the day, both went to sea together each morning. I almost thought Rolf was going to do himself in when my father disappeared.

"What are you doing here, anyway, Chisel? I'm not trying to pry. It's just been so long and I haven't seen you down here. Not once. Not once since …"

I was hoping he wouldn't say it. And he didn't.

"Shoot, Rolf. I don't know what I'm doing here."

"Pilgrimage," Ramona said. "It's a kind of personal pilgrimage, I think."

Rolf looked puzzled. He probably didn't know many people who went on pilgrimages. He nodded, puffed a little air out of his mouth, coughed once. "Whelp," he said. "You arrived safe and sound in Mecca. I got a big extension cord I can run over from my place. Give you lovebirds some electricity in case you want to listen to music or whatever."

I wanted to tell him not to bother, that we'd probably only be around for today and gone by late afternoon. But he had already turned and waved a hand, indicating that his mind was fixed on it and there was no changing it. And then he stopped, turned around, looked at Ramona again and then at me.

"Oh, and Chisel. About the boat. Your father's boat. I kept it up. I've leased her out a few times over the years so I could keep it in shape. But it's still down the wharf. It's yours, I believe. I always hoped you'd come back." And he was gone.

8

Ramona looked at me. "You have a boat?"

"That's news to me. If it was my father's boat, that must be one very old vessel."

"You gonna take me out to sea?"

"I haven't driven a boat since I was a teenager. We'd have to be crazy."

"We are," she said. "We are crazy. Besides. Boats, cars, bicycles. Once you learn you never really forget, right? This one have an engine or do you have to row?"

I laughed, realizing she had envisioned something like a little rowboat or a dory. "This one has an engine. Or it did, anyway. A very old engine. I'll look it over. If it seems safe, maybe we can go out."

"Maybe. That's all I get is a maybe. I still don't get it. You didn't know about the boat all these years?"

I shrugged. Maybe I knew about it, but I just didn't think about it. After I left, I had really shut down pretty much all of my thinking about this place. In truth, I had just walked away and never looked back. Well, almost never. Some things about my life back in Stewart Harbour haunted me when I least expected it.

"What about that brother you mentioned? How come he didn't take over the fishing?"

"Pete was like me. He left. Went out west. Ended up at Fort McMurray, working in the tar sands. Married a girl out there. Neither one of us wanted to be a goddamned fisherman."

"You stay in touch with him?"

"Yeah. We send each other a Christmas card unfailingly each December."

"Christ, you're a hard one."

"Guess there's some things I'm not good at."

"I had a brother once," she said, looking down at the worn pine floorboards.

The "once" part threw me. I thought maybe I should just say nothing. Whatever "once" meant, it wasn't going to be good. But she was looking at me, waiting for me to ask. "What happened?"

It looked like she was about to explain but she stopped herself. "Let's save that for another time."

"Sure." We were getting to know each other, one story at a time. The more stories, the more we were becoming linked in that most human of ways. I couldn't help wondering how far this was going to go. Who would be the first to draw the line? To stop whatever was starting.

Rolf was banging at the loose pane in one of the windows now, holding up the end of an extension cord. I smiled, lifted the window sash, and he slipped it through. "You got power now," he said. "Now you can stay the night."

I had no intention of staying the night and I'm sure Ramona didn't. But standing there in the room that was both kitchen and living room, the sunlight spilling in through the open door, I suddenly wished that this little interlude in my otherwise dismal and dim existence could stretch out for a very long time. Lost in thought, I must have had a stunned look on my face.

"Now what?" Ramona asked. "What do people do when they get to the destination of their pilgrimage?"

"Pray maybe."

"Okay. Who do we pray to?"

It'd been a long time since I prayed, a long time since I believed in praying. My upbringing had not been very religious. Church was an Easter and Christmas thing. My father was a staunch pragmatist but never would have used that word to define himself. My mother seemed to have her own quiet spiritual sentiments but never spoke about it much. Yeah, who *do* we pray to?

I saw an old radio sitting on the counter. Yellow, cracked plastic housing. Shortwave, AM/FM. My father used to tune it in to the marine weather forecast. I could almost hear it in my mind. Forchu. Banquereau. East Scotian Slope. Laurentian Fan. Wind and tide and sea state. I could almost feel the static in the air. Who to pray to? "Let's pray to the god of sex and drums and rock 'n' roll," I said, quoting the lyrics of an old Meatloaf song I remembered from high school. Then I plugged in the radio and turned the FM dial until I found an oldies station. The song was "Message in a Bottle" by The Police. It seemed somehow fitting.

Ramona started swaying to the tinny music. I was afraid she was going to try to dance with me and I knew that would be a disaster. I couldn't dance. Instead, she turned the radio down. "Sorry, I don't mean to ruin such a pious moment but I have to pee again. All that coffee. Where's the, um, washroom?"

I pointed out the big picture window in the bedroom. The old outhouse was still standing. No doubt Rolf had rescued it after a storm or two. But it was still upright and it still had a door. "You got to be kidding," she said.

"My father was not big on plumbing," I said. "He was kind of old school in that way."

Ramona looked a little flustered, even a little perturbed as she walked past me and out the door. I wondered if that was it. Maybe the honeymoon was over.

But when she returned, she had snapped back into her old witty, vivacious self. "Cute spiders out there. Probably had the place all to themselves for quite a while." Then she rubbed her hands together. "Enough housecleaning. The place looks great. Let's go get some lunch."

"I'm buying," I said, instinctively.

"You're broke, idiot."

"Oh yeah. I guess you're buying. There's a little café not far off back on the mainland."

"No. I have a better idea. Let's get supplies." She pointed to the old two-burner hotplate on the counter. "Buy something to cook, maybe a pot and a frying pan. I'll make you a home-cooked meal. None of that restaurant shit."

"I didn't take you as the cooking type, being a movie star and all that. I figured you had people who cooked for you, cleaned your house and pool, did landscaping."

"I told you. I was an actor who did a couple of movies that went nowhere and then bowed out. I wasn't a movie star."

"Then you can cook?"

"Yes. Just watch me, Chisel."

The nearest store was a little general store in Burntwood. It seemed to have everything. And I do mean everything. The guy behind the counter, a young man, watched us closely as we walked around the crowded aisles — Ramona picking up cooking gear and food, then handing things to me to carry. When my arms were full, I walked to the counter, spilled my goods, and walked back to her. She had picked up a towel, sheets, and a blanket. That threw me, threw me good.

Even I knew that there were times when it was best to keep your mouth shut, to not ask a single thing. This was one of those times.

I took another load to the counter. The guy there was ringing up the first load and looking at me now with a little smile on his lips. He nodded toward Ramona and raised his eyebrows a notch. She was studying the meagre wine selection and I was thinking it more than fortuitous that this little ramshackle store had an NSLC licence. Ramona came toward us with a couple of bottles. "This'll do," she said.

Ramona paid cash and buddy was all smiles now. He even helped us haul some of the stuff to the car. "You folks aren't from around here, are ya?" he asked.

"Actually I am," I said. "Grew up in Stewart Harbour."

"No shit. What's your name?"

"Charles. Charles Howard."

"Howard?" The name had triggered something in his head.

"You probably remember my father, Desmond. Or at least stories about my father." My legendary father. He'd been gone all these years. But he was still remembered.

The guy looked puzzled, troubled even, but then said, "Oh, yeah. Sure."

He nodded and gave one of those furtive sidelong glances at Ramona, the kind men do when they think they are being coy. But women always know. "You both have a good evening," he said. "Thanks for the business."

"Cheers," I said. "Thank you." And wondered, was there really going to be an evening?

9

Ramona made sandwiches for our rather late lunch, and I took her for a long hike out to Prosper Point and out around Falcon Head. It wasn't easy going, walking on those loose rocks, but she didn't seem to mind. There were shiny fat seals sunning themselves on the ledges offshore and filling the air with those otherworldly moans. Gulls swooped down overhead and spindly-legged shorebirds — sandpipers or plovers maybe — tricked in and out with the waves along the sandy stretches.

"Heaven," Ramona said. "This makes me think that this is what heaven must be like."

I laughed. "It didn't seem that way when I was growing up here. And the sun wasn't always out. In fact, we have more fog here than probably any place in the province."

"Shh. Just let me hang on to this. This illusion or whatever it is."

I picked up a really flat stone and tried skipping it on the waves. It skipped once and then sank. Ramona picked up a stone and made four good skips with it before it sank. "It's all in the wrist," she said.

"Show-off."

"I'm an actor, remember? I play my roles well."

"A lot of stone skipping in your movies."

"No, usually just a lot of bad dialogue in coffee shops or bars. I got real good at holding a cup of coffee or a beer in the air while delivering my lines."

"Why didn't you stay with it? The acting?"

"Times changed. Filmmaking in Canada was on the decline. I didn't want to stay in California. I guess it'll sound like a cliché, but I found the whole business just a bit too shallow."

"No?" I said, pretending to be shocked. "So you just quit?"

"Yeah. There was some money in the family that came my way and I'd saved a fair bit. Unlike the other people I worked with out there, I kept a fairly low-key lifestyle. It seemed to work for me. Kept me grounded."

"Sensible girl." I pointed to her feet. "You even wear sensible shoes."

"Yeah, when I put them on this morning I was thinking to myself, *Hey, maybe I'll meet a nice man who will take me hiking on an empty beach somewhere.* How romantic is that?"

"Very. So you think I'm nice?"

"Nice enough."

"Enough for what?"

But she didn't answer.

We were rounding the tip of the headland. The hillside was badly eroded by the sea — red dirt cliffs and large rocks sticking out in places. "The sea just keeps carving away at the land," I said. "This is an old drumlin, a pile of mud and rocks left here by retreating glaciers."

"Ah, the professor is back."

"I used to play out here all the time. Pete and me. I thought of myself as the king of the drumlins."

"Cute. How did you know what a drumlin was?"

"I read books. Lots of books. Books on anything. Poetry to geology. Books made me want to leave all this."

"Big wide world out there and all that."

"I only got as far as Halifax. Dal. Then journalism at King's, the job at the *Tribune.* The rest, as they say, is history."

"That sounds all too tidy. I'm still trying to figure you out. You just left to go to university and you never looked back. Just left friends, family, and girlfriend all behind. People don't do that. It's not human."

"I did it. It's what I had to do. Pete was already gone — out west. Pretty soon we didn't have anything to return to."

"But now you're here."

"Yep."

I led her up a trail toward a gully at the top that would loop back toward the harbour. As soon as we were away from the sea breeze there were mosquitoes and blackflies we had to shoo away. "One of the things I liked best about Halifax was that there weren't any mosquitoes or blackflies."

She gave me a strangely curious look and then said, "Let's run. Let's get the hell out of here." And she started running. I was sure she was going to trip on a root or rock but she didn't. She ran like a woman who knew her way around obstacles. I could barely catch up to her, but I loved watching her run.

When we came back along the sea, we were both breathing hard. I reached out and grabbed her hand. "Stop, please. I gotta catch my breath." For some reason I didn't let go of her hand.

"Wow. I'd never seen bugs like that before. It was like a scene out of *The African Queen*."

"Bogart and Hepburn," I said. "That's us."

"All we need is the boat."

"Well, apparently we have that too. Let's go check it out."

It seemed incomprehensible to me that old Rolf had kept my father's fishing boat in repair. An old Cape Islander like that needed annual maintenance, and many fishermen in Nova Scotia had given up on them years ago and bought expensive fibreglass boats. But then, being there was like going back in time. Not all that much had changed since I'd left. I guess you *can* go home again. It all just seemed so bloody weird.

The stones rattled in a most pleasing way as the sea shoved them up the steep shoreline and then sucked them back. It was a sound I had become familiar with as a kid whenever I'd slept over at the fish shack. Something straight out of a poem.

A few men stared at us as we walked past the other buildings and out onto the old wharf. I didn't recognize any faces. There wasn't much activity. Just a few boats already in for the day, men in oilskins gutting hake, joking, drinking beer, gulls swirling above shitting on them.

The boat was unmistakable. Pretty much like all the others but the name stuck out. It never made much sense. Still didn't. *Sheer Delight.*

"Your father had a sense of humour."

"Sometimes. Nothing about fishing was anything but hard work as I recall. Hard. Wet. Cold." But I wasn't really thinking of the fishing. I was thinking of him out there on his final day at sea. Me, gone to Halifax. Not looking back. Not caring.

"Why did he do it then?"

"Fishing? It's what he did. What his father did. Work was work. Nobody much questioned it."

"Father to son. But not to you."

"Not Pete either. He got the hell out of here the day he graduated from high school."

"Were you and your brother close?"

"No." End of story. "Come on. Let's get on board."

The boat was clean and looked like it hadn't been doing any fishing that season, that was for sure. As we stood on the deck, I was haunted by old feelings, old memories. I was thinking about that day Pete went overboard. I figured I had to tell *that* story. If nothing else, to get it out of me.

"Right there where you're standing," I said. "That's where Pete was standing when he went overboard."

"Really? What happened?" She looked at me with a sudden intensity. So I told her every last detail. The whole thing played out before my eyes as if it was all happening over again.

"We were both young — teenagers fooling around, really getting on our father's nerves. Total jerks. My dad was tossing lobster traps overboard. They had stones in the bottom to help them sink. Me and Pete were pushing at each other. Roughhousing like we did all the time, but sometimes it got nasty. Pete had just knocked me down into a big tub of bait. I was pissed. So I got up, wiped off the slime and charged at him just as one of those big traps was going over the side. I didn't even knock him over, but he lost his balance and his leg went into the coil of rope. He tried to shake his leg out, but the rope tightened; he got slammed into the gunwale then dragged over it, feet first into the water. He looked like some kind of rag doll.

"He went in and down, those rocks in the trap pulling him toward the bottom. My father screamed and grabbed for the rope, but it had just yanked the marker buoy out of the boat and into the drink. I stood there paralyzed. My father screamed again. Not at me but at the water, at the sea itself. 'You motherfucking ocean,' he yelled. 'You're not getting away with this.' He said he hated the sea on some days. This was one of them."

I had to stop then and take a breath. I hadn't told this story in a long time. Ramona studied my face.

"What happened to Pete?" she asked.

"My dad grabbed the peavey, the long pole with a hook on the end. He hooked the buoy, lost it, then caught it again. I stood watching like a little shit, not able to do anything but feel the hot panic in my head. My father pulled the buoy in, began yanking on the rope. Hauling and cursing. It seemed to take forever. It seemed an eternity.

"I broke out of my trance and went over to help but he pushed me away. And then I saw my brother, still under the water, his body limp. My father, still holding the rope with one hand, reached down with the other and grabbed Pete's foot. He yanked Pete up and over the side and took out his knife and cut the rope to the trap.

"Pete was unconscious and my father stood there for a second and stared at him. I saw the fear in his eyes. And the anger. He'd seen drowned men before. All of us there in the Harbour had seen them. He knelt down and turned Pete on his side, began pounding his back. I wanted to say something about artificial respiration but I didn't know how to do it. And I knew he didn't.

"So I just watched him pound. Pound and curse. Then I saw Pete's body go into some kind of convulsion. Then he crunched up into a fetal position and began to cough and vomit — spit and seawater and the breakfast our mother had made us eat before we went to sea.

"My father was leaning over him and saying over and over, 'You're gonna be all right.' I knelt beside them and uncoiled the rope from around Pete's leg. The twisting of the rope had torn through his pants and had ripped right through his skin. His leg was raw and bleeding. Pete kept coughing and heaving even after there was nothing left in him to heave.

"'Watch your brother,' my father said, then he pulled up anchor, charged into the wheelhouse, fired up the engine, and turned the boat back to shore. He pushed that old engine until it roared loud enough so I couldn't hear whatever my father was saying. But he wasn't speaking to me. He was looking out at the water. Maybe he was praying. Maybe he was still cursing. I don't know. But he never took the two of us out to sea ever again. Could have been my mother's doing but it never ever even came up in conversation."

"Maybe that's why Pete wanted to get as far from this place as he could."

"That and other things. How do you like the boat so far?" I asked, realizing what a dumb jerk I was to be telling her that story at a time like this.

"I like it. And I'll take the story as a warning, a cautionary tale. I'll steer clear of any coils of rope I see. Anything else I need to be wary of?"

"Come on. Let me show you inside the cabin."

"Said the spider to the fly. Do you always try to seduce your women with stories about your brother's near drowning?"

It had never occurred to me to try and seduce Ramona. I was still thinking she was way out of my league, didn't have a clue why she was even hanging out with me or even why I had brought her to Stewart Harbour. Everything just sort of happened on its own.

Those few seconds of thought probably came off as stunned silence so I had to say something. "Works every time."

"Every time?"

"Well, most."

The door to the wheelhouse wasn't locked. I lifted the little latch and we walked in. It was just as I remembered it. The wood still shiny with its clear varnish, the wheel, the salt-stained glass windows, the compass, the tiny sink, and single propane burner with an old kettle still sitting on it. And the narrow uncomfortable bed where I fell asleep a couple of times after being seasick, resting there since my father refused to take me ashore until he was finished with his tasks. All before the Pete incident, of course.

"It's no luxury yacht, is it now?" I said.

"I've never been on a luxury yacht."

"I thought all you California starlets liked to get wined and dined at sea on them with billionaires."

"Not to my taste," Ramona said. "I was more of a dry land with a dry martini kind of starlet."

God, I liked this woman. I liked her smile. I liked her mannerisms, I liked the way we could banter back and forth like this. I even liked her goddamn shoes that allowed her to dance her way across those shoreline boulders that would have made most city women go racing back to level sidewalks. I wanted to say all this to her. And maybe I should have, but now someone was addressing us from the wharf.

"Yo, Rolf?" a man's voice said. "Is that you in there? What's goin' on? You have some ole floozy with you, you son of a bitch?"

I waved for Ramona to sit on the bed where I had once thrown up so violently. I poked my head out. I didn't recognize him at first. And he didn't recognize me.

"Hey, buddy," he said, now sounding a little arrogant. "This ain't your boat. What are you doing here?"

I studied him before I said anything. He was studying me too. He seemed to be practising at making a fist now. Is that what men did when they felt threatened? And then it clicked. "Joe?" I asked. "Joe Myatt?"

He was still trying to figure out who I was. And maybe I thought he was going to break into a smile when he recognized me. But I was dead wrong.

"Charles? Charles Howard." Nope. He wasn't the slightest bit happy to see me. "What the fuck are you doing back here?"

10

Ramona was peeking out from the small window in the cabin. I was trying to figure out why Joe looked at me like he hated my guts. We'd never been close in school, but I'd never done anything much to make him despise me.

"I don't know, Joe. I just thought it was time to reconnect." Bad word choice. A bit too intellectual for a guy like Joe.

"What the fuck is there to reconnect with?"

After I left, after I *disconnected* with Beth Ann, I'd heard word that Joe had moved in. They seemed like such an unlikely couple. Joe Myatt, the wrestling jock, none too bright but considered a small-town hero after he won some provincial title. Joe, destined for a career in Saturday afternoon Grand Prix Wrestling or some such thing. It had thrown me when I heard the news, made me think about what a crazy backwater world I'd come from. And they had a kid too. I lost touch after that. Maybe the idiot thought I was after his wife.

"I don't know. Truth is my life was flushed down the toilet. Lost my job. Lost most everything."

Joe gave me half a smile, huffed, and shook his head. "So what'd you expect to find back here? Pot of gold or something?"

"No, just trying to make sense of things." It's funny what you say when you really don't know what you're looking for and when your life really has had a good flushing.

"Screw that. No point to it."

"How's Beth Ann?" I ventured.

He huffed again, spit a gob of something into the oily water around the boat. "That bitch? We broke up a long time ago."

"Sorry to hear that."

"Not me. Discovered I didn't really like being a husband. Made me want to puke at the thought of settling down. Coming home every night sober. Washing dishes. Mowing a lawn."

"Yeah, guess that would be pretty tough on anyone," I said, and had my little moment, my flash into the world of what might have been. Me and Beth Ann settling down. Sobriety, dishes, and lawn mowing didn't seem all that bad from where I stood.

"Anyways," he said, stretching out all three syllables, "we're both better off." He nodded across the wharf. "That's my boat over there. The big one."

And it was one hell of a big-ass boat, with a really wide hull and a super-deluxe-looking cabin. "Fishing must be good," I said. "Maybe I should get back into it."

"Fishing's crap, really. Bank owns that thing, not me. They're just too chicken-shit to take it from me. They tell me to just keep making payments, but I'm nearly a year behind."

"Must be tough."

"Fuck, yeah. But ya gotta make a go of it." He spit again, hitting the exact spot in the dark water where his first gob had landed. The man had obviously had a lot of practice. All the venom had gone out of him with the spit. "Can't believe Rolf kept this old thing shipshape all these years. And, you know, we all felt bad about what happened to your father. You weren't around so we couldn't say it to you." That was a little dig. He just couldn't help himself, I guess. "You and Pete stay in touch?"

"Barely."

"He still out west?"

"I think so."

Joe laughed again, added a little snort. "Anyways. See you around, I guess."

"Thanks for stopping by."

And Joe, a slightly worn and beaten-down blast from my past, galumphed off the wharf, him in his high rubber boots. But not before he gave a half turn and caught a glimpse of Ramona just as she was opening the cabin door.

"What was that about?" she asked.

"High-school reunion," I said. "Joe was voted most likely to run his car off the road in a drunken haze. Looks like he turned out to be one notch up on me."

Ramona switched on that radiant smile, the one I was getting used to, the one I found myself eagerly waiting to happen. She liked me. She liked the language that I used. She liked something about the little boy lost in me. And on top of all the other good things on my checklist I had for her, maybe I liked her most for liking me.

"So now the word will be out," I warned her. "Mystery woman in town. It's gonna go viral. When they find out you kissed Tom Hanks, everybody's gonna want to check you out."

"Bring 'em on," she said. "I'd like to get to know the locals."

Taking the boat out into the ocean would have to be for another day. She'd asked, but I said no. Figured we might get caught in a storm and die. I decided to get Rolf to coach me about engines and tides and shit like that sometime. Then maybe.

"Head back to the villa?" I asked.

"Sure. I think I'm ready for a glass of wine."

I almost reached for her hand as we headed back down the wharf, the boards clunking in a most pleasing rhythm as we walked. The impulse was there, but I held back. I kept thinking, one false move on my part and it'd be like the gun and the deer. Slow and steady was my plan. If you could call it a plan.

Rolf was waiting for us when we arrived back at the shack. He had fish. "You city folks eat haddock?"

Ramona was all smiles. "I love haddock. How much?"

Rolf looked insulted. "Not selling it, dear. Giving it. I got a Jesus complex. I need to feed the masses. Or in this case, you two starving gringos."

I opened the door and invited Rolf back in. He immediately spied the two wine bottles on the table. "Now, she's talkin'," he said.

"Sit. I'll pour you a glass."

Rolf sat, sprawled, accepted the Mason jar with a splash of wine in it, then pulled a hip bottle of something from his side pocket and doubled the liquid in the glass. My guess would have been rum. "They call it fortified wine in the liquor store," he said.

"The boat looks amazing," I told Rolf. "The lady was impressed. Thanks so much."

"My pleasure. I did it more for your old man than for you to be honest. But I did get a bit of satisfaction over the idea that if you take good care of something, it can last one hell of a long time."

The life lesson was not lost on me.

Ramona poured some wine for me in an old Esso glass from the Olympics and poured some for herself into what I presumed to be an old Smucker's jelly jar. Rolf offered to "fortify" it, but we both covered our respective glasses.

The wine tasted good. The fillets of haddock sitting on the counter seemed more than a good omen. Rolf gulped down what was left in his glass and thumped the table with his hand. "Kids, thanks for the wine and for the conversation. A guy like me gets tired of his own company, but I need to go home and feed the cats, have a nap, and then go to bed. Just bang on the door if you need anything. You know where I am."

"Thanks again for the fish," Ramona said and kissed Rolf on his unshaven salt-and-pepper bearded cheek.

And then we were alone. I think it was another one of our awkward moments. The wine had not kicked in yet. Our glasses emptied quickly and she refilled them.

"Why does the second glass of wine always taste better than the first?" I asked.

"Does it? Maybe because the wine has had time to breathe."

"Bullshit. How could that be?"

"Just is."

We had wine, we had fish that we could cook in an old frying pan, and I had this brilliant woman sitting across the table from me who had had the foresight to buy a small bottle of olive oil from the young man back at the general store.

"Guess you know about expensive wines and such, huh?" I said, just trying to keep the small talk rolling.

"Maybe. But hey, knock it off. I'm not the person who you seem to think I am. In some ways, I'm a whole lot like you."

True, I had been playing the game of labelling her. Movies, money, fashion. Unfair. "That's good to know. I'm surprised, though. You got to know quite a bit about me today. Thought I would have scared you off by now. But I still have a shitload of unanswered questions about you."

"Save them. A woman likes to hang on to at least a little mystery if she can."

"But I don't know enough about you to even begin to connect the dots or figure out how all roads lead to Stewart Harbour."

"Well, all roads didn't lead here. You did. And here we are. And I like it."

"Little Miss Sunshine," I said.

"Yeah. That's me. Do you like her?"

"I like her a lot."

She took another sip of wine. "Ready for fish?"

"Not yet. C'mon, give me something about you. Anything. Family stuff maybe."

"Sure. Fair enough. Where to begin? Born in Halifax. Mother was a schoolteacher. Father was a lawyer who dealt in shipping matters and a bit of real estate on the side — all incredibly boring stuff but lucrative. Good parents, they were. Mostly. I had a brother, a couple of years younger. Trevor. A good kid. We never fought. My parents never fought."

"How boring."

"You want the real story or do you want me to make up something?"

"Sorry. Really." I suppressed a laugh and nearly shot some wine out of my nose. "Continue."

"Parents sent us both to private schools. Armbrae Academy. I had to wear short plaid dresses. Boys seemed to like me, but I liked to keep to myself, had a way of keeping them away when they came sniffing. Got labelled as a cold bitch."

"No way. I can't see it."

"Call it self-defence. I had a look, a line, a couple of close friends who were quite excellent cock blockers."

"Jesus," I said. "In high school?"

"It allowed me be more of who *I* wanted to be rather than what boys wanted me to be."

"Parents still alive?"

"Mom's in a home on Oxford Street. My father died of working too hard, making too much money, ditching his family, and then having a heart attack."

"Sorry."

"Me too. He's the one who left me the loot so I could do whatever I wanted with my life. But I'd have been happier if he had lived and kept his money."

"So it's coming into focus. Young South End Halifax girl, goes to private school, fends off all the horny boys there, has a rich ole daddy who can buy her anything. What next?"

"Well, it wasn't quite that superficial, but you're close. So then I do the circuit. Go to university in Toronto. U of T. Get my first jobs as a model, modelling lingerie for Sears catalogues."

"No way."

"Yeah. That was me trying to be independent. But it was just for money, money that I could say I earned on my own."

"No longer just daddy's little girl."

"Still was, really. But my mom was a little embarrassed when her friends went shopping for bras in the Sears catalogue and saw me there in a 34C."

"I guess she was."

"But that was nothing. I soon gave it up and got into theatre. Shakespeare, Beckett, Pinter. A string of boyfriends around then but nothing serious. Truth was, I liked the gay guys in the theatre scene more than most of the men who wanted to date me."

"But were any of these boyfriends one of the serious ones?"

"Only one. Blake. And only because he was the best actor I'd ever met. He taught me to memorize lines and I thought I could never do it. He taught me to fight all those demons of stage fright and fear. He was older, smoother, wiser. But he was, as they say, married to his craft. And so was I, perhaps. Or so I thought. He left for London and I left for California. An amicable parting of the ways."

"What, no drama, no story?"

"No, there wasn't. In Toronto I got in with some independent film people, starred in a couple of short films on the festival circuit, got noticed by a couple of TV producers. You ever see *Downtown East*?"

"You acted in that?"

"One season. It wasn't much. Then I was in a couple of independent features based on literary novels. Really depressing stories. They made the movie houses in Canada, but people walked out of those theatres psychologically damaged, I think. Nonetheless, I followed a couple of those directors to California because that's where the action was."

I sat silently and just looked at her. The sunlight was coming in off the harbour now and lighting up her face in a coppery glow. I'd never seen a more beautiful fifty-year-old woman before in my life.

She suddenly seemed like she was tired of telling me her story. Maybe she thought I was bored by it. Maybe she thought that adoring gaze of mine was boredom. "Anyway, I had a few bit parts in commercial movies, kissed Tom Hanks, and then decided to go home."

I was still in the dark about relationships. She had really glossed over that and given me a version of her curriculum vitae without the insightful or juicy bits. But I was wise enough to not ask more about her personal life.

"What about that brother?" I asked, hoping to just hear a little more family history and then leave it alone.

"He died," she said. "He went to university in Montreal. But he didn't come back." Ramona turned away and looked out the window at the sun sparkling on the water.

I'd said sorry too much already today. So I sat silently and waited for her to come back.

When she did, she touched my hand resting on the table. She gave me a sad soft smile and said, "We've all had losses. All of us."

11

When you pass a half century in your life and you're getting to know someone for the first time, you can't tell your whole life history in one sitting or one day or even one month. We sipped our wine and probably both made a silent vow to stop talking about dead brothers, fathers, mothers. "I've never known anyone named Ramona before," I finally said, wanting to take us back to small talk. "Wasn't there some kids' books with a girl that name?"

"*Ramona the Pest* was one of them. The girl's name was Ramona Quimby."

"Never read it. I was more of a science fiction kind of guy. I liked novels set in the future. I couldn't wait to get there. The future, that is. And look, here I am. And what a disappointment. No flying cars, no jetpacks, no vacations on the moon."

"Is it really so bad?"

I looked at her, studied the way she held her wine glass. "No. I take that back. Not at all. I look around and I see paradise. That's only because you're here." I was getting bolder but I still said it like it was a tease, a joke. Just in case I had gone too far.

"Thank you, kind sir. I'll graciously accept any compliment you can throw at me."

"And I bet you cook one hell of a piece of fish," I said.

"So that's it. Boy gets hungry. Boy gives girl a compliment in hopes she'll cook him some haddock."

"Damn. You can see right through me."

I think I mentioned food because I just wasn't sure where things would go next. Deep down I was scared. I was having a great time with this woman, but I was still scared out of my wits, diving down, out of my depths, and certain I would screw every-thing up somehow. But, when in doubt, eat.

"I'm gonna clean one of those pots and boil some potatoes," she said. Ramona had bought a bag of new small potatoes at the store. "I guess I should have bought some vegetables."

"Fried haddock and boiled potatoes. The perfect meal, according to my father. He detested vegetables. I don't know why. He considered them evil. He'd tolerate cabbage and pota-toes but seemed to have a grudge against anything green. Funny, eh?"

"We all have our quirks. Maybe he could have patented it and made a fortune. The Stewart Harbour Diet. Fish and spuds. Protein, omega-3, and carbs. Lose weight, make friends with fishermen, live long and prosper."

"Well, we did eat a lot of fish, Pete and I. And we were hardly ever sick."

"Lucky you."

The potatoes were boiled, the fish was fried, and a happier meal could not have occurred on the planet that day. The sun was going down and the second bottle of wine was opened. And then I looked over at the supplies she had bought and saw the carton of eggs. Had I not fully taken the hint when she had been so bold to buy sheets at the general store? Sheets and eggs. Ramona was planning on staying the night with me.

I turned on a little lamp and lit a couple of candles I found in a drawer, candles my mother had made. She'd save stubs of burned down candles, melt them, add a wick, and make new ones. I never thought of us as being exactly poor, but both of my parents prided themselves on being thrifty and not wasting anything.

I don't fully remember what we talked about for the rest of the evening. All I know is that we kept it light as we flirted and joked. We became casual and avoided heavy topics. And we both became weary. Weary but comfortable.

The wine might have hit her a bit harder than me. Her cheeks were flushed and her eyes were squinty and she was talking about how she had always wanted to live by the sea. "Right by the edge of the ocean," she said. "So you could walk out your door and it would be right there. You could smell the salt air and hear the waves. Nothing between me and France except the Atlantic Ocean."

I could have told her about the disadvantages of living by the ocean — the fog, the wind, the nor'easters, and the hurricanes. But it was not an evening for logic or negativity.

As she drifted off, two men were having an argument in my head. The horny guy was screaming that now was the time to make a move. *Lure her into bed and screw her brains out. It has been a long while, buddy. A mighty long while.*

The other man, the shy one, the gentleman, said, *Look here, Bosco, she's already had a bit too much to drink and you'd be taking advantage of her. Go slow. Now's not the time for pushing things too far.*

And, of course, the gentleman was right. The wine was gone, the sun had dropped below the horizon. The eggs were waiting for breakfast.

"Time for bed," I said softly.

"Really? I'm not even tired." Her eyes were fully closed now, her head slightly slumped over.

I unwrapped the sheets and tossed them over the old mattress we had smacked with a broom outside earlier that day. I led her to the old fisherman's single bed where my father had so often sacked out at night, only to awaken in the dark hours before sunrise, preparing to go to sea. I tucked her in and placed a blanket over her. She immediately slid toward the wall, making just enough space for me to lie beside her and curl into her, both of us still with our clothes on.

In the morning the sun was shining as I opened my eyes and realized I was alone in the bed. I could smell coffee.

Ramona was standing by the hotplate cooking eggs. "Sorry I fell asleep on you, cowboy. Guess it shows I can't hold my liquor. Anything crazy happen that I should know about?"

I smiled, sat up. "Not a damn thing. Nothing crazy. It was all good. Most fun I'd had since I don't know when."

"Welcome to the future."

"What?"

"The future. No flying cars, no jetpacks. But you have to admit, it was better than a vacation on the moon."

"It was indeed. We had way more oxygen. And gravity. I rather like the combination."

There were scrambled eggs and coffee and small talk. And I kept waiting for the bubble to burst.

And it did.

"I've got to go back to Halifax this morning," she said after we had finished eating. "I have this appointment with a lawyer concerning the trust fund. Papers I need to sign. He claims it's really important and if we don't do this now, I'm gonna be hit with a shitload of taxes."

"Oh," I said, feeling a little stunned.

"You wanna come?"

I had this gut feeling that if I returned to Halifax, it would be some kind of weird rewind thing and all of this would go away. She'd go her way; I'd go my way back to my truly unappealing jobless rathole of a life and I'd end up standing alone on the pier on another foggy morning, looking into the abyss.

"No, I think I need to stay here," I said.

She immediately detected my mood swing. I guess it was pretty obvious. "You sure?"

"Yeah, I'm sure." What I was sure of was that Ramona, who had suddenly dropped from the clouds into my life, was about to ascend back into them and disappear.

Ramona walked over to the stained and faded mirror above the sink and began to put on makeup. "I'm really sorry but I have to do this," she said, all businesslike suddenly.

"I'm sorry too." I had reverted to being a hurt little boy. It was like my birthday was over and I had to go back to being a sorry-assed, snot-nosed brat who had to wake up and go to school.

"I'll be back," she said unconvincingly.

"I'll be here."

"I'll call you."

"I don't have a phone."

"No cellphone?"

"Nope. Not even sure there's reception here."

"Crazy. But here. Keep mine. Hold it up high in the air or climb a tree or something. Gotta be a signal somewhere around here."

"You really gotta go?" I could feel her slipping away. My own cocky and somewhat confident self from yesterday had fled the scene this morning. Mopey man in the aftermath morning. Where was my day-after pill?

Ramona, on the other hand, was back to looking like the movie star she had once hoped to be. I wondered, with my newly deflated self-esteem, how I could ever have thought she'd want to have a fling with me, let alone a relationship.

"Charles," she said, taking my chin in her hand and looking me directly in the eyes. "I'll be back. Stop trying to read anything into this." But then she added something that really threw me off. "Some of us have responsibilities, okay? Do you know what happened to my keys?"

She got a little flustered then and flitted around the little cabin, looking for the keys until I held them out to her. They'd been in my pants pocket. I'd been the one driving the car.

And then she took her cellphone out of her purse, set it on the table. "I've got another one in the car. I thought I had lost this one, but later I found it. I'll call you later. Or you call me.

Number's in the phone. Thanks for a great day yesterday." And she kissed me in the middle of my forehead and walked out the door. I sat there stunned as I listened to the car start, the tires churning on the loose stones of the road. And she was gone.

12

Alone again. A little dazed. More than a little confused. Broken man? Not quite. What would the headline read? "Man Watches Woman Leave. Picks Up Pieces of Himself." "Charles: The Human Rubik's Cube." "Enigma Man Returns to Boyhood Home. Ponders Life. Wonders About Mystery Woman." Etc.

I walked out the door and headed toward the water. The harbour was gleaming in morning sunlight. The wharf looked empty. The fishermen all at sea on a grand morning like this. I wondered how many of these so-called fishermen's reserves were left in Nova Scotia. It was truly an odd sort of place. Almost no one actually lived out there in the shacks, except for maybe a couple of the fishermen whose wives had kicked them out of the house. And Rolf, of course, who said he'd never survive on the mainland. But most of the men lived a few miles inland, in real houses with real yards and real families, drove their trucks to the wharf and their boats; maybe occasionally they might sleep out in their shacks to get an early start or spend the night having a roaring party, the likes of which you didn't want to chance on the mainland.

Life on the land was tenuous. Hurricanes had swept through there, waves right up under the sheds, even floated some of them around. No one actually owned the property their building was on but they could still hand it down to their kids. And it wasn't just men anymore. I'd written articles about women in the fishing business. Fisherwomen. No, actually they just wanted to be referred to as fishers. Like Ramona. Not an actress, she'd said, but an actor.

The whole crooked finger of a peninsula, this ridiculously narrow thread of land, was lashed to the mainland by a man-made causeway that would be nearly underwater in a seasonally high tide. The truth of the matter, I admitted to myself, was that global warming and annually higher tides and heavier storms would wash everything away sooner or later. There was no doubting it. Meanwhile, life went on out there, much the same today as it had in my childhood. Fishers out to sea before the sun comes up, back by late morning or noon.

I sat on the rocks by the shore and let my mind wander back in time; eventually it just wandered off to the day before. To Ramona. Had she truly disappeared from my life as suddenly as she'd appeared out of the fog there in Halifax? Is that the way women did it these days? Nah. She wouldn't have left her cellphone even if she did have more than one. Leaving a cellphone was a kind of commitment, I tried to convince myself. I wondered if I should call her. *Hell no, man,* a voice in my head said. Too needy. Women don't want a man who's too needy.

I looked out to sea and saw two Cape Islanders headed back to port. A morning like this, sunrise at sea, would have been grand and dramatic. Thoughts were now swirling in my morning brain like artistic gulls, feathery paintbrushes against the sky.

What I'd lost over the years of working for a newspaper — chasing stories, interviewing politicians and union leaders and all the rest — was the ability to have meditative moments like this. It just didn't seem to fit the lifestyle. So, for decades I'd more or less given up on that mode of thinking. No pondering, no real reflection. Just doing. Working. Writing. Socializing at night in bars, even though it was never my thing. It's what a single man in the city does. Even long after he realizes that hanging out in pubs and meeting new women night after night is the most depressing of routines.

How come I could never step out of myself for all those years, those decades, and see that life was about something else?

The wind was coming up off the water now, a cool breeze out of the south, bringing with it the smell of the open sea. I watched as those two boats pulled up to the wharf, their captains tying them up, the gulls arriving to spiral above, waiting for unwanted parts of the gutted fish. I couldn't quite see the *Sheer Delight*, but I knew it was docked there, waiting for me.

I was falling into a kind of a trance, I guess. Had to stand back up, shake my head. I turned to go back inside.

Worn wood floors, unpainted walls, the black and rusting woodstove, the sink, the little bedroom where Ramona and I had slept. Did I really wake in the middle of the night to find her arm around me? Or did I make that up?

I'd left the door open, letting the morning sun spill in and paint the floorboards with solar radiance. Welcome home, the walls seemed to say. We knew you'd find your way back here one day. I walked inside.

I heard footsteps first, then someone was blocking the sun in the doorway. "Knock, knock," a man's voice said. All I could see at first was a silhouette. But he was holding something in his hands. What the hell?

I shifted toward the side of the room and discovered that it was a youngish, heavy-built man holding aloft two live lobsters. "Thought I'd stop by and see who the city boy was," he said. He had a scruffy beard, long shaggy hair that stuck out from under a Harley-Davidson cap. He wore a dirty flannel jacket and heavy workboots.

"Hi," I said. "What's up?"

He nodded toward one and then the other lobster. Their claws were working the air. "Wondering if you'd care to buy these two beauties here. Couldn't get anything more fresh. These guys were scuttling around on the sea floor just an hour ago. Now they're here wondering what the fuck? Bet you never tasted lobster this fresh."

"Probably not," I said, though I had of course. You couldn't grow up there without eating so much freshly caught lobster that you became sick of it.

"So what do you think? Ten bucks for the both of them."

"You catch them?"

"Hell, no," he said. "I bartered."

"What did you barter?"

He just shrugged. It was then I noticed the tattoo on his neck. Some kind of death mask. But then who didn't have some grotesque tattoo these days? No big deal. No Russian mobster. Just a hangashore with a couple of squirmy lobsters.

"C'mon, man, what do you say? Ten bucks for the two of them."

I laughed. "Funny thing is, I don't have any money."

He was walking around the room now. I hadn't exactly invited him in but then fish shacks were pretty much public terrain to anyone in the community. He must have spied the little pile of bills on the table at the same time I did.

I didn't get it at first. Then it sunk in. Ramona had left me money.

"Jesus," I said out loud, picking up the cash. Three twenties and a ten. "'Up on Cripple Creek.'"

He kind of snorted. "Excuse me?"

"Oh, nothing. An old seventies song I remember. About a woman. A woman who takes care of her man."

"Sounds like my kind of woman."

I handed him the ten and set the rest of the bills back down on the table.

He placed the lobsters down on the floor, tucked the bill in his top pocket. "They're all yours."

The lobsters started crawling around the room. I didn't have a clue what I was going to do with them.

"You staying around for a while?" the guy asked.

"Don't know yet."

"Need a little something to get you through the day? Or night?"

"Not sure what you mean."

"C'mon, man. Everybody needs a little something." He held out a small plastic bag with some white powder in it. Another with some pills. Lucky me. I'd just bought two lobsters from the local drug dealer.

"Not just now," I said. "I'm just settling in."

He shook his head. "Understood. Anyway, I'll let you be. I'm Brody by the way."

"Charles," I said.

"Like the prince, right?"

"Yeah."

"Okay, Prince Charles. Nice to make your acquaintance. You need anything, just ask around for me. I'm usually not far."

Brody left and the room was suddenly quiet except for the scuttling of the two lobsters scratching away at the floorboards. What the hell to do with them?

It wasn't like I was opposed to eating lobster. But I wasn't about to boil their sorry asses. And I felt kind of bad for them. They seemed so sad, so lost, so out of their element that I totally identified with this pair of crustaceans. I gingerly picked them up, gripping their backs as the claws flayed the air. The memory of being pinched by a big bugger of a lobster came back.

When I had a decent grip on both, I walked them outside and down to the edge of the water. "Pass it on," I said to them as I carefully set them down on the pebbly bottom of the shallow water. The water felt cool and soothing. They immediately started poking their way along the bottom into the deeper water. T.S. fucking Eliot, I thought. "I should have been a pair of ragged claws," or whatever it was.

I stayed down on my haunches watching the ripples on the water well after the creatures were gone from my sight.

When I stood up, I could see that I had an audience on the wharf. Five fishermen had seen me deliver the lobsters back to the sea. The look on all their faces was the same: *Who is that crazy fuck and where did he come from?*

When I turned around, I saw Rolf standing there. "I get it," he said. "I totally get it. Lobster rights activist, right? Bunch of Swedish women came over here a couple of years ago, started protesting. Beautiful women, the whole lot of them. But they hated our guts. Said we all killed things because we had tiny dicks or something like that. They got to you, didn't they?"

"Something like that," I said.

"Where's the missus?" he asked, changing the subject.

"Had to go to town," I said.

"She coming back?"

"I sure as hell hope so."

Rolf turned to go. "Let me know if you need anything," he said yet again. "And let me know when you want to take the boat out." Rolf had it fixed in his mind that I was going to take the *Sheer Delight* out to sea.

When I walked back into the shack I noticed the three twenties that I'd left on the table were gone. So much for living in a community where no one locks their doors.

13

I think that missing sixty dollars bothered me almost as much as the forty thousand I had given to that young man who was supposed to go help out in Haiti. I stewed on it for a bit. Decided to let it go. Then stewed some more and decided to do something about it.

That's when I noticed there was a text message on Ramona's phone.

> Charles, missing you already. Will see you later
> today. I'll bring supplies.
> Love Ramona

Yeah, she used the word *love*. Hmmm. Just a word, right? Way to end a message.

I barely knew how to send a text message. But I fiddled with it until I could.

> Ramona, life's just not quite the same here with-
> out you. Hurry home.
> Love Charles

I guess if I said those words to her out loud I would have made it sound facetious, like a line from a movie. But there, I did it. And I found myself staring at the phone, waiting to see how she'd respond. But there was nothing.

So I sat down at the bare wood table and stared off into space. A flood of memories poured over me. My mother and father and long-distance brother. Childhood memories. Charles Howard, the boy who just packed up one day and went to town and never came back until he was fifty-five years old. What kind of person does that?

The same kind of guy who never maintained a long-term relationship. The same kind of guy who can't finish the novel he started over ten years ago. Walk-away Charlie. I thought of myself as Charlie when I wanted to poke fun at myself, when I saw myself as a bit of a clown, a laughable fuck-up, a twenty-first-century male buffoon. That's when I slammed my fist on the table. *That bastard with the lobsters. How dare he?*

Rolf was mending a fishing net in front of his shack when I walked back out. And he was smoking a pipe. "Jesus, Rolf, you doing that for the tourists? The province pay you to look like that?"

"Like what?" he shot back.

"Like an old weathered fisherman mending a net. Like a postcard from the nineteenth century."

"Must be the pants," he said. "Or the shirt. Both pretty old, worn 'em for a few years. Pretty authentic looking, you say?"

"And the beard. How long you been growing that beard?"

"Since I was twelve, I believe. Me and the beard go a long way back and we've shared quite a few adventures. The women seem to like it."

"I don't see any women around. You mean those Swedish animal rights girls?"

"Yeah. Them."

I guess we could have gone on like that all day. And I admit it felt good to shoot that kind of shit. Reminded me of the beer talk after working all day at the paper. Gossip. Jokes. Beer and verbal baloney.

"Rolf, you see that young guy who came by this morning?"

"Yep. I wondered what that was about. Then I saw you let those lobsters go. Figured there must be a story."

"You know him?"

"Of course. Can't say I approve of the lad but he's one of us."

"Brody, right?"

"Brody Myatt, Joe's son."

"No way."

"Yeah, 'tis true. But he and his father don't get along worth shit."

"I want to find him. He stole sixty bucks from me."

"I thought you were broke."

"I was. Ramona left me some cash."

Rolf stopped mending and looked up into the sun. "You that good in bed?"

"Hell, yes."

"I gotta get me to Halifax one day and find me one of them women. She gave you money?"

"It's not like that. So, where can I find Brody?"

"You're not gonna like this."

"Like it or not. Where's he live?"

"He lives with his mother."

"Are you shitting me?"

"I shit you not."

"Beth Ann?"

"Yep."

It kind of hit even harder as it sank in. Beth Ann, who I had dropped like a hot potato when I went off to Dal. "No?"

"Yep. She and Joe got together not all that long after you walked off the face of the earth, remember? He'd been waiting in the wings so to speak. They had a kid, things seemed to be okay at first, but then something happened. Joe always had a bit of a temper, of course. Beth Ann didn't never take much shit from anyone, including him. I don't know if she gave him the boot or he moved out of his own accord. But they haven't been together for years and years. And, like I said, Brody and his father don't see things eye to eye. Me, I try to see the good in everybody, but he's a bad one. It don't surprise me he took your money. Or your lady's money, that is."

Rolf was smiling, the old devil. Everything was funny to him. Even this.

A voice inside me said to give it up. Sixty bucks. Burned, but lesson learned. Give it up. But for some reason I couldn't. "Where's she live?"

"Back on the mainland. Third house in from the causeway." He left his net and walked past me, looking toward the wharf. "Her boat's in so she might be home by now."

"She fishes?"

"Pretty much the only work you can get around here. Old Joe Myatt, the skinflint, he wasn't going to support her and she had to raise that brat mostly on her own."

I wished it was anyone but Beth Ann's kid. But there it was. Grown up, of course, but still hers. He must be in his thirties.

I just should have dropped it. Maybe Beth Ann would still be pissed off at me for running out of her life. Another good reason not to go there. But I just couldn't seem to let it go.

The long walk across the causeway gave me plenty of time for second thoughts. The anger I felt toward Brody eased off and curiosity set in about Beth Ann. In some alternate universe, I knew I had stayed home, married her, taken over my father's boat, and gone fishing. Lived my life in Stewart Harbour.

The house was set back from the road. It had bright yellow vinyl siding. Two trucks sat in the driveway. My body kept trying to turn around and head back out the causeway but my feet just kept walking toward her door. I tapped on the aluminum storm door and the glass rattled in the frame.

A woman came to the door. A good-looking woman who wore her age well. Beth Ann.

I think she thought at first I was selling something. She had that look. She didn't recognize me at all. I wanted to say something but my mouth was dry. My brain froze. She kept looking and then it hit her.

"Charles," she finally said. "Jesus, God! Charles!"

"Beth Ann."

That couple in the alternate universe probably got dizzy right about then. Worlds were colliding. Maybe suns were imploding, planets being sucked into black holes. I don't know.

"Come in," she said. "Come in."

I followed her into the living room and then she waved me to follow her to the kitchen. All serious talk about anything takes place in the kitchen on this shore. She pointed to a chair and I sat down. She poured coffee, didn't ask me if I wanted cream or sugar. She remembered I drank it black.

"It's been a while," she said. Understatement of the year.

"It's been a lifetime."

"I know. But here we are."

"Funny, eh? All that water under the bridge. I hear you have a boat, do some fishing."

"It's what I do. When we were young, no one ever thought about women going to sea to fish for a living. But here we are."

I sipped the coffee. It was strong. "Guess I should start by saying I'm sorry."

She waved her hand in the air. "Let's not go there. It was so long ago. We were so young. I think I always knew I couldn't hold onto you or hold you back once you left. You're a writer, right?"

"Was," I said. "Paper closed. Big corporate decision in Toronto."

"Sorry to hear that. You back for good?"

"I don't know."

She sipped her coffee, hesitated. "You with someone?"

That word. *With.* Was I *with* someone? "Hard to say." I cleared my throat, wanted to change up the subject. "I, uh, I met your son today. He brought me some lobsters."

Beth Ann scrunched up her brow. I wasn't sure what she was thinking. "That's nice," she said. "He just turned thirty-seven last month."

"All grown up."

"Sort of. But in some ways he's just like a kid."

I guess my brain was at least partially functioning because I decided then and there not to mention the fact her "kid" had stolen money from me. I looked around. "Looks like you're doing okay," I said flatly.

"It's a life. I'm getting kind of weary waking up before dawn and hoofing it down to the dock. The sea just doesn't seem as inviting as it once was."

"I can't quite envision you ..." But I didn't finish the sentence. I was remembering the Beth Ann from high school. Young, pretty, feminine, long silky hair and a smile that could light up the darkest days. She was still a fine-looking woman.

"We all do what we have to do."

"So you and Joe Myatt got married?"

"We did."

"He stopped by the boat yesterday. Wasn't that happy to see me."

"He's not much happy to see anyone. Got a big ole chip on his shoulder." She paused, looked more than a little concerned. "What did he say to you?"

"Not much. Surprised to see me. I can't quite believe Rolf kept my father's old boat going all these years."

"It's old. A good boat but old. Not sure I'd want to go out to sea in it myself now. But Rolf leased it to me when I was starting out."

"You fished in my father's boat?"

"Otherwise, it just would have sat there and got dry rot." She sounded defensive.

"No. I mean, that's kind of ironic." Maybe *ironic* was the wrong word. "I mean, it was just kind of, um, curious." I didn't know what I meant.

"It's a small community. I needed a boat and it was available. It wasn't like you and Pete were around to take up where your father left off." There was a bit of an edge in her voice now. I don't think she meant anything, but there it was. "Besides, when Rolf found it, it was adrift in the sea, remember? By salvage rights, it was his at that point."

"I guess so," I said. "I didn't mean to imply you didn't have a right to use it."

"Don't worry. I have my own boat now. Almost paid for too. Another couple years and I won't owe the bank a cent."

I wanted to apologize for the way I had screwed up our conversation but didn't know how. "Brody, he fish too?"

She rolled her eyes. "Not exactly."

"What's he do?"

"Cause trouble."

"How's the pay?"

"Don't ask."

And that's when Brody walked in the door and into the kitchen. He was big. Funny, I hadn't really noticed how big before. Big and tall and his head barely made it under the door frame. He looked stunned when he saw me sitting there at the table.

"Here's my boy," Beth Ann said.

"Hey," Brody said.

"Hi again," I said.

"Want some coffee, Brody?" Beth Ann asked.

"Nah. Just came to get my truck."

"You've met Charles."

"I did. Gotta go," he said. And he left.

Beth Ann looked at his back as he walked away, then she looked at me. "After Joe and I were over, I had to raise Brody by myself. I'm not sure I was the best mother in the world for him. But I tried to do what I could."

"I'm sure you were a great mother." I felt like I had overstayed my welcome. Awkward conversation and all that. "Thanks for the coffee," I said. "I'm gonna head back to my place. Let's talk again. Let's remember old times."

She smiled a soft smile and placed her hand on mine. "Sure. Old times. Good times." Then she rapped her knuckle on the table. "Let me give you a ride back."

I wanted to say no. I wanted to escape from there, escape from the past that I pretended I wanted to talk about. But she'd already grabbed her keys and was walking toward the door.

I followed, got into her pickup. She backed out of the driveway and headed us toward the causeway. We drove in silence. And then she came to a stop in front of my shack.

"Thanks," I said. "It was great to see you."

"Charles," she said, leaning on the steering wheel, the engine still running. "I promised myself never to tell you. But I have to tell you this."

More worlds colliding, more planets imploding. Shit. "Tell me what?"

"Brody. He's your son. He doesn't even know it. I never told him. Joe accepted the fact I was pregnant. He knows Brody is yours. He tried his best to accept Brody as his own and did okay at it for a while. But then we broke up. He never told a soul. And I never told Brody. Maybe it's best to just leave it that way. But I had to tell someone. And when I saw you today, I was just bursting to tell you." She paused and flexed her fingers on the steering wheel. "And now I told you. Just thought you should know."

14

I sat down on the old narrow bed and watched dust particles ascend to the ceiling in the bright morning sun. Denial was my best buddy at that moment. Couldn't be. No way. She would have told me back then. No one keeps secrets that long. Maybe this was her idea of revenge. Now get out of town before someone makes up some other blarney.

But.

But, I knew in my gut it was true. And it was just like the old Beth Ann that I knew. Make the best of a bad situation and don't hurt anyone.

I didn't have to get a DNA test. It fit the story of my life. Get involved. Make a commitment. Then walk away. And walk away I did. Deadbeat dad of the worst kind.

There was a noise. I didn't know what it was at first. Oh, the phone. Buzzing, vibrating on the table. I got up and looked at it. Text message.

Ms. Danforth:
We've booked your next appointment for next
Wednesday at 2 pm. Please confirm.
Dr. Jenkins

It was Ramona's phone. Made sense someone might contact her on it. I was about to give her a call, but I was afraid of what I might say. Maybe say the wrong thing. And I was afraid to text here, afraid she wouldn't respond at all. I was feeling manic. Just like yesterday on the pier in Halifax. Was that only yesterday? Fuck me.

Sleep seemed like a wonderful option. Curl up and take a nap. But my brain was on fire. I got up and tromped out the door, headed for Prosper Point. Used to go there when I was a kid. I walked past the wharf, heard voices, laughter. Possibly at me. The lobster thing. Good story to spread around. If only they knew the rest. *So, he knocks her up when he's a teenager, leaves town and comes back decades later, the boy sells him a couple of lobsters that he lets go back in the water. And get this, his kid, his own flesh and blood, steals the only money he has in the world and walks off.*

I swear I could still hear them laughing as I walked past the last shack, an abandoned one that used to be owned by Jess Kinsey. The windows were all boarded up and the door was off its hinges. Beach rocks and sand had been driven by a really high tide and waves into the front room. One day, all these old buildings would have the same fate. So long Stewart Harbour. Only a matter of time.

Fortunately, it was low tide.

Prosper Point was once a fairly substantial headland, but it had been washed away on both the east and west sides and was now a long spit of rocks leading to a wedge-shaped narrow vestige of the headland with dirt cliffs on both sides. Another drumlin. Used to go out there all the time as a kid. King of the Drumlins. Place to daydream, dream of a magnificent future. Marine biologist was the goal, until I discovered I didn't have math or science skills. But the teachers said I could write.

By university, I wanted to be a novelist. Write the great Canadian novel. Set it in Stewart Harbour and dig down deep in my psyche, nail down all the universal truths that all those other writers were too wimpy to scratch at. Three false starts at it and

I signed up for journalism at King's College. Kept trying to find my way back to fiction but the facts kept getting in the way. Straight out of school and into a job at the *Tribune*. Interviewing MLAs, covering city council meetings. The odd interview with visiting important people. Met Bill Clinton once after he was out of office. He told me a couple of jokes, pretended like we were old buddies. Even invited me to play golf with him and the premier at Ashburn Golf Club. I bowed out. Knew nothing about golf.

Wrote words on a computer screen for all those years and then suddenly the job disappeared. And the novel, the latest one, the one I'd been working on for at least ten years, the one I never gave up on, but could never find my way to the end of — well, it sat in a drawer back in Halifax.

Lots to ponder. Father of the Year. I climbed the embankment and sat on the edge. The top of this diminishing peninsula was covered in wild roses, thistles, mostly things with spikes and thorns. But it brought back good memories. Memories I'd walked away from. Put in a drawer that I forgot to open again. Until now.

The image of Ramona swam up in my head. I pictured us having a life. Doing things. Travelling. Laughing. Kissing. Daydreams. All of them. Just like the ones I used to have there. The anything-is-possible daydreams. So fresh and vivid at one time. Too bad real life keeps chipping away at them until there's nothing left.

Two fishing boats were passing by me now, headed in to the wharf. Most of the boats looked alike. An old guy waved at me. I swore it could have been my father. I waved back. And I suddenly ached. I missed him. I missed him and I missed my mother.

She went first. That summer after I graduated high school. She was diabetic and had taken good care of herself all her life. And my father was always asking, "Did you take your insulin? What's your blood sugar?" He loved her and watched out for her. Then, one day when he was out to sea, something went wrong. She missed her insulin maybe. He was at sea; I was at

Prosper Point. That was why this was coming back. I was out here on the Point with Beth Ann. Maybe if I had been there, I could have done something, got her to the hospital on time. Something.

It destroyed him. My father. Never the same after that. Kept going out fishing, but he must have been charting his own course to disaster. But not before he tore down the house that fall.

I looked across to the little treeless chunk of land called Goat Island. Supposedly, a French ship sank off the coast here a long time ago. Only survivor was a goat, who swam to that island in the sea. A local fisherman found the goat and took it home. Male goat. White one. Sired a couple of dozen baby goats and was locally famous. Too bad no one raised goats anymore around there. There were seals, though. A big, fat family of seals lounged on the ledges off Goat Island and provided a musical soundtrack for my reveries.

Memory is a funny thing. So much I had forgotten, but it was all stashed away. Not at all sure what good any of it did me.

I looked away from the seals and back toward the mainland. Someone was walking this way, picking his way from dry rock to dry rock, over what would be the sea floor a few hours from now. Beth Ann and I had to wade our way back sometimes on those summer days. Came out there to make out and sometimes we forgot all about tides. The moon would tug the sea back toward the land, not really having the slightest bit of concern for horny young lovers. We got wet, soaked on the way back, but we figured it had been worth it, of course. It always was.

The guy coming this way. Couldn't be. But the cap, the red flannel jacket. Brody.

Come to see his old man? Had she finally told him? Or was he just coming to rip me off again? He'd be disappointed. I was broke again. Nothing to do but sit in the sun and see what was up.

He walked to the base of the dirt cliff below me, looked up, didn't say anything. Then he scrambled up toward me, kind of clumsy, getting footholds on protruding rocks and handholds on the roots of scrubby spruce trying to survive on the side of an eroding drumlin.

"Fuck," he said when he got to the top, somewhat out of breath. "Fuck." He plopped down beside me, breathing hard.

I said nothing. Waited. His move. Whatever that might be.

"Was wondering why you were at the house," he said. "Why were you speaking to my mother?"

"We used to know each other."

He nodded. "You tell her about the money?"

"Nope."

He nodded again. "Sorry about that."

"You come out here to give it back?"

He shrugged. "No. Spent it. Kind of guy I am."

"Darn. It was all I had."

"How come you didn't tell her?"

I shrugged.

"Why?"

"Just didn't. Didn't see the point." I looked off toward the seals again, listened to them moan.

"I came to pay you back," he said, reaching in the pocket of his flannel jacket. He held out a baggy with what was unmistakably weed in it. "I brought you this."

I just looked at the bag of weed and gave him my best scowl.

"I'm truly sorry," he said. "I was tempted, you know. All my life, I see a thing I want and I just take it. Guess it's kind of a bad habit."

"You should probably get that fixed."

Brody laughed. My son laughed. He thought I was funny.

He set the baggy down on the ground after making what looked like a little nest for it in the weeds. He took out some Zig-Zags and started to roll a joint.

"Look," I said, "I haven't smoked pot in a long while."

"Pot. That's funny. I haven't heard anybody call it that for a long time."

He concentrated on his work, filling and rolling the most elegant and fattest joint I'd ever seen. "This one is called Tuna Kush. Don't know what that means, but it's very relaxing."

"So, you selling this stuff?"

"A bit. There used to be a pretty good market for it, but now, you know, people can legally grow their own and they can buy it too. Nowhere to buy it here, but you can buy it online. It gets mailed to you just like buying from Amazon. So, not much point me working hard trying to sell it."

"You still enjoy smokin' up, though."

"Yeah, I get a nice buzz. Hey, I've got other goods if you're interested. More powerful stuff."

"No thanks."

"'Kay." He lit the joint with a Bic lighter and took a big hit, handed me the doobie. I took it from him and just stared at it for a second. I didn't really have the slightest desire to get high. But there *he* was. There *I* was. Father and son smoking a joint. It made me smile. How crazy was that? I took my first hit of weed in a long, long time.

I can't say I smoked more than three hits before I felt my head expanding. The seals were singing their mournful tune, the sun was warming the top of my hair in a most benevolent way, and the waves were moving shoreward like tiny dancers.

I felt myself dozing off and thought I'd better say something to keep myself awake. "So," I asked, "how's life here?"

At first Brody looked at me and gave a kind of grunt — half laugh, half snarl. "You really want to know about life here?"

"Yes," I said. "Enlighten me."

"Enlighten you?" he repeated sarcastically and then took another hit from the joint, after which he coughed hard, exhaled smoke, and then broke out into a goofy smile.

"Okay," he said, "you asked for it."

Brody started talking about himself. Told me he was a loner, a screw-up at school. Barely graduated, kept wanting to leave town and go to Toronto, find a stripper there for a girlfriend. Maybe make one big score, one big fat sale, and go legal after that. Put it all behind him and settle down.

Mostly garbage talk. My son, the drug dealer. I wondered how deeply he was involved. Looked like just weed and pills maybe. If his mother could keep him from going to Toronto, he might just survive to be an old man.

"You don't fish?" I asked. "I thought all the men here fished."

"I hate boats. Hate being at sea. But I sell to the lads. They all count on me."

I nodded. "Kind of providing a community service, eh?"

"Something like that."

"Do you read?"

"Read?"

"Books."

"Not really. Why?"

"Just wondering."

"You a big reader?"

"Yep. And a writer. Or was."

"No shit. What do you write?"

"Wrote for a newspaper. Been trying to write a novel."

"You should write screenplays. For movies. That's where the money is."

"Maybe I should give it a try. I'm dead broke."

"Hey, like I said, I'm sorry. If I had the sixty bucks, I'd give it back."

"What happened to it?"

"Beer. I bought beer."

"Good choice."

Brody laughed. It was a stoned laugh. He punched me gently on the shoulder. "Man," he said, "this is really great. Just sitting out here like this, me and you, shooting the shit. Not a soul around to hassle us."

I guess I was stoned too, but he was right. This wasn't bad. Father and son and a bag of weed, sitting atop a dying headland on a warm summer day. I tried to envision a quality in Brody that suggested he had inherited something from me. Certainly not his looks, his body build, or the things he was interested in. All I could detect was that we were both classic screw-ups in our own way and in our own right. And, be that as it may, we were growing closer, even if he didn't know the truth.

15

I was staring off into the sparkling water for several minutes when it occurred to me that this weed we were smoking was maybe ten times more potent than what I'd put in my water pipe back at Dal and King's. I sure hoped that Justin Trudeau knew what he was getting Canada into when he legalized the stuff.

I sat there lost in my thoughts, enjoying the high and the sunshine, letting time slip away. Sure enough, by the time Brody and I could pull enough brain cells together to realize it was time to head back to the mainland, the tide had come up and we had to wade in hip-deep, icy-cold, North Atlantic water back toward the fish shacks and wharf. I think we giggled the whole way.

Brody asked me again if I wanted anything stronger — "on the house," as he put it. But I said no way and told him to be careful.

"Don't worry about me," he said. "Shit happens, but I always seem to come out okay. My mother says I have guardian angels."

"I wish I was so lucky," I said.

I think I had bread and peanut butter for my evening meal. It seemed to do the job. There were messages on the cellphone from someone — Ramona, I supposed. But I couldn't figure out how to retrieve them, even though I'd already listened to one before. I thought of calling her, but was afraid I was too stoned. I was still obsessed with the idea that I would blunder and screw up this good thing.

So I did what any good stoner would do at a time like that. I fell asleep.

Deep, deep asleep. Dope dreams to boot. Some kind of "Kubla Khan" Samuel Taylor Coleridge sort of thing. There were no Abyssinian maids, but there were plenty of underground caves and waterfalls, and there was a lot of weirdness. Like Coleridge, I lost most of it by the time I woke up. In fact, when I awoke, I thought I was still dreaming.

It was still dark. I heard the tires of a car on the gravel outside the door. A car door opened right away and then slammed. Footsteps on the gravel, the door to the shack opening.

"Hello?" It was Ramona.

"In here," I said, groggily.

She flicked on the light and walked into the little bedroom.

"I was worried," she said, her voice a little shrill. "You didn't call me back. You didn't answer the phone."

"Sorry," I offered. "You drove all the way out here at night?"

"I had to. Like I said, I was worried."

I tried to organize a few sensible words to string together. The weed had mostly worn off, but I seemed to have a fuzzy nimbus cloud where my brain once was. "I haven't had anyone to worry about me since my mother stopped fretting about my well-being. But I'm sorry I made you worry."

She took a breath, looked tired and rattled. "Well, I'm here now."

"I missed you."

She walked close to me and put her head on my shoulder then pulled back. "Phew. What were you smoking?"

"I was out on the headland. This guy came along, the one who brought the lobsters, the one who ..." I thought I better not go there. Way too much. Way too soon.

"What lobsters, what guy?"

"Later. Much later. But, yes, Your Honour, I was smoking some mighty powerful weed. Didn't know it came that way."

"Doesn't quite fit the profile I had of you."

"Believe me, it was a one-off thing. I may have my faults, but most of what I know about pot is from old Cheech and Chong movies."

She smiled. Ramona smiled. I wanted to write a song about that smile. I wanted to write a novel about it, make it into a movie. I wanted to take that smile and build a life around it.

"Let's get some sleep," she said. And we fell into bed together, our clothes on, me reeking of weed and peanut butter. Ramona smelling like sweetness and light.

———

In the morning she made breakfast again. Rolf had leaned in through the open window and dropped a freshly caught and filleted mackerel in the sink. He winked at us but didn't say a word.

"I want you to take me out in your fishing boat," she said.

"Okay. If the engine starts. If she seems seaworthy."

"She?" Ramona teased.

"You know a boat is always a she."

"Of course." Her eyebrows went up. "I'm just wondering if you can tell how a man treats a woman by the way he treats his boat."

"I never thought about it. But probably."

"Then I'll be watching."

The weather looked good. I flicked on the radio to the marine weather channel. It brought back a wave of memories. Not all good. But the marine forecast looked just fine. Light north wind. High pressure system stalled on us. Not a cloud between here and Sable Island.

"Oh!" I said. "There was a message from a Dr. Jenkins. About an appointment. What's that about?"

"Nothing," she said. "Just a check-up."

"How did things go back in dirty ole Halifax?"

"The lawyer stuff went okay. Turns out my father's investments did better than we all expected. I have more money than I thought. Too bad he didn't care about his family as much as he cared about his money."

"Sometimes it works out that way. Oh, and Miss Moneybags, thanks for leaving me some cash. That felt kind of like, well, you were looking out for me. Taking care of me."

"I was. I am."

"That doesn't exactly make me a gigolo, does it?"

"No," she said coyly. "Not yet."

Damn, I'd found myself a good woman.

"What'd you do with the money?"

I hesitated. "I lost it," I lied.

"No. Really?"

"Really. I think it blew away."

"Liar. My guess is you spent it on that weed."

"No. The weed was a sort of gift. From that guy who showed up."

"You're a piece of work, you know that? I'm going to have to keep my eye on you."

"Please do. Now, what else can you tell me about your day in town?"

"I visited my mother. She's not doing so well. She wasn't quite sure who I was. We talked mostly about the flowers in the room. I need to do more for her. The home is just great. Expensive, but great. But I'm not being the best daughter in the world. I need to go see her again. Soon."

"I'll go with you. We'll go together."

"Okay. Day after tomorrow. I have more business in town."

"Ah, you're going to drag me back to Halifax."

"You don't have to come if you don't want to."

"I want to. I want to meet your mom."

———————

Some of the men hanging around the wharf gave us the serious once-over as we walked the loose thick planks and hopped onboard *Sheer Delight*. I wasn't sure of my boating skills and was looking for a reason to say I wasn't ready to take her out to sea, but the hull looked solid, the deck was freshly painted, the key was right where Rolf had told me it would be — in an old cigar box in a drawer. And the V8 engine fired up like a dream. We had a full tank of gas and a spare can on deck. I had no excuses.

As the engine idled with a satisfying thrum, I cast off the lines and we began to drift. Then I took the wheel, adjusted the throttle, and we were headed out into the blue Atlantic. I instinctively knew where the channel was, remembered each rocky shoal that could tear the bottom off the boat if you weren't careful. Soon we were passing Goat Island and I pointed out the seals lolling on the rocks like old fat cartoon characters.

I took us two miles out to sea, not so far that I couldn't get us back easily, but far enough to feel we were free of the mainland and in our own private haven of sea and sky and gentle rolling waves.

When I cut the engine it was like another world. The air grew quiet except for the little splashing of wavelets against the hull.

"I can't believe you gave this up for life in the city."

"It ain't always like this, darlin'. Picture a mean November morning, freezing rain, choppy seas, nor'east gale, and you've quickly converted heaven to hell."

"Understood. But this. This is amazing. Being out on the water like this makes everything seem so uncomplicated."

When she said that word, a lot was going through my head. Like Ramona, I was blissed out by the moment, intoxicated with being there at sea with someone like her. But my mind refused to stay in the moment; it kept wandering, and wherever it went there were complications. I had already dipped a toe back into the turbulent waters of the community and people of my youth. Prodigal son returning. Beth Ann. Brody. What else? What happens, I wondered, when that all comes out in the wash?

"Where'd you go?"

"Oops. Sorry. Uncomplicated. You bet."

A seal popped up just then, pushing the head of his shiny wet body up out of the depths. He looked at us directly with those deep dark eyes. Questioning. I remembered that fishermen used to shoot them for fun. Or revenge. Claiming that seals were eating all the cod, reducing their numbers and ruining the amount they could catch. I thought that was all bullshit. Shooting seals I regarded as an example of just how crude and barbarous the men of Stewart Harbour could be.

"*God damn them all,*" Ramona suddenly said. "*I was told we'd cruise the seas for American gold.*"

"*We'd fire no guns, shed no tears* ... and the rest as they say is history. But I don't feel like a broken man anymore. And if you think we'd make good pirates, I'm ready to cruise those seas if you are my shipmate."

"What would we hijack first?" she asked.

"Probably would be one of the big container ships coming this way from Europe."

"That sounds messy. What would we do with all the empty containers once we looted them?"

"You're right. Let's scrap that plan. Think of something else."

"I can think of only one thing." And she nodded toward the little cabin.

At first I thought we were still playing word games. But as she began to unbutton her blouse I could see she was serious.

"It's been a long while," I said nervously. Yes, I was nervous and a tad scared. Did she really want me to make love to her? There on the high seas?

"I'll coach you if you forget how. I'm a really good teacher."

"I thought you were an actor."

"I'll act any way you want. Just let me know."

I swallowed hard. Was I ready for this? Performance anxiety, maybe. I can't say I had fond memories of the sexual encounters I'd had in recent years. There had not been many. I'd lost my edge, lost my interest in the whole routine of going to a downtown bar, meeting a woman looking to get laid, taking her home, doing the deed, and then waking up the next morning to that awkward conversation. After a while, I had decided the whole silly sexual charade just wasn't worth it. But this was different. Dare I say, this was shaping up to be the real thing.

I looked out at the sea, off toward the coastline that was fading from view. "We're drifting," I said.

"Is that bad?"

"Maybe I should toss over the anchor."

"Don't," she said. "Let's drift. What's the worst that can happen?"

"We hit the Gulf Stream and end up in Ireland."

"Sounds like a plan to me," she said, and finally, probably realizing that I was acting more shy and nervous by the minute, she took my hand and led me into the cabin. We sat down on the narrow bed where I'd once lay moaning with seasickness. She continued to undress.

"Is this where I should put up a hand-painted sign reading, 'If the boat is rockin', don't come knockin'?" What a stupid thing to say.

"I think you should just relax," she said as she unzipped my jeans and slid her hands down into my pants.

We kissed and our tongues met. We embraced. It was awkward at first, trying to wrap ourselves around each other on the narrow bed. My shyness, my nervousness, and my modesty suddenly abandoned ship. I lifted her up, tossed the dingy mattress onto the cabin floor, and lowered her onto it.

In my unfinished book, a terse, Hemingwayesque novel of lost idealism, lost identity, lost love, I'd tried more than once to write a decent love scene. It always came out either like a bad

Harlequin passage, a porno paragraph, or a sickly sweet dollop of candied prose. So I won't attempt to describe the next twenty minutes of that glorious day.

Let me just say that we were linked, biologically and emotionally. We were completely in synch at every point, with every move.

Okay. It was just this: it was good. It was great. Afterward, lying there on the mattress on the floor, dizzy from the passion, my first words were, "Thank you."

She lifted herself up on one arm. "You're welcome. But thank you too."

"I feel like I should spend the next ten years thanking you."

"Be my guest," she said. "Are we in Ireland yet?"

16

So, "going to Ireland" became a kind of code to us. Everybody should have their personal code words for things like making love. Yes, I would like to call it that. Making love, not just sex. I wanted to believe there was still such a thing. I had had sex (not all that often, mind you) in recent years, but it had been one hell of a long time since I'd made love — or "gone to Ireland." Thank God for the Gulf Stream.

And yes, we had drifted. Miles and miles from shore. But the compass in the wheelhouse — a real beauty installed there by my father — told me what I needed to know. We had drifted south and west, I was pretty sure. All I needed to do was steer us north and a bit east. Or at least I hoped that would work. If I needed guidance, there was a radio on board and some other electronics, but I really didn't know how to use them.

To the south I could see storm clouds. Time to fire up the old Chevy engine and get us back to shore, back to the so-called real world.

Ramona was in a kind of dreamy, post-coital mood, and she was wearing nothing but my old flannel shirt. "All's well, Captain," she said.

"All's well," I said.

And we really didn't say much after that. In fact, I think we now both felt kind of shy. She walked to me and I put my arm around her beautiful body and held her close as I peered through the cabin window, praying that my instinct was correct and that any minute Nova Scotia would come into view.

"*A man is never lost at sea,*" I said, quoting Hemingway.

She must have recognized it. "They forced us to read *The Old Man and the Sea* back at Armbrae Academy."

"And?"

"I hated it," she said. "I felt sorry for the old man, but I thought it was a dumb story. I especially hated the shark. The shark was like God. He gives you something and then he takes it away. Bit by bit until it's all gone."

"Ouch," I said. "The dark side of Ramona."

"You know what I mean. Time. Aging. I guess I'm thinking about my mother. Somebody should change the rules."

"They should. But don't blame Ernest. He was just an honest novelist."

"No such thing. They're all liars."

"Well, true."

"When are you going to tell me about that novel of yours?"

"Never."

"Why not?"

"I've written three hundred pages and it hasn't gone anywhere yet. My narrator is a whiner instead of a protagonist."

"Let me read it."

"No."

I felt guilty for refusing her and so I focused on looking out the window. It was then that a thin line appeared in the distance where I guessed Nova Scotia would be. I hoped it wasn't my eyes fooling me. As it thickened, I heaved a sigh of relief. Land.

In the days after, I kept wishing that I had made a mistake. I wished that I'd gone in the opposite direction, slipped us over the horizon and taken our chances with those dark clouds, high seas, or whatever else the wet world of the Atlantic could throw at us. I just kept wishing we had not gone back to Stewart Harbour.

But we did.

My seagoing confidence grew large as I saw the first marker buoy at the mouth of the harbour and the farthest tip of Prosper Point called Falcon Head. As we sailed past Goat Island and those lazy, moaning seals, Ramona tucked herself into me. "*O Captain! My Captain!*" she said and slid her hand down into my pants again.

I smiled the kind of smile that indicates a man has lost every worry in the world and has a brain pumped up on serotonin or dopamine or whatever floods into brain cells when you are so happy that you are about to explode.

But I should have listened to the tiny, shrill voice of doom shackled in the back room of my brain instead of drowning in all those hormones of happiness.

I was taking deep breaths. Feeling great. Ramona put her clothes back on and came to stand beside me. She was still acting shy and quiet.

"Shit," I said out loud when I first saw it. The ambulance at the wharf. Its top light flashing.

Ramona looked up. "What is it?"

"An accident of some sort, maybe. Fishermen are always getting injured. Hooks and winches and machinery. Fuck."

The wind was coming up now, shifting so that it was out of the southwest. I had a harder time steering the boat into the wharf than I expected. I could see two paramedics, a man and a woman, aboard one of the fishing boats now. One had an oxygen mask over someone on the deck of the boat. Another was administering CPR.

I struggled with the boat, going forward and reverse, trying to get it docked at the same berth from where we had left. Finally, I bumped it up against the wharf. Ramona threw the rope over a post at the rear of the boat and then at the front. Just like she had done this a thousand times before. I killed the engine, and we both jumped onto the wharf and began walking toward the boat where the paramedics were.

Rolf saw us and came our way, waving for us to stay away.

"Scooter Deacon," he said. "Overdosed on some drug he took. OxyContin, I think. Just stopped breathing."

"He gonna be okay?" Ramona asked.

"I don't know. This drug thing is getting kind of crazy. Scooter's just nineteen. Brian Deacon's youngest kid from that second wife of his."

I remembered Brian. He'd been class president our graduation year in high school. Everybody expected he'd go into politics or get a job at something big. Funny to think that he'd stayed there, became a fisherman like his father. Had a kid who does opioids. "Jesus," I said, "I guess things have changed around here after all."

Ramona was clinging to my arm. I felt her hand squeeze a bit tighter. "Anything we can do?" she asked.

At that moment, I could see that the paramedics had stopped working on Scooter. They lifted him onto a stretcher and with the help of some of the men on the wharf got him off the boat. I could see he was breathing.

"Where the hell would he be getting OxyContin?" I asked. I knew all about kids using all kinds of drugs back in Halifax. I'd written stories about the influx of coke, ecstasy parties, doctors who overprescribed painkillers and other meds. But somehow I always thought that was an urban issue.

"I think you've already made his acquaintance," Rolf said, scratching at his beard.

I was going to say something but stopped myself. Damn.

As Scooter was being loaded into the ambulance, a woman who must have been his mother was getting in with him. There was a man there too, standing by the ambulance pounding his fists on the side and letting out an ungodly roar. I barely recognized him. "Brian?" I asked Rolf.

"Yep."

Brian also tried to get into the ambulance with his son, but the paramedics put up their hands and told him no. Brian looked like he was going to smash the man, but he held back and just stood there with his clenched fists and red face.

The lights continued to flash and the siren let out one loud shriek as the ambulance spit gravel, speeding away.

There was quite a crowd at the wharf now. It seemed like maybe everyone in Stewart Harbour had come out for the action. Brian was still in a rage. He looked around at those who had gathered — fishermen from the wharf, housewives, and kids as well. "What the fuck are you looking at?" he screamed at them.

"He's not the first person to OD here," Rolf told us. "Pretty soon the shit's gonna hit the fan."

I looked at the faces of the people of Stewart Harbour and I thought I could recognize a few. But, more than anything, they reminded me of the people I'd seen gathered at car accidents and tragedies I once covered for the *Tribune*. Concerned faces, yes. But also curious faces. The bad kind of curious. People who want entertainment value from others' tragedies. Fuck 'em all.

Brian was studying those faces. Then he noticed Joe. Joe Myatt was walking away from the wharf toward his truck. Brian locked onto him and started running. The gawkers were still watching as he caught up with Joe, who was just opening the door to his old Ford truck. Brian slammed the door shut and starting cursing at Joe.

I didn't need to hear what he was saying. Nobody did. Brian screamed at Joe. Joe threw his hands up in the air. Brian planted a fist in Joe's face. Joe just tried to cover his head at first, but then he was fighting back. He shoved Brian up against his truck and started punching him hard with piston-like fists. Four men left the crowd of onlookers and ran over to pull Joe off.

"Let's get out of here," Rolf said. "Pretty lady shouldn't have to be exposed to a scene like this."

Rolf put a hand on Ramona's arm and one on mine and began to lead us away from the wharf. I knew that it wasn't Joe that Brian was really after. It was Brody. Brody was nowhere around, but I was pretty sure he was the one who had sold the

Oxy. Unless there was more than one drug dealer working the wharf.

Ramona looked really upset. I mean really upset. I wished so much that we could have missed the drama. Should have stayed at sea.

"I need a drink," Rolf declared when we got back to the fish shack. "Damn! I never got a chance to get to the LC this week."

Ramona took out her car key and hit the remote that opened the trunk of the Lexus. "No problem," she said as the trunk lid lifted.

In the trunk was a case of wine.

"Holy Mother of God," Rolf said, looking like he'd just seen the gates of heaven swing wide open.

"I gotta get me a woman like her," he told me again as Ramona lifted the box of wine from the car and headed for the house.

17

The wine was red and it was from South Africa and the first bottle seemed to empty itself.

"What's with the hard drugs?" I asked Rolf. "It doesn't make sense."

"When does anything make sense?" Rolf said. "Chisel, everyone thinks that it's just the young ones, but it's not. Some of the older guys just go to sea, work hard, make good money, and then want to blow off steam. Used to be a case of Moosehead would do the job. But now the drugs are cheaper and easier to get than the beer. And the game seems to be — what's up next? What do you have that's more powerful than what you had last week?"

"And Brody?"

"Yeah. Brody'll get you whatever you want."

I took a slug of wine and worried. Only three people alive knew that I was really Brody's father — the one who'd brought that little son of a bitch into the world. Me, Beth Ann, and Joe. Not even Brody. Not even Rolf. And, God help me, not Ramona. Did I really have some responsibility there? I was beginning to think it was time to get the hell out of Dodge. Before Ramona found out.

"Someone's gonna get killed," Rolf said. "Could be another one like Scooter or it could be Brody."

"Somebody's gotta do something," I found myself saying.

"Oh, somebody will. But it ain't gonna be pretty."

Rolf left us after that and Ramona and I sat in silence. This whole thing seemed to have hit her pretty hard. "Do you know this Brody?"

I told her about the lobster, about the money. I didn't tell her anything else. I wanted to change the subject. "I think we should go see your mom tomorrow. I'd really like to meet her."

"Sure," Ramona said. "I'd like that."

I tried my best to bring back some of the magic from earlier in the day, but it was no use. And the wine didn't help. We gave it up and walked behind the house to sit on the stones and watch the sun going down across the water. When the sun slipped below the horizon we went back inside.

It was looking like a sombre, quiet, suddenly all-too-sober evening until Beth Ann arrived. I heard the knock on the door and opened it.

"We need to talk," she said.

I didn't know what to say. I let her in.

"This is Ramona," I said. "Ramona, Beth Ann."

Ramona was wide-eyed.

"Hi, honey," Beth Ann said.

I think Ramona winced at the word *honey* but she remained polite. Trying to break the ice, Ramona offered a few kind words about the village and asked Beth Ann some innocuous questions. The two women exchanged a short, decidedly stilted back-and-forth of small talk. Then it suddenly stopped.

Beth Ann turned now and looked directly at me. "Does she know?"

I shook my head.

"Know what?" Ramona asked.

Beth Ann looked at me again. I nodded. It all had to come out, I knew. One way or the other. I figured it was better if I spoke first. "Brody's my son," I admitted. "I'm his biological father."

Sorry, but I don't have the proper adjectives to describe the look on Ramona's face. I don't think anyone in the room was breathing right then.

Beth Ann was first to speak again. She looked straight at Ramona, not me. "Listen, Joe and I raised Brody. After Joe left, I did most of the raising. I take the full responsibility for how he turned out. Brody doesn't even know who his real father is. But that doesn't really matter. Joe and I knew what we were getting into and it really didn't matter to us, well not at first, who the real father was. Truth is, after a few years, we never expected to see Charles ever again. Family all gone here. Not a trace. Kind of a shock to see him back here."

"But now I'm here," I said. What label could you put on me at that moment? Deadbeat dad? Father of a monster? Ill-fated, stupid-ass man who chooses the perfectly wrong time and place to be?

I was wondering if Ramona was about to jump back into her Lexus and make a run for it again. I wouldn't blame her.

Instead, she took Beth Ann's hand and then gave her a hug. Beth Ann began to sob and a tear fell down her cheek before she pulled away.

"You have to do something," Ramona said to me.

"Talk to him," Beth Ann said, wiping her face with a Kleenex. "You tell him who you really are. Tell him why he's got to stop what he's doing. I've talked to him. Joe's talked to him. When that didn't work, Joe beat the crap out of him. But he doesn't listen. He thinks he's untouchable. He's been accused before, but he's never even been charged. And he just won't stop."

I remembered what Rolf had said. Yeah, someone was going to get killed there.

The funny thing about that moment was, I was remembering the afternoon of smoking weed with Brody, getting high with my son, and I really liked him. We had, in our own stoned way, bonded. I had to at least talk to him.

"Where is he?" I asked.

"Home watching television."

"Does he know what happened today?"

"He knows. Says it wasn't his fault. Says he explained to Scooter what was a safe amount to take. Says that it was Scooter's own damn fault for never doing what he's told." Beth Ann threw her keys at me. "Take my truck. Better if I'm not there."

We all have zombie moments in our lives and this was one of mine. I caught the keys. I held them in my hand. I walked out the door in slow motion, leaving behind the first real girlfriend I ever had and Ramona to get acquainted with each other while I drove off to give my son the first serious disciplinary lecture he'd had from his real father.

Brody was watching a movie when I walked in. I didn't knock. I recognized the film. *127 Hours* with James Franco. "Good film?" I asked by way of salutation.

He nearly jumped out of his skin. "Jesus, man!" Brody said. "What are you doing here?"

I sat down across from him, grabbed the remote, and switched off the TV. Brody looked nervous now. Scared maybe. Then he gave a little hint of a smile like this was some kind of joke. "No. Really, man, what's up?"

So I told him who I was and how he came into the world. I told him I didn't know all these years about it, but that I was still one of the world's biggest assholes and had a plaque on my wall at home that said so.

He wasn't nearly as shocked as I thought he would be. In fact, he laughed out loud. "I knew it, man. I knew all along that Joe Myatt was not my real father. I could feel it in my bones." He got up and walked around the room. "This explains quite a bit. But why are you telling me this now?"

"Your mother asked me to talk to you."

"She's always yammering away at me about something, but I don't pay that much attention to her."

"You should. She's a wise woman."

"So where did you two do it? In a car? Out in the woods?"

"It was my old bedroom. One afternoon. No one else was at home."

He puffed out a little burp of a laugh. "Too bad the old place is torn down. I'd like to go there and take a look at the scene of the crime, so to speak."

"Yeah, too bad."

Then I got to the point. Yes, he knew what happened to Scooter. And yes, he had warned him. In fact, given him a serious lecture. "You see, this was some new stuff," he said. "It wasn't really just Oxy. It was mixed with some new shit. Fentanyl. Comes from China. Dirt cheap and it puts a real pop onto whatever it's mixed with. You just have to go light on how much you take. I told him that."

"But Scooter didn't listen?"

"Scooter never listens to anyone. That's his problem."

"And you don't feel responsible?"

"I feel bad, yeah. But you know, *buyer beware*. If he didn't buy it from me, someone else would come along and sell the shit. Hey, I would have been happy to keep selling weed for the rest of my life. But Justin fucking Trudeau came along and legalized bud and I got to keep up with the times."

"Even if it kills someone."

"Scooter didn't die. He just fucked up."

It was like talking to a brick wall, as my father used to say when he lectured me. I began to see that Brody really didn't hold himself to blame. And he couldn't get it into his head that someone, primarily Brian Deacon, might take it upon himself to come seek revenge.

"I think, given the circumstances, that you should take a little vacation."

The smirk. The laugh. "Great," he said. "Where to?"

I pulled a key out from my pocket. The key to my rathole apartment. "Halifax," I said. "Go stay at my apartment for a bit."

"Really?"

"Really."

Brody reached out and took the key. I told him the address. Then I watched as he put on his running shoes and picked up a grey hoodie. He looked at me with a crooked grin. "Thanks, Dad," he said. "Tell Mom I won't be home for dinner."

And he was gone. I listened as his truck pulled out of the driveway and I sat there, stunned. Totally stunned at what had just happened. I flicked on the TV and saw James Franco, still trapped in a deep Utah chasm with his fingers locked in place by the rock that wedged them to the wall. The words on the screen said he'd been stuck there for seventy hours.

18

O kay, so I probably was not thinking entirely rationally. It was a short-term solution that would probably come back to bite me in the ass. But I at least got him out of town before he killed someone or someone killed him. I'd read about how many people were dying from overdoses of fentanyl in Vancouver. It wasn't that they wanted to die. They just didn't know they were taking a drug many times more powerful than what had been on the street before. Buyer beware was not good enough.

And I really didn't care if I ever lived in my old apartment again. Rent was overdue. I didn't know how long my kindly landlord would let me hang on to it without paying. Maybe Brody would have a party and trash the place. Maybe he'd try to set up shop and deal in the city. If so, that would definitely get him killed. Dealers guarded their turf and would make short order of a wharf rat like Brody.

Hell. The guy was a walking accident waiting to happen.

All this and more was on my mind as I drove Beth Ann's truck back to the wharf, grinding the gears like a high-school kid with a learning permit. *Shit. Fuck.* I said the words out loud. The windshield was not the least offended. What next?

I reluctantly opened the creaky door to the fish shack. There was Beth Ann and Ramona sitting at the bare wood table drinking tea. I could not read the look on either of their faces.

"Tea?" Ramona asked.

"Please."

Ramona looked around the sink but couldn't find another cup. She poured me some tea from the old cracked teapot into an old jam jar. I sat on a wooden crate and sipped it Japanese-style. I explained that I'd packed Brody off to Halifax.

"Did you convince him to stop selling drugs?" Beth Ann asked.

"I tried. I don't think I got through. But at least I got him out of Stewart Harbour for a bit."

"Brian won't let it go. He and Joe already had a bad thing going. Both of them had a hate-on for each other."

The tea was bitter. Right at this moment, life was bitter. And just a few hours ago, it had all been so sweet.

"Brody has to be stopped," Ramona insisted.

"I know that. I just don't know how."

"Problems have solutions," Ramona added.

Beth Ann got up. "I'll leave you two alone. Ramona, it was good getting to know you. I'm gonna go find Joe, if he hasn't had his face bashed in, and see what he has to say about this. But he and Brody don't really talk much, so I doubt he has any clout. Still, he helped me raise the kid when he was little."

Beth Ann looked tired. There was a hint of defeat in her voice. A weariness in her eyes. She pulled the door closed behind her as she left and then drove off.

A numbing silence fell over the room. Ramona nailed me to the wood I was sitting on with a look. I was expecting anger, rage maybe. I stared at the Lexus keys on the table. All she had to do was pick them up and drive off. That would be the end of it.

Instead, Ramona cleared her throat and gave me a hard look. "I find it hard to believe you never found out that you had a son all these years."

"I didn't know until we came back here," I said in my own defence, the voice echoing in my head like that of a guilty little boy.

Ramona just looked at me.

"It's true. Beth Ann and Joe were the only ones who knew. And they told no one."

"This is a weird little place you grew up in."

"You don't have to tell me that."

She picked up the keys and threw them to me. "Let's get out of here. I think I need to sleep in my own bed tonight."

Not more than ten minutes later we were driving across the causeway, past Beth Ann's house and headed back toward Halifax.

"I like her," Ramona said, breaking the silence. "She's had it tough, but she's made a life of it. She stuck with it."

"I don't know what was wrong with me. Leaving like I did. Never looking back. How could anyone do that?"

"You did. So do a lot of men. Women too, probably."

"There should be some kind of law," I said.

It got me a hint of a smile. "Like that would work."

"How come *you* didn't just get up and leave *me* back there. Look at the rat's nest I got you into."

"That's a good question. In fact, after hearing what Beth Ann had to say, I almost did. I would have been gone before you got back."

"But?"

"But she talked me out of it. She said she still believes you have a good heart. She forgave you a long time ago. I think it was the first real heart-to-heart conversation I've had with a woman in a long time."

"Thank you," I said. "Thanks for not ditching me and riding off into the sunset."

"I think Beth Ann convinced me to stick it out. There's plenty of exits if I need them. But maybe you'll need me around for moral support. You seem to be up to your earlobes in shit."

"I love the image. I believe it describes my situation perfectly. And I would appreciate the moral support, but you might get your hands dirty in the process."

"And I'll have to put up with the stink."

"I think we should leave the metaphor there and not pursue it," I countered. "But here I am again, totally dependent on you. No money. No place to stay now that I gave Brody my key."

"See. That's why I can't just hoist up my anchor and leave. You need an ally. But promise me you'll find Brody tomorrow and talk to him again. Convince him to give up selling."

"I will," I said, although I was pretty sure it wouldn't do any good.

"But first we have to visit my mother."

"Yes."

"And you have to be nice to her even if she doesn't make sense."

"Hey, I was a newspaperman, remember. I interviewed dozens of politicians. Most of them didn't make much sense, but I always gave them the time of day."

"That's the spirit."

We had dinner at the pub in Porters Lake. It was quiet. The food was okay. Our table was by the door and there was a near constant parade of smokers leaving the video gambling room, going outside for a smoke, coming back in with a desperate look on their faces as they prepared to squander whatever weekly wages had come their way. The look on Ramona's face was what I'd call quiet resolve.

"What's going to become of your mom?" I asked. I was trying to prepare myself for tomorrow.

"It's all downhill. It's a form of dementia and it doesn't just go away. And it doesn't really get cured. Hers started to come on when she was only in her fifties. Her name's Brenda, by the way. She likes to hear the sound of her name, but sometimes she forgets it. She forgets many things and she gets mixed up easily so work with it."

"Well, I forget things and get confused easily so we already have a lot in common."

Now Ramona gave the look. The look I was getting familiar with. A pursing of the lips (those beautiful lips) that said I was an idiot, my joke was idiotic, but despite all that, she thought I was cute and funny. Yes, that was what that look meant. I was sure of it.

―――――

Her apartment was as luxurious as I expected. Clean, neat, opulent. Movie star digs. We were both very tired. She took a bath while I thumbed through some of her books, reading passages here and there out of context.

When she came out, she had a robe on and her hair was still wet. I couldn't read her look this time. "Want me to sleep on the sofa?" I asked.

"No," she said. "Keep me company."

I showered and soon we were in bed. But it was nothing like the afternoon. We were both dead tired and drifted off to sleep quickly, more like brother and sister than lovers.

―――――

Brenda Danforth did not look like a woman with dementia. She looked much like Queen Elizabeth, in fact, which rather startled me. She looked old, but she was elegant and well dressed, and had excellent posture for an old woman.

"Mom, this is Charles," Ramona said. And I almost laughed. Because of my name, that is. Because of the association I had just made with the queen of England. And because of what the queen had named her son.

"Nice to meet you, Mrs. Danforth."

"Call me Brenda," she said, looking me directly in the eye.

I was beginning to think Ramona had tricked me. Her mother seemed completely coherent. But then things quickly began to change.

"I'm expecting company today," she said. "My daughter is coming by."

Ramona waved at her. "That would be me."

"Oh, yes. Of course," Brenda said, with a hint of doubt in her eyes.

"Charles is a writer," Ramona told her.

Brenda's eyelids lifted. "An author?"

"More like a reporter. A journalist. Or was."

"But you have a love of language."

"Yes, I do have that."

"Have you read the classics?"

"Some."

"The Russians? Tolstoy? Dostoevsky? Gogol, Solzhenitsyn?"

"Yes, yes, no, and yes," I responded.

"They're all very dark and dreadful, are they not?"

"Mostly," I admitted. Most of my reading of the likes of Dostoevsky was back at Dal, when I was honing my skills at being pretentious. As I grew older, I lost my skill set in that department.

"I listen to a lot of audiobooks now," Brenda offered. "The words are like music to my ears."

I thought we were doing pretty good with the small talk, and I was keeping up my end of it nicely, but then there was another shift. She looked away out the window and then back at me. Her face lit up. "Trevor," she said. "You finally came back to visit your old mother."

I looked at Ramona. I wasn't sure what to do. I knew there had been a brother and he was dead.

"It's good to see you," I said. "How are you doing?"

"I'm doing much better now that you're here. Who is that with you?" she asked, nodding toward her daughter.

"Ramona," I said.

"Ah, yes," Brenda responded, but I don't think she recognized her. "How are things in Montreal?" she asked me.

"Good. Life is good in Montreal."

"And how are things at the university?"

"Just great. I have good grades."

"That's my boy. Keep it up." She turned toward Ramona and asked, "Could you please get me some water?"

"Sure, Mom." Ramona got up and walked into the small bathroom.

Brenda leaned toward me and whispered, "Who did you say she was?"

"Ramona," I whispered back. "Your daughter."

"But I don't have a daughter. At least I don't think so."

Ramona returned with a pink plastic cup and handed her mother the water. She sipped it loudly.

"Mom," Ramona said, trying to re-establish contact, "I'm going to try to come visit more often. I'm sorry I haven't been around as much as I should have."

"Oh, that's okay, dear. It's always nice to have visitors, though."

There was a quiet spell just then. I kind of tuned out while Ramona tried to continue to make small talk with her mother, asking about meals, health, prompting her to remember things from when Ramona had been young.

In the midst of it, Brenda turned back to me as if just seeing me for the first time. Her facial expression suddenly changed dramatically. "Goddamn it, Stanley," she spit out at me. "Where have you been? What have you been up to?"

"This is not who you think it is," Ramona insisted. Brenda remained angry.

Ramona leaned toward me. "Stanley was my father. Things did not go well in their final years."

"Do you still only think about money?" Brenda asked me accusingly. An odd question to ask a man who is totally broke. I thought it best not to play along on this one. I could pretend to be a son but not a husband, one who was obviously disliked by his own wife.

Ramona turned toward her mother. "Stanley is not here. This is Charles."

That confused her. She studied my face again. "I thought it was Trevor."

"Charles," I repeated gently.

Her puzzlement gave way to a slight hint of a smile. "Of course. You always said you wanted to change your name."

I nodded and let go a little nervous laugh.

Ramona drew her back into a conversation about the staff and the nursing home and her favourite TV shows. I faded into the background as best I could, and after about forty-five minutes, with Brenda getting tired, we left. We helped her lie down on the bed. A nurse showed up shortly and said, "She usually has a nap around this time of day."

Ramona kissed her on the cheek and asked me to do the same. I dutifully kissed Brenda lightly on her powdered cheek and we made our exit.

We went for coffee at the Just Us! coffee shop on Spring Garden Road. It was busy in there and noisy and I liked the hustle and bustle after the oppressive quiet of the nursing home.

"Tell me about Trevor," I said.

Ramona held her cup with two hands and stared into it. "Trevor was a lot like you. Maybe that's what my mom detected in you. He loved to read and he loved words. He wrote poetry, had some published in Montreal literary magazines. He went to McGill to study literature. Wanted to be a university prof. Wanted to write books. I think he started a novel once or twice like you did. He was the sensitive type. Too sensitive. Got in with a girl from Laval. I don't think he'd ever been in love before. But she wasn't good for him."

"What do you mean?"

"She was like us. She had a habit of just walking away."

"We should all have a sign stitched on our shirts. *Beware of this one. Heartbreaker.* Something like that."

"He didn't commit suicide. It wasn't like that."

"What happened?"

"Drug overdose. Not OxyContin, not fentanyl. But it was some kind of opiate. Some kind of mix of things. I'm sure he didn't know what he was taking. But my mother and father started to come apart after that. Maybe it had already begun. But things were never quite the same with them after that and my father started spending more time at his work and away. I wasn't much help, off trying to chase my own celluloid dreams."

"So that drama back in the harbour must have brought back bad memories."

"It did. I tried to hold it together. When Beth Ann told me about you and about her son, I secretly hoped someone would find Brody and beat the living daylights out of him. Sorry."

"I'll do whatever it takes to get him to stop."

"Promise me?"

"Yes, I promise," I said, although I didn't then know what I was promising to do.

"Thank you. And, if you don't mind, I don't want to speak any more about my brother."

"Okay. Let's change the subject."

"Oh. But there is one more thing. I lied to you."

"About?"

"About my father. He's not dead. He's very much alive, the bastard."

19

The coffee shop seemed to empty just about then. The room grew quiet and I felt like I had yet again been thrown into another dimension.

"After my brother died," Ramona continued, "things started going badly for my parents. I went into a period of depression myself and started taking antidepressants. But they screwed up my acting. And I didn't feel like myself. So I stopped, let the pain sweep over me, and, yes, it eventually began to fade. I got on with my life. But I was beginning to see that the whole acting thing was not the dream vocation I thought it was.

"But my mother was trying to put Trevor's death behind her somehow and threw herself into charity work. My father, meanwhile, had created a little real estate empire and had other investments. He started travelling a great deal as part of his work. And when they were together, they fought. Each blamed the other for something they did wrong in raising Trevor, I think.

"And then my mother started to show symptoms of early-onset dementia. I didn't think anything of it at first. She'd always been absent-minded, forgetful, a bit quirky with her way of doing things. By the time it was finally diagnosed, my father already had one foot out the door."

"How old was she at the time?"

"Only fifty-four. I didn't know such a thing could happen. And my father refused to accept that it was a medical condition. Besides, he was already at work on firming up the classic male cliché. He had found another woman. A younger one, of course. Someone who liked him for his cash."

"Did they divorce?" I asked, hoping to sound sympathetic.

"No, they didn't. My father was just away more and more. My mother claimed she didn't care. She was happier when he was gone. I eventually moved back to Halifax. My father moved to Toronto to be closer to the big money. The other woman was soon replaced by a second and a third. There was a trust fund to take care of Mom and me. There was never a divorce. Mom got worse. I did a bit of modelling again since it wasn't as stressful as acting. But I grew to hate it. Standing around in those lights. Posing. Pouting. Pretending."

"But you don't talk to your father."

"No. I tried for a couple of years. But I hated him. He'd walked away when she needed him most."

"I guess some men can be pretty callous."

"Actually, the way he treated us really coloured my feelings toward men in general. I found myself being attracted to women again. But I soon came to the conclusion that men and women are pretty much the same when it comes to faithfulness and loyalty."

"Is that what you want? Faithfulness. Loyalty? Did you ever think of getting a dog?"

"Idiot."

"Sorry."

"Yes, it is." And then she paused. "Well, now you know more of the story. What do you think?"

"What do I think about what?"

"About me. About my situation."

"Well, I think you have wounds that haven't fully healed, but then you seem to have gotten on with your life."

"No. That's just it. I didn't get on with my life. I stalled some-where along the way."

"You had all that guilt money to live on, so why worry about a career or anything else?"

"Because it always felt like something was missing. And then you came along."

That last line threw me. "I didn't exactly come along. I was just standing there minding my own business."

"But you were there at the moment I was about to break out of my shell."

"Two lost souls on a Halifax pier."

"Something like that. I was drawn to you. I don't know why."

"Right time, right place. Right stranger staring into the fog."

"Yes, I thought you looked lost. I wanted to help."

"I think I read it somewhere on the internet. If you want women to like you, see if you can arouse their pity."

"Maybe there's something to that. You did look lost. You looked like you needed a friend. And I needed something too. I needed to walk out of my comfortable dead-end life."

"But then you stumbled into my suddenly complicated coastal world of fish, drugs, and fucked-up folks."

"Yes. And that was not what I expected."

"But now that we're rooting around in each other's sordid past, what next?"

"The past always, always catches up with us. I don't think my father has figured that out, even now. He never comes back to visit. I've cut off communication with him."

"But the money is still there."

"Yes. The bloody trust fund. A well-invested trust fund that seems to keep growing, even though Mom's nursing care is paid for and I can dip into it whenever I want."

"Poor little rich girl."

"That's exactly what I say every morning when I look in the mirror."

The coffee shop was completely empty now except for Ramona and me. And it was like a scene from some movie. What was it? Not a romantic comedy. Not a tragedy. Not an action thriller, that's for sure. Something independent. A tad melodramatic. But not exactly predictable.

The silence was suddenly deafening. "Do you think there's any chance we could make this last?" she asked. "I don't want to use the word *love* so soon, but —"

I held up my hand to stop her right there. There was something in her eyes I didn't understand, but I didn't really care what it was. "Yes, Ramona. Whatever you need. Whatever you want. I think I already do ... love you, I mean." And as soon as the words were out, I knew this was not acting. This was what my heart forced my mouth to say.

It wasn't the classic *Do you love me?* But it was one hell of a line. There was a director somewhere — the barista maybe — looking my way, waiting for me to deliver the line of the big scene in the movie.

Maybe I was expecting some great romantic moment to follow, some clever, sexy comeback line, the next invitation to hop into her posh Halifax sack and make love. But it didn't play out that way.

"Then you need to do something for me," she said.

It was some kind of test. Bring it on. "Okay. What?"

"You need to make sure Brody never sells another pill, another bag of coke, any other drug ever again. You need to do this for my mom, do this for Trevor, and do this for me."

20

After we went back to Ramona's apartment, she told me she had a couple more appointments in the afternoon. She gave me a key to the place and said I would be on my own for the afternoon. After lunch she took a shower and then was gone, leaving me with a kiss on my cheek and a squeeze of my hand. Then she put her car keys in my hand again. "I can walk to where I need to be. Take the car for a spin. Go down to Point Pleasant Park or something."

I had this feeling that something wasn't quite right between us. I'd met her mother, she'd filled in some gaps in her life, admitted to lying to me, taken me many miles deeper into her tangled life, and then delivered a kind of ultimatum. And it was just that. It was an ultimatum, not a request. It seemed strange for her to leave me like that. I didn't like the feel of it. Had I been coyly manipulated yet again by an attractive woman? Or had she stated something so obvious that it had to be done?

I tried to psych myself up for the impending father and son talk, but I knew it was not going to go well. I had detected a stubbornness in Brody, a willfulness, a naive certainty that whatever selfish and destructive actions he took in life, he'd wiggle free and go about his life just like before. No one had ever put the proverbial fear of God in him. There simply was no God or replacement for God in his life. I had brought a boy into the world who thought of drug dealing as a noble profession. Now I had to teach my boy a life lesson that would stick. And I was not the slightest bit prepared to do it effectively.

At first Brody did not come to the door of my old apartment when I knocked. I could hear music inside, some kind of loud rap music, the sort of gangsta rap that always made me squirm and yearn for the days when lyrics meant something and there was such a thing as melody. I knocked louder. Still no answer. I tried the door handle and it was not locked.

Brody was nowhere in sight. The place was a mess. He'd thrown my mattress on the floor for some reason and there were books scattered around. I could tell Brody was not exactly the model house guest. It was a small apartment so it wasn't long before I discovered him. He was lying naked in the tub taking a bath. He nearly jumped out of his skin when I walked in.

"Holy fuck, man! What are you doing here?"

"C'mon, Brody. Put some clothes on. We need to talk."

"Perv," he countered, standing up and reaching for my old bathrobe hanging from a nail on the wall.

I walked into the living room, turned off the music, and waited for him to come out of the bathroom.

"Nice tattoos," I said, referring to the death mask I'd seen on his chest.

"You should see the one on my ass."

"No, thank you. Please, I just had lunch."

"Why are you here? I thought you were staying back in Stewart Harbour."

"Had some visiting to do here in town."

"Guess you want your apartment back. I hate to tell you, but this place is a dump. And the people who live here are creepy."

"I always thought the neighbours were nice."

"Some don't have teeth. Some of them like to shout at two a.m., and the kids are like little weasels running up and down the stairs."

"But they're truly nice when you get to know them."

"No thanks."

"So how do you like it here in the big city?"

Brody did that signature snort laugh of his. "The truth is, Halifax has been good to me. But I might as well get going. I got a little business deal to finish up and I'm gonna head back later this afternoon."

"What kind of business deal?" I asked.

"The kind you don't want to know about."

"Brody, you gotta quit what you've been doing."

"And do what?"

"You saw what happened to Scooter."

"That wasn't my fault. Besides, if he didn't get the stuff from me, he'd get it somewhere else."

"You don't care that you gave him something that nearly killed him?"

What Brody said next really threw me. He gave me a half-smile. "Not really."

This from the damn kid who was my son. I knew then that Ramona was right. Someone had to stop him.

"What if Scooter's father decides he wants revenge for what you sold to his son?"

Brody gave me another half-grunt of a laugh and walked over to my dresser drawer. He lifted out a small gun, a Ruger, not much bigger than the size of his hand. He held it up. "Like I said, Halifax has been kind to me." The kid was full of surprises.

"What can I say to get you to stop dealing?"

"You can't say nothing," he said flatly, pointing the gun at a lamp. "Instead, you can kiss my hairy tattooed ass." And then he playfully pointed the gun at me and pulled the trigger. I heard the click of the Ruger. Thankfully there was no bullet. He saw the look of shock on my face.

"Don't worry, man. I couldn't kill you. You're my father, remember? That would be, um, what's the word for it?"

"Patricide," I said.

"Oh, really. I thought it was revenge."

"I'm gonna leave now. Get rid of the gun, Brody. Before someone gets hurt. Go home and be good to your mother if you can and come up with a plan for your life."

Brody just stood there, looking at me. "Nice lecture, Pop. Hey, I'll be nice and clean the place up before I go. Maybe leave you a little present. And I do appreciate the sentiment and all, but don't worry about me. I got this far, didn't I, without your help or anybody else's."

He flipped me the key to my apartment. "I'll lock up on my way out later. Thanks."

21

I called Ramona from the car. She answered in a hushed tone.
"I need to drive out of town this afternoon. Can you come with me?"

"No. I told you I have appointments."

"Can't you break them?"

"No. What's so important?"

I told her about my encounter with Brody. I didn't mention the gun, but I told her I knew I hadn't succeeded at persuading him to quit dealing.

"What are you going to do?"

"I'm gonna make him stop."

"How?"

I tapped the phone's off button. I was hoping she'd think we were cut off. It rang again almost instantly. I didn't answer it. The *how* part was still troubling me. I had thought maybe Ramona would come with me and together we would sort out Plan B. But she had her appointments and I had to do something. Anything. I was pretty sure Brian Deacon would be on the lookout for Brody as soon as he was back in Stewart Harbour.

I opened my wallet and found the business card that Tom, the Mountie from Musquodoboit, had given me. I called him and he answered on the third ring.

"Tom, it's Charles Howard."

The name didn't seem to register.

"Uh, huh," he said and then paused.

"The deer thing, remember?"

"Of course. What's up?"

"Are you on duty this afternoon?"

"Yup. In my cruiser on the road until seven tonight. Why?"

"Can I meet you in, say, an hour?"

"Sure. But I'd like to know what this is about."

"I need your help," was all I said.

He didn't say anything at first. Then he said, "Okay. Meet me by the old train in town here. In an hour."

I shut the phone off and tossed it in the back seat. I nervously drove through the city traffic, jammed up because of construction, and crossed the MacKay Bridge, heading east yet again. I hit red for every light on my way through Dartmouth. I got gas at the Esso station in Cole Harbour and drove on.

Tom was waiting for me in the parking lot by the train museum. That old train looked sadder and rustier than the time I drove by before. I got out of the Lexus and tried to open the passenger door of the patrol car, but it was locked. Tom was looking at me warily as he rolled the window down. "You gotta sit in the back if you want to talk. Rules."

I sat in the back, behind the bars separating us. The doors locked when they shut. It was like I was being arrested.

"What's this about?" he asked.

So I told him about Brody. "He'll be coming through here sometime soon. I want you to arrest him."

"What did you say he was dealing?"

"I'm not sure what he has now. But he's been selling OxyContin and I think it's been cut with fentanyl." I explained about Scooter's overdose. I explained that Brody felt invincible. I didn't tell him about the gun. I was hoping that my Mountie friend would be as gun shy around Brody as he was around an injured animal. And then I added, "And by the way, Brody is my son."

I think it took a while for it to sink in. Tom sat there tapping his fingers on the steering wheel. "We had a call yesterday. I didn't take it but I heard the story. Woman from down your way called and told us the same thing. She wanted us to arrest her son. But she said he wasn't around. She was asked if she had any evidence about him dealing and such, but she said she didn't. We told her to call back when he returned, but she never called back. We wrote it off as a crank call. Mother pissed off at her little boy."

"Do you remember what her name was?"

"I think she was a Myatt. A lot of Myatts down that way."

"That's Brody. She raised him. But I wasn't around. He didn't take my name."

"Look, I can't just go stopping cars on impulse or anything. I need to get someone to authorize it."

"I'd rather you didn't. This is me calling in a favour. Look, he'll be coming by here sometime this afternoon. I'll sit here in my car and watch. Call you when I see him. You stop him and if he's clean, this never happened. If he's not, I'll be there to make sure he doesn't do anything stupid."

"What do you mean by that?"

"I mean like run off or something."

Tom pondered all this. "Okay. Look. I have some paperwork to do back at the office, so I'm right around the corner. You see him, you call me. Same number. I'll catch up with you and I'll stop him and see what he's up to. And that's it. Game over."

"Thank you," I said. And I heard the lock click. I opened the door and got out.

―――――――――

If you'd driven by that afternoon you might have seen a nervous-looking guy parked in front of a rusty train engine that had seen much better days. He was looking at every pickup truck that passed by and praying that everything was going to turn out all right.

It was late afternoon when I saw Brody's truck rolling toward me on the highway. I was parked behind the train so he'd be unlikely to spot me. I waited for him to pass by to make sure it was him. As he slowed near the intersection for traffic, I could see that one of his tail lights wasn't working. That helped.

Tom took my call on the first ring. I told him Brody was headed east from Musquodoboit on 7 and that one of his tail lights was out. I gave him the licence plate number I had written down.

"Okay," he said, not sounding at all like this was something he wanted to do. I started up the car and took off in slow pursuit of my son. I was pretty sure he was headed straight home to Stewart Harbour, but I wanted to be sure we didn't lose him. Like in the movies, I stayed behind two cars and it was easy enough to keep a bead on him. All the while, I was thinking about that damn gun he'd bought in Halifax. Gone were the days when you had to go over the border into Maine to get your mitts on a handgun.

The cellphone was ringing and I could see it was Ramona. I didn't answer.

About ten minutes into it, I saw the Mountie car pass vehicles and come up behind me. When he passed me, he looked over and nodded. I could still see the doubt in his face. But not more than a minute later, he had his lights flashing and had pulled Brody over. I guess I could have just kept on going, kept my nose out of it, and if he was busted, no one would be the wiser that I was involved.

But I was involved. I got Tom into this and, while I didn't have any real plan of action, I knew I needed to be on hand. So I pulled up behind the police car and watched as Tom walked up to the truck window. There would be the classic tail light story for starters.

I watched as Brody protested. I got out and walked toward them as Tom was asking him to get out of the truck. Brody saw me and was furious.

"What the hell?" he shouted. "What the fucking hell?"

Brody was out of the truck now, but cursing and elbowing the Mountie. Suddenly, he took a swipe at Tom, but Tom ducked out of the way. Nonetheless, I could tell that Tom wasn't used to this sort of thing. I was beginning to think I had gotten him in over his head. Tom was having a hell of a hard time as he tugged Brody toward the police cruiser and tried to get his hands behind him.

I scooted past them and leaned into the truck cab. The gun was there in the glove compartment. I stuffed it into my pants pocket. I looked around for the drugs. Not in the cab. I could hear Brody shouting, "I didn't do anything," sounding like a little kid. *My kid who I'd never been around to help raise.*

I looked under the seat. Nothing. Shit.

Tom had Brody handcuffed now and was pushing his head down as he shoved him into the back of the car where I had once sat. Kid in a cage now. Seething. Hating me.

Tom gave me a look. A what-have-you-gotten-me-into look. I shrugged. There was a tool box in the back of the truck. It was locked, but there was a hammer back there too. I smashed the lock and opened it. A package of something. Brown paper wrapping. I tore part of it off. It looked like flour. But I knew what it was. I figured I was breaking at least ten rules of legal protocol, but I convinced myself I had to do this to get the job done.

Tom tried to look calm as he walked toward me, Brody now safely locked in the back-seat cage. I showed Tom what I'd found. He shook his head and took it. Brody was looking at me now, screaming something unintelligible. He'd never, ever forgive me. So much for father and son reunion. I stood there by the side of the road as Tom got behind the wheel and drove Brody away, the kid still screaming at me through the window.

And there I was again, standing alone by the side of Highway 7 in the middle of nowhere. Alone. But this time with a gun in my pocket. I rolled up the window of the truck and left the keys on the seat. The Mounties would have it towed. I needed to get back to Halifax.

22

I hit rush-hour traffic on the way into Halifax. I called Ramona and told her I was on my way.

"Where have you been?" she asked.

"I'll tell you when I get there. Let's go somewhere for a beer."

"Meet me at the Split Crow," she said. "Happy hour."

Not exactly what I had in mind. But I wanted to see her. Badly. I wanted her to hear my confession and confirm I did the right thing. The only thing.

I left the gun under the car seat. Glove compartment seemed too obvious. Where do criminals usually hide their weapons? What does it say in the handbook? Me and guns. Seems we kept running into each other. Before I got out, I pulled the Ruger out from under the seat and checked it. Damn. It was loaded. And the safety hadn't even been on. Somebody could have been killed. I clicked the safety and stashed it back under the seat, not sure if I should tell Ramona about it. Tom hadn't seen it. One less thing Brody could be charged for.

It was crowded in the Split Crow. Mostly college-age kids. I'd been one of them once. Saturday afternoon. Tables full of twelve-ounce glasses of beer, sunlight glinting in through the glass, rowdy crowds singing to a pop song on the sound system.

"Sorry I put so many miles on your car," I said by means of salutation.

"Now you gonna tell me where you went?"

"I went back down the Shore," I said, "to have my son arrested." And I told her about the stakeout, about Tom, about the arrest, and about Brody watching me through that window from the back seat of a cop car with a look that said he hated me more than anyone he'd ever hated in his life.

"But you did the right thing."

"Did I?" I had real doubts. What if he had pulled out that damn gun?

"If you couldn't convince him, you did the *only* thing you could do."

"It's gonna get messy." Messy wasn't the half of it.

I pulled the phone that Ramona had given to me out of my pocket. I dialed the number.

Beth Ann answered on the second ring. "Hello?"

"Beth Ann, it's Charles."

"Charles?"

"Brody's been arrested," I blurted out. "I had him arrested."

A tableful of enthusiastic young men and women suddenly shouted out and cheered. A TV was on, a hockey game and somebody scored. Life went on. As the roar subsided, I waited to take whatever Beth Ann was going to throw at me. The line was silent at first.

"Beth Ann?"

More silence.

And then she spoke haltingly. "Thank you. I used to dread such a thing would happen, but now that it has, I'm relieved."

"I don't know. I just don't know."

"I do. You did what had to be done. You are a good man." It was just like Beth Ann to forgive everyone, including me. *What happens next?* I wanted to ask. But didn't. I didn't want to think about whatever happens next.

"Joe won't see it that way, though, I'm sorry to say."

"I didn't think he'd take this lightly."

"I'll talk to him. Get him to understand. He didn't like Brody dealing either. He and Brody had a couple of fights over it. Nasty fights. On the wharf. Men laughed at them when they got going at it. Wasn't anything to laugh at. Both of them have a mean streak."

"What are you going to do now?" I asked her.

"Get up tomorrow," Beth Ann said, "and go fishing. Thanks again."

And she hung up.

I handed the phone back to Ramona. She took my hand, squeezed it, and gave me a sympathetic look. A waiter appeared then — skinny kid with rimless glasses and something that looked like bolts in his ears.

"A pitcher of IPA please," Ramona said, "and two glasses."

He nodded.

The beer came. It was cold. It was good. Somebody scored again in the hockey game. Sports fans cheered.

"Tell me about your day," I said.

"Not now. It's not important. Thanks for visiting my mom."

"Tough thing to see your mother slowly lose her memory."

"The only good thing about it is that you forget the bad as well as the good."

"Glass is half full, you mean."

"Something like that."

"I got an idea," she said after that, taking another sip of beer from her glass. "What if you and I go get some supplies, go back to my apartment, turn off the phones, close the drapes, and just have nothing to do with the world until, um, Thursday."

I had a hard time remembering what day of the week it was. Monday. "Just you and me? Tuesday. Wednesday. All day."

"And night," she said.

"And night," I repeated.

———

I should tell you about Tuesday and Wednesday. But I won't. It's private and it's personal and every single thing we did drew us closer together. But so be it. We found each other in a way that went beyond anything I had experienced before. Again, the words fail me as they so often do whenever I want to express in writing something of great importance.

I got to be the hero in the story for once. My heroic act: taking one minor dope dealer off the street, or, in this case, off the wharf. Ramona assumed the role of lover, mistress, mother, and caregiver. I got to be a man with no past, no guilt, no allegiance to anything but himself and his woman. I think I'll leave it at that.

The days passed quickly and suddenly it was Thursday.

"Now what?" I asked. "More of the same?"

"No. You can only hide from the world for a limited time."

"Why? Who said that?"

"I did."

23

Thursday. Fucking Thursday. If you leave the world for whatever time you can get away with, you inevitably have to find your way back to it.

Ramona's phone rang around eight o'clock in the morning. "Don't answer it," I insisted.

Ramona leaned up on her elbow and looked to see who was calling. I peeped out from under the covers and wondered how any woman could look so damn good when she first woke up in the day.

"Gotta take it," she said. All business.

I could hear the voice. A familiar voice. *How did she get Ramona's number?* I wondered. Then I remembered that I'd called her using the phone on Monday.

Ramona listened. "Okay. I will. I promise." That's all she said. Then she hung up.

"Please tell me this is still a dream."

"No dream, champ. We gotta get up. We have to drive to Burnside."

"Burnside? In Dartmouth? Why? Is there a sale at Payless Shoes or something?"

I perhaps forgot to inform you, dear reader, that Ramona had a closet full of shoes. Yes, a shoe closet. A closet for nothing but shoes.

"Sexist pig," she said fondly.

"Did you call me a sexy pig?"

"Idiot. This is serious."

"I was afraid of that. That was Beth Ann, wasn't it? You girls getting together for coffee at Starbucks this morning or what?"

"I can't believe I've been sleeping with a man with such insipid thoughts."

"Sorry. Listen, I just had the two most wonderful days since …" As my voice trailed off I realized I had no information to complete that sentence. *Since? There was no since.* I corrected myself. "I just had the two most wonderful days in my life."

She lit up like a birthday candle. "Me too. How did we do that?"

"I don't know. I give you all the credit."

"Well, now we have to stop being carefree sexy teenagers and go back to being responsible adults."

"Those are the two worst words in the English language. I hate them both. I don't know which one I hate more. *Responsible* or *adult.*"

"Tough titty."

"I can't believe you said that."

She looked at me, no trace of a smile on her face now.

"Sorry. This must be serious."

"Brody is in Burnside at the Central Nova Scotia Correctional Facility. That's where he's being held. He got roughed up by someone in there. We need to get him out of there before something worse happens. Beth Ann doesn't have the money. Neither does Joe. We have to post bail."

"But I don't have any money, as you know."

"How convenient." Was that real sarcasm I detected? "I can do this," Ramona said. "In for a penny, in for a pound."

"I think my mother used to use that phrase."

"Mine did too," Ramona said. "It's been so long since I had a sensible conversation with her, I almost forget what a good mother she was. Let's do this for her. Besides, my father made the money. Didn't do her much good. So it should do someone some good."

We got up like a couple of normal human beings getting dressed to go to work. Only I was still wearing the same shabby shirt and dirty jeans I'd been wearing for days. And, get this, we brushed our teeth side by side at the twin sinks in her stylish bathroom. "We gotta buy you some new clothes," she said.

"I love you," I said. It was the playful *I love you*. Or maybe it was the real thing.

"I love you too," she said. "We play an old married couple real well." And then she spat toothpaste into the sink.

"Old?"

"Not so old."

As we walked into the Burnside jail, all eyes were on Ramona. She was dressed like the movie star that she once almost was. I was dressed a bit like Jed Clampett and I hadn't shaved for days. I had tried shaving with Ramona's lady razor, but it tore my cheek and I gave up.

The desk cop or whatever he was gave her the once-over, me the once-over, and had a puzzled look. I could see how we did that to people, the two of us. I'd seen it already more than once. What the hell is *he* doing with *her*?

I cleared my throat. "We are here to post bail for Brody Myatt."

"Ahh. Okay. You related?"

"I'm his father."

He gave me a look of pity. I could read his thoughts: *Don't tell me she is his mother?*

He pulled something up on his computer. "Sorry, it's a little slow," he said, then looked up at Ramona. "You look familiar. TV or something?"

"Maybe," she said.

"Okay. Here it is. Let me print this out. You'll need to sign and take legal responsibility."

I nodded.

The cop handed me a sheet of paper with the amount on it. Ramona produced her debit card.

The cop processed the transaction and handed Ramona her receipt. And then we waited. And waited.

Then we finally heard doors, metal doors, opening. The desk cop and Brody appeared. He had bruises on his face and one eye was swollen. He took one look at me and nearly exploded. Then he got control, realizing what was at stake there.

The cop sat him down by his desk and opened up a large Manila envelope, handed him a wallet and a watch. I noticed it was a Mickey Mouse watch. There were some keys and some bills, which the cop counted out in front of him and handed to him, like he was getting change for some purchase he just made.

Once we were outside, Brody went volcanic. "Look what you did to me!" he shouted, pointing at his face.

"I didn't do that to you," I insisted.

"Who the fuck do you think you are that you can come into my life and screw it up like this? I should kill you."

Patricide again. I was determined to keep my cool, take whatever shit the kid could throw at me, and deliver him to Beth Ann's doorstep. If he skipped town, Ramona would be out of a shitload of money. Strangely, it seemed that didn't concern her very much.

Brody looked around the parking lot. "Where's my truck?"

"Impounded probably," I said. "They wouldn't have towed it here. Probably down the Shore near where they picked you up."

"Take me fucking there, asshole."

We were walking toward Ramona's car at that moment. Her heels were clicking on the pavement. She suddenly stopped, turned to Brody, put her face up to within inches of his. "Look. We're taking you to your mother. Like it or not. You run and we call your keepers back there at the daycare centre."

It was a role perhaps. A good one. Tough-love mother in a movie of the week or something. She was good.

"Fuck," Brody said. A boy with a limited vocabulary. "Fuck. Fuck. Fuck."

But the funny thing was, he followed her toward the Lexus and heaved himself into the back seat.

Brody was hungry and wanted hamburgers. We stopped at the Burger King in Dartmouth. We bought him a big greasy bag of food at the drive-thru window. I watched as seagulls soared overhead, wondering how they liked their lives inland, searching for garbage at places like Burger King and Kentucky Fried Chicken. I remembered the first time I'd seen a fisherman shoot a seagull with a rifle just for sport. Seagulls and humans. They both had a bad habit of drifting away from what they were really intended to do in life.

Someone had made the highway much longer than before. The drive down to Stewart Harbour was interminable. Ramona refused to stop at the RCMP headquarters in Musquodoboit Harbour to find out about Brody's truck. Better for him to not have wheels. Not that this would stop him if he decided to run.

Brody settled a little after he finished two Whoppers and a giant bag of French fries. He was about to throw his garbage out the window when Ramona turned around and grabbed his wrist. "Not on your life, buster. You do that and I'll poke your eyes out."

Brody laughed just then. He crumpled up the bag and put it on the floor in front of him. Then he looked up into the rearview mirror at Ramona. He looked long and hard. He laughed again. "Wait a minute. I don't believe this."

Ramona was stone-faced.

"I thought I recognized you," he said. Here we go again, I was thinking.

"You were in that porno film. What was it? *Hung Well in Hollywood*?"

"You are so mistaken," she said.

"I could swear that was you. A younger you, maybe, but you. A guy doesn't forget a ... well, you know."

"I assure you, you've made a mistake. You don't know anything about me."

He looked again. "I guess not. I just wondered why a babe like that would be here in Nova Scotia hanging out with this loser." That would be me.

"My sentiment, exactly," she said, ending the conversation.

Sated on cow meat and greasy potatoes, Brody slumped back in his seat and closed his eyes. "Man, this eye is giving me trouble. Anybody have anything for pain?"

Ramona opened her purse, took out two Tylenol and handed them to Brody, who wolfed them down. "I was hoping for something a little stronger," he said.

"Sorry. Suck it up," she said.

The paved stretch of the highway finally gave out and we were nearing the causeway. Beth Ann's house came into view. As we pulled into the driveway, I watched as she came out the door. She had the look of a worried mother, a distressed mother. But I could still see the high-school girl in her, the one who had been so good to me in my last difficult years of high school. How the hell did we end up in a situation like this?

Brody opened the door, swung himself out. If I thought a thank you was in order, I was sadly mistaken. "This isn't over," he said and slammed the door.

We sat there for a minute and watched as he walked slump-shouldered to his mother.

"What do we do now?" I asked.

"We drive away."

"Okay."

"I don't want to go back to Halifax," she said.

"Okay. Where to?"

"How about out to sea?"

The wiser part of me thought we should drive off to Cape Breton and check in at the Keltic Lodge for, say, five years. But another part of me was saying that going anywhere right now was still just running away. I guessed we'd have to play this out and see how it went.

We went to my fish shack. There I remembered that Ramona had asked me politely to stop calling it a shack. We hadn't come up with a more genteel moniker for it yet.

It wasn't locked, of course. We went in.

We weren't inside for five minutes when Rolf let himself in the front door. "Heard what you did. Ballsy. Real ballsy."

"How's the boy?" Ramona asked.

"Scooter? They pumped his stomach. Said it was enough of that drug to kill a horse. I don't know the full story. It was bad, but he pulled through. His father still wants to kill someone. Him and Joe have a kind of standoff. Might cool down or maybe not. You never know about these things."

"I remember grudge matches from my childhood," I said. "Real doozies. Over much less than this."

"Jesus, yes," Rolf said. "Billy Young nearly killed Kyle McGregor over stealing the lobsters from his lobster traps."

"Caught him red-handed if I recall," I said.

"Green-handed, really. Lobsters don't turn red until they're cooked."

"Ah, the good old days."

"They was. What about Brody? Where'd they send him?"

"He was in Burnside, but now he's back."

"Back? How could that be?"

Ramona cleared her throat, explained to Rolf about the not-so-happy return of the wayward boy.

Rolf scratched his head. "You young people," he said. "You play by a whole different set of rules. Crazy upstairs is my guess. I think it's holding those damn cellphones to your head all the time. Electromagnetic waves twisting about your brain cells or something."

"Something," Ramona echoed.

"Anyways, I was hoping you'd come back, come hell or high water. I gassed up the *Sheer Delight* just in case."

"Thank you so much," Ramona said, lighting back up now, dropping the tough-mama role. She walked to Rolf and planted a big sloppy kiss on his grizzled cheek.

Rolf nearly cracked his face smiling. "That's it, Jesus. You can take me now," he said, made a little bow and shuffled backward out the door.

That's when I remembered the gun. "You two lovebirds catch up," he said, "while I go make sure the boat's ready to go."

Rolf winked. Ramona rolled her eyes.

But that gave me my little window to go the car, tuck the damn thing down into my pants and pull my shirt over it like a bad guy in a car-chase movie. I would have tossed it in the water, but eyes were on me the whole way from the car to the boat. So I hid it inside the cabin, in a tool box, the one my father kept his boat tools in. "Never know when you gonna break down at sea," he'd say. He had plenty of tools.

I hoofed it back to the shack and Rolf was already gone.

"Let's go," I said. "The sea awaits."

24

Things were quiet at the wharf and that was good. We walked to the boat, boarded, threw the lines. I fired up the engine and confirmed that indeed we had a good supply of gas. At idle, I slipped away from the wharf and into the channel, past the poles of spruce that marked the deeper water.

A light wind from the southwest made for some chop and a bit of spray on us, but soon we were at sea, far enough from land that it was just a thin dark line to the north. I cut the engine and dropped anchor. I liked the idea of just drifting, but my father was in my head just then. Drifting could be a funny thing in a wind like this. If you weren't paying attention, you could hit a current, or an even bigger wind could come up, and soon you'd be a long way from home. And you didn't want that.

We hadn't said a word since I'd started up the engine. Now all was quiet except for the wind and the waves lapping against the wooden hull.

"Why are you sticking your neck out like this?" I asked as gently as I could.

"You mean Brody and the bail."

"Brody, me, the whole shebang?"

Ramona sat down on the wooden engine cover. I sat beside her.

"Well, I had been looking for something to change in my life. One day was becoming a bit too much like the day before."

"You could have just hopped on a plane. Gone to Paris. Australia. Rome. Whatever."

"Been there. Done that. Not as much fun as you'd think when you're on your own. I was looking for something more."

"Well, lucky me. Right time. Right place."

"Something like that. But not quite. You know what you had going for you?"

"Shoot."

"Vulnerability."

I had to think about that one. "You felt sorry for me. Standing there all alone by the water."

"Not exactly. Vulnerability is a little different. Not weakness. But possibility."

"Explain, professor."

"When you are vulnerable, you can be easily hurt, but you are also open to possibility. Perhaps you have some empathy, are willing to let someone into your life."

"You saw that in me?"

"I thought I saw it or the possibility of it."

"Funny, I always thought women want to see men who are strong, men who can take charge."

"That went out of fashion shortly after people stopped living in caves."

"I didn't know that."

"Not many men do."

"Okay, so that was my hook. My vulnerability. But you're still hanging on to Mr. Sensitive. Why?"

"Because, so far, most of it has been good. Not easy. But good."

"You sure don't scare easily."

"No, I don't."

"There's gotta be more."

"There is."

A fish jumped then. And then another. She seemed surprised.

"Fish," I said, "the ocean's full of them. Or was. John Cabot said the fish were so thick it slowed down his ships. Not quite that many left."

"What were they?"

"Cod, probably. But forget the fish story. I said there's gotta be more. And you said there is. So what is it?"

"Commitment."

"There's a word you don't hear much of anymore, unless you're about to put your wife or husband into the loony bin. What exactly do you mean?"

"I decided that you are my experiment."

"That's makes it sound like I'm being used."

"You are. It's a commitment experiment. I'm trying to see if I can stay committed to you even if things get, let's say, complicated."

"And they have."

"Indeed."

"And?"

"So far, so good. Like I said, over and over, I would get close to someone and then suddenly just walk away. It would always be that easy for me."

"So, you still might do that to me?"

"Might."

I thought about it. But I realized that Ramona was indeed the best thing that had ever sauntered into my life in lady shoes, so what the hell. "I can live with that. How am I doing so far? In the experiment?"

"It's not just you. It's us. And we are doing more than okay for a couple of human lab rats."

"Lab rats. I like that."

We were good talkers, she and me. Our conversations had rhythm and content. The very opposite of bar talk and pickup lines. I think part of it still had to do with her being quite the fine actor who could shift her roles in conversation. All I had going for me was that I was a word man, looking for nuance, thinking about what was peeking out from under the meaning of a word based on how she used it. But enough musing about that.

"Okay, I remain curious. Can I ask more about you?"

"Absofuckinglutely."

"Back in Burnside, the cop seemed to recognize you. Then, while driving home, Brody said something."

"I was afraid you were going to ask."

"You weren't really in a porno film?"

A few more fish jumped into the air and splashed back down. "Yes and no," she said.

"I don't believe it."

"Do I have to tell you the whole sorry tale?"

"Yes. We stay out here until you do."

"Hey, I could stay out here forever. So, no threats. But, yes, I will tell."

I got up and walked to the gunwale, leaned back in front of her so I could see her face. She was more than a little embarrassed.

"I had just arrived in California. I did a couple of commercials. I auditioned for some indie producers who were working on art films. A so-called agent had latched onto me and said there was a hot young filmmaker working on some very non-commercial projects — all character driven, all about relationships. Did I want to be in one?

"I was wary, believe me. I was pretty good at detecting all the bullshit lines of film people. But I said I would meet with the director. And did. He was intellectual. He showed me some clips of his work. He didn't try to hustle me or put the make on me."

"I take it that was rare where you were."

"Very rare. So I read the script. Said yes. Practised my lines. And he shot a very low-budget film about a young couple falling in love who came from completely opposite worlds."

"Romeo and Juliet?"

"Romeo and Juliet in New Jersey was sort of the drift. My romantic interest was a young and upwardly mobile investment hotshot headed to Wall Street. I was, get this, a young ingenue from the sticks. He decided I could be a young ingenue from Nova Scotia."

"No?"

"Yes. So we shot it. I got paid. But then I never saw an edited version. I'd call him up and ask, and he told me he couldn't afford to finish editing it or that the time wasn't right to release it or some other bullshit line. And after a while I forgot about it.

"A couple of years later, one of my actor friends, a gay guy named Julian, told me that he'd seen me in a film, a porno film involving bis and straights."

"But wait. Did you do, um, sex scenes that you thought were tasteful?"

"No. Not even that. It was strictly clothes on. Romantic buildup. Two strangers falling in love. But no sex."

"What happened?"

"Film is all smoke and mirrors, right? So he took what he shot of Romeo and me and, I don't know quite how to explain this, but used other actors for the body shots."

"So those were not your boobs on the screen?"

"And not my private parts either, shall we say."

"You mean some woman got hired to stand in as the most intimate portions of your anatomy?"

"Yes. And thank you for using polite language."

"Couldn't you sue or something?"

"Could, but what's the point? But it gets worse. The film ends up on the internet. Not the whole film, just the seedy parts. But, of course, it looks like me with the bare bum, the voluptuous breasts, and the fully shaved you know what. And so I started to get Googled, tagged, and tracked down, and, best of all, get slobbering emails from teenage boys."

"That's terrible. What did you do?"

"I actually wrote back to some saying it wasn't me. I tried to locate the director, but he'd moved to Peru and was making nature documentaries for Animal Planet. I talked to internet privacy consultants. All to no avail."

"That was a violation of your human rights. The fucking bastard."

"Calm down, champ. I did all I could do and then I gave up. I still get men looking at me, thinking it was me in those video clips. But I ignore it. I hold my head high and get on with my life."

I stood silently for a moment looking at her. Then, as usual, I shared a sliver of my sparkling wit. "I never thought I'd be out at sea like this in my father's old fishing boat with a porn queen."

She mugged a look of disgust and then came to stand beside me on the rail of the boat. When a small wave pushed up against the hull, she dipped her hand over, scooped some water and as I leaned toward her, she splashed the cold salt water into my face.

"Let's never speak of this again," she said. And kissed me on my wet salty lips.

25

I took Ramona's story about being conned into acting in a porno film at face value. I got it. She with a pretty face had been lured into acting in a movie and then a lass with a lesser ethical code was lured into doing the dirty parts. Clearly there was no honour or dignity in the movie business. Surprise, surprise.

Each time we told stories about ourselves, our bond deepened. She hadn't heard all about me yet. Nor had I heard all about her. Maybe that would take a lifetime. If so, I was in for the long run.

"What's that?" she asked, pulling me back from staring at the water.

I looked up and east. Dark skies, bumpy horizon.

"A little weather coming this way," I said.

"Should we be worried?"

"Not yet. It's a long way off. Wind's still light. We're okay."

"Isn't that what they said in *The Perfect Storm*?"

I'd seen the movie a dozen times. Much of it didn't ring true. But some of it did. The fear of an ocean gone mad.

"Ever kiss George Clooney?"

"No. Now I'm sorry I told you about Tom Hanks."

"Don't be. I was just asking. Shall we pull anchor?"

"Weigh anchor, isn't that what they say?"

"Only in the movies, sweetheart." My best Bogart.

At that moment, the wind dropped entirely. Both of us wanted to stop all clocks from ticking, seize the moment. Freeze it and live it. Quiet. Peaceful. Two people breathing almost in synch. Doing nothing but being here and now. Total Buddhist blissed-out behaviour.

Weather. Fisherman's friend or foe? I understood this stillness. Calm before the storm, city people say, but fishermen have a lot more understanding. Like my father, I could feel it. You didn't need a barometer. Pressure dropping. Low pressure system moving in from the northeast. Old wharf rats could tell you a day or so in advance. Back would hurt, bad knee would announce it like a finely tuned weather instrument.

Along the coast of Nova Scotia, some things are written like laws in the sky. Southwest wind at morning. Raining in Yarmouth. Get out your umbrellas in Halifax by noon. Rain in Stewart Harbour by evening. Cape Breton by midnight.

Wind from the east was another matter. Starts with a bright tingly morning and a glass sheen on the sea. Whole thing bright as a shiny penny. Back in the days when we still had pennies. Clingy, coppery morning. Then the ripples. Then a still patch again.

Like now.

Then increments of wind puffs from the east. If you're tucked in on the west side of a finger of land like Prosper Point, you don't notice it at first, but pretty soon, the wind, the storm will hit. Then you wonder, holy shit, where'd all that rain come from. But at sea, you're given fair warning.

Like now.

For the moment, we had time. Plenty of time. Storms like that tend to be slow moving. My father never came in early if there was still fishing to do. "Always just keep your eyes on it. Keep steady. Know the wind. Know the boat. Don't take short-cuts in the harbour or you'll kiss your keel on the ledges, do some serious damage."

I had forgotten altogether about the radio in the cabin. About how my father would always turn it on at a time like this, even though he claimed he never trusted marine forecasts. "Just use your eyes. And your nose," he'd say. My father could sniff out a storm within two hundred miles before Environment Canada even knew the wind had changed.

So I turned on the radio. It crackled. I fiddled with the dial. There it was. That familiar voice. Damn if it didn't sound like the same monotone announcer from fifty years ago. I left it on but went back to Ramona, who was still looking toward the darkening sky.

"Write me a poem," she said. "Write me a poem about all this."

"I want to write about you instead."

"Then do it."

"Now?"

"Why not?"

"I haven't written a poem since college."

"Bullshit. You said you were writer."

"But not a poet."

"Why?"

"There's no money in poetry," I said.

"But there's no poetry in money," she countered. "Somebody said that. I remember it from my university poetry course."

A thought blipped in my head. "Wow. What if we had met back then?"

"Hmm. You are forgetting. You would have been twenty. I would have been fifteen."

I laughed. "At twenty I would have been so full of myself you wouldn't have liked me."

"At fifteen, I would have been so teenage gorgeous that you couldn't have resisted me."

And that led to me grabbing her and planting a kiss to end all kisses. No poem could have captured it properly.

I heard it before I saw it. A boat. Headed this way. At first, I assumed it was just somebody from the Harbour out to top up the day's catch with a little afternoon handlining. Common enough.

But the thrum of the engine was a pitch too high. And nobody, absolutely nobody did any joyriding with their meal ticket. Boys who liked to cowboy, if they struck a good lobster season, would buy a big, wanking Cape Islander with a big Volvo engine, blast away for a season, and then let it go with failed payments.

I went looking for my father's old Bushnell binoculars and there they were, hanging on the same nail as when I was eleven. Man, this boat was like a museum of my childhood.

The first big whiff of the easterly wind lifted Ramona's hair, touched her cheek like a gentle finger of air. Maybe I did have a poem in me.

"What, pray, dost thou see?" she asked.

I held the binoculars up to my eyes, but then had to wipe the dust off. "Better not go the Romeo and Juliet route. Remember, that got you in trouble last time."

"Who do you think it is?"

"Whoever it is doesn't care about saving fuel." I didn't want to say until I knew.

It didn't take long. It was Joe Myatt; he was barrelling this way in a boat much newer than this one and with an engine almost big enough to compensate for his limited intellectual abilities. I thought about the gun in the tool box. No way would it come to that. Clearly, Joe would understand what I did was for Brody's own good. Besides, I'd been told the two of them didn't get along.

I thought of at least heading back toward land, arcing wide around Incoming Joe. But it wouldn't look good. Probably burn him even more.

"Joe Myatt," I said. "You mind if I ask you to go in the cabin, just lay low and see how this plays out? Joe and I go way back. I think we can work this out."

Ramona was reluctant to play the school marm role and get out of the way like a good little lady. She scowled and said, "You want to do your boy thing, I'll acquiesce." Yeah, she used that word. It was a hint. "But I'm not far. And I'm part of whatever this is. Don't tell me I'm not."

As the sky darkened more, the wind was rising and there were shafts of sunlight stabbing down from the broody clouds, painting silver swords on patches of the sea.

Joe cut his engine and turned his boat sideways, till he smacked up against *Sheer Delight* on the port side. He let his engine idle as his boat nudged us against the waves. He quickly tied the two boats together and yanked on the knot.

Joe wasn't in a pretty mood. Fortunately, though, Rolf was on board with him also. Joe snarled something at Rolf and Rolf went into the wheelhouse and took the wheel, held the boat steady. I waited for whatever was coming my way.

Joe jumped over onto my deck. It wasn't a social call.

"You fucking sent my son to jail," he snarled.

"I did. For his own good."

"They sent him to Burnside for God's sakes. A boy like that could have been raped. Or worse."

There was nothing I could say to that.

"You leave here decades ago. Don't give a shit about any of us, including Brody, then come back to town and fuck everything up in just a couple of days."

In his mind, I had brought pain into paradise. But things had not been pretty in that dysfunctional family for a long time. Anger produces its own perverse logic, however.

"Scooter almost died," I said. "Brody was dealing stuff so strong he didn't even understand what he was doing." I didn't know yet exactly what was in those drugs. Brody had said it was fentanyl, which was bad enough, but it could have been almost anything. It was all over the news. But now wasn't the time to lecture a guy like Joe on pharmacology.

"Yeah, and that was pretty typical of Scooter, or his old man, for that matter. Never able to know when enough is enough."

"This wasn't backwoods hooch Brody was selling."

"Scooter knew what he was doing."

I couldn't believe Joe Myatt was saying that. Beth Ann had admitted to me that Brody just kept moving on to the next thing and the thing after that, never questioning what he was selling.

We were still sparring with words. But I was pretty sure that wouldn't last. I didn't stand much of a chance against Joe. I'd been punching keys on a computer for thirty years. He'd been hauling traps and nets.

I could see Rolf giving me some kind of hand signals. "I see you brought Rolf," I said to Joe.

"I was gearing up to go. Coming after you, dickhead. I didn't see him get on board. When I turned around and saw him standing on my deck, I was ready to heave him in the channel. But I knew the stupid old fuck couldn't swim a stroke. I had no choice."

I nodded to Rolf. Not sure he had anything helpful in mind, but maybe he'd have a plan to stop Joe from killing me.

"On the way out, I decided that if I succeeded in killing you, I'd be willing to drown the old dimwit and the world would not have lost much."

"I get it. Two men lost at sea. Death by natural causes, I suppose." I nodded to the dark skies still on the horizon and heading our way. "Mother nature doing her thing, they would say. Me, inexperienced at sea in his father's old tub. Rolf, well, he was just along for the ride and not much use."

"That's pretty much it."

I kept waiting for Joe to take a swing at me. Instead, he jumped back into his own boat. But he wasn't about to sail away. He picked up a crowbar and climbed back into *Sheer Delight.*

My radio was crackling away, repeating the storm warning. But I could hear a different radio on Joe's boat. Shortwave? Marine band?

Rolf looked worried. He was biting his lip. I thought about Ramona. What was she making of all this?

I was beginning to think that words as weapons against a crowbar was not a good enough plan. Joe was serious.

"Your boy. My boy. Sweet Jesus, he needs help. Not this. Put the fucking crowbar down, Joe."

"You know, I don't really give a shit what happens to me anymore. You fucked it all up for me at the very beginning. Beth Ann could never quite get over you leaving. I could never quite feel right about us raising your kid. But I tried, goddamn it. I tried. I was good to him. Brody fought me the whole way. But I still hate the fact you ambushed him and let the cops arrest him. The only thing I hate more than you is the fucking cops."

And that's when Joe made his move. He swung the crowbar in a short arc that would have smashed my skull had I not ducked and darted. I shifted to the other side of the boat so I had the engine between us. He leaned forward and took another swing. I felt the steel nick my earlobe as it swept by.

Rolf was shouting something now. Screaming at Joe at the top of his lungs.

Joe had been an angry violent kid in school. Beaten by his father on a daily basis. I think he'd always tried to pretend it didn't happen. But he carried it in everything he did. School. Business. Marriage. Life. He had enemies and he treated them just like that. I was Enemy Number One right now and nothing I could say or do would change that. And, I understood that he really didn't care what happened after this. He wanted me punished.

Swing number three was low. And that was a surprise. It caught me in the gut and I toppled. Once down on the deck, I wouldn't stand much of a chance. Out of the corner of my eye, I could see Rolf had left Joe's wheelhouse and was scrambling to come save my sorry ass. But I'd heard what Joe had to say. Rolf would get it too.

And that's when I saw Ramona open the cabin door and point Brody's gun at Joe. "You move, motherfucker, and I'll pull this fucking trigger." The line was not original, but the acting was good.

Joe just looked at her and laughed. Ramona didn't know anything about guns, I was pretty sure of that. And I knew she was holding an empty gun. I'd taken the bullets out of the gun and hidden them in a drawer. Fuck.

Just as Joe started walking toward her, she raised the barrel up into the air and pulled the trigger. The blast was deafening. I guess she had found the ammunition. She aimed the gun at Joe and he froze in his tracks.

"Go ahead, bitch. Shoot me. I bet I can still get to your boy-friend before I go down."

I was ready to dive for Joe's feet. I figured he'd get in another blow with the damn crowbar, but I had to do something. A strange silence settled for a split second. But, before I could get up the courage to make my move, there was a voice on the radio. Not mine, but the one from Joe's boat.

"Joe! Can you hear me, Joe? Come in!"

Joe cocked his head, eyes still fixed on the gun. I realized I wasn't going to dive for his legs. Ramona was ready to fire if she had to. I saw the determination in her eyes.

"Joe, damn it. It's Kent Webber. Brody's stolen my boat. About an hour ago. He's headed out to sea."

Something drained out of Joe just then. He looked at the gun again, at Ramona, not at me. Then he jumped back into his boat and got on the radio. I walked toward Ramona and cautiously took the gun from her. She was shaking.

When Joe walked back out onto his deck, he looked at me, showed me a fist, but then threw the crowbar over the side. "Brody stole Kent Webber's new boat. He doesn't know shit about boats. Somebody spotted him east beyond Fiddler's Point."

We both looked east then. Brody was headed straight into that oncoming storm. Sure, Brody was trying to escape, but he knew enough about the sea to realize a dirty blast of weather was coming. It was crazy, but he seemed to be headed right into it, like he was doing it on purpose.

"I gotta go," Joe said. "Rolf, get your sorry ass off my boat."

Rolf scrambled toward the gunwales and crawled over into *Sheer Delight*. He started to untie the two boats, but I stopped him. I jumped over into Joe's boat and looked back at Rolf. "Take her back to the harbour and get there before this storm hits."

Perhaps the *her* was ambiguous. I'd meant Ramona, of course. And I knew following Joe in my old boat would be of no use. Too old. Too slow.

But just then Ramona walked toward me, crossed over into Joe's boat and undid the rope that tied the two boats together. "No. Go," I said.

She looked at me with defiance.

"Get the bitch off my boat," Joe said.

"The bitch is staying," Ramona said.

"Fuck me, Jesus," Joe said. He gunned the engine and the boat leapt forward, heading toward the east and an ever-darkening sky.

26

Even though Joe's attention was focused on the ocean, his fury at having us aboard was palpable. We hung back outside the cabin and let the spray from the waves we were hitting rain down on us. The chop was increasing. The wind was coming up. Fiddler's Point was maybe ten miles east. High dirt cliffs, rocky shoreline, no harbours, no easy place to go ashore.

I wondered if Joe had any clues as to what Brody's plan was. Could be the boy didn't have a clue about geography and thought he was headed to Sable Island or Bermuda. Who could know? Whatever it was, it was a dumb idea. And this storm coming in looked like the real thing.

I gave Ramona a hug. "Why didn't you go with Rolf? God knows what this is going to be like."

"I figured you needed me for moral support," she answered. "Also to make sure Joe doesn't kill you. Or Brody for that matter, if you find him."

"Seems like there's never a dull moment when you're around."

"I thought it was the other way — never a dull moment when *you* are around," she said.

"Hey, that gun thing. I had made sure the gun was unloaded."

"I found the bullets in a drawer in the cabin. What are you doing with a handgun on a boat, anyway?"

"It was Brody's. I took it from his truck when he was arrested. Otherwise, there would have been stiffer charges. Or something worse."

"That boy is trouble."

We both looked ahead at the gloom. The seas were continuing to rise. The waves were now a few feet high and we heard a loud *whump* each time Joe slammed the speeding boat into the larger ones.

"Let's see what the captain has in mind," I said, lifting a hatch cover and finding three floater jackets. I put one on Ramona, one on myself, and carried the third into the cabin to hand to Joe. Ramona came in with me.

Joe was staring straight ahead, keeping the bow straight into the waves. I handed him the jacket and he waved me away. "Bad luck, those things. Never wear them."

We both stood there listening to the marine weather again. The word *intensifying* kept coming up. "Shit, shit, and shit," Joe said under his breath. That pretty much summed up the weather report.

Kent Webber came on the radio. "Joe Myatt, you out there? You hear me, you son of a bitch, over."

Joe picked up the mic. "I hear ya, Kent. I'm gonna get your boat back, over."

"Damn you, Joe. That kid of yours. Why'd he have to pick my boat? I just bought the damn thing. And I don't even have insurance on it yet, over."

"How much gas was in the tank, Kent?"

"Not a whole hell of a lot. Quarter tank, maybe. Why?"

Joe didn't answer the question. He switched off the radio and I could see he was making some kind of calculation in his head.

"I reckon he should be running out of gas within the next twenty minutes," Joe said matter-of-factly, as if his recent attempt to plant a crowbar in my brain had never happened. He was a different man entirely. But I understood. I'd seen it at sea with my father and a hired hand. One minute, my father would be screaming at the guy about being a lazy, worthless son of a bitch, and the next minute something would happen, something would go wrong, or there was need for a cool head, and he turned serious and professional.

I guess I had a curious look on my face.

"I know what you're thinking," Joe said. "I never was very good at math in school."

"No. I was just thinking what my own father might do at a time like this."

"Your father was a damn good fisherman. Too bad he went nuts like that at the end."

Ramona looked at me with a big question mark hanging there between us.

"He didn't go crazy, Joe."

Joe shrugged. "Anyway, like I was saying, he was a damn good fisherman. And I liked the guy. He never had a bad word to say to me."

We hit a bigger wave just then, head-on, and a shudder went through the boat as the spray flumed up into the air.

"You gonna help me save my boy?" Joe asked, still looking straight ahead.

He was right. It was *his* boy. He may not have fully raised the kid I'd helped bring into the world, but he'd been around all those years. Someday, I'd hear the whole story.

"Yeah. You tell me what to do. I'll do it." I held out the floater jacket again. "You sure you don't want this on?"

"Nope," he said.

"What can I do to help?" Ramona asked.

Joe spit something onto the floor. "Just stay out of the way, lady." Sexism was a long way from dead on the Shore and especially at sea.

And then the rain started. Squall is the term often applied, but it's a weak word for the conspiracy of wind and wave and downpour from the heavens. On shore, you can plant your feet in one place, get soaked to the core, but the storm usually won't knock you over. At sea, the forces conspire to make air and sea one. They team up to knock you off your feet, wreck your vision, soak you through to the marrow in your bones, and then do something to your innards that will make you want to throw up until you get the dry heaves.

So far we were inside and dry and nobody was puking. I took all that as a good omen. Steady as she goes.

Joe leaned a little my way as if confiding some kind of secret, but I guess he was just thinking out loud. "I figure it this way. If Brody got past that headland there ..." I couldn't see any headland. The rain made vision almost impossible. But Joe knew this territory, or so I hoped.

"If he made it past the point over there, he'd not get far, because he'd be straight into the wind. Wind and wave would start pushing him back. He'd end up on the east side of Fiddler's. Nothing out there but rocks and dirt cliffs. Nobody lives out there anymore. Best hope is that he gets Kent's big-ass boat grounded close to shore and he gets ashore to sit it out with the seagulls."

"So that looks good, right?"

"I didn't say that. If he drifts past the tip of Fiddler's then he's screwed. No engine, no decent way to steer into the waves or away from the waves. He'd get swamped for sure."

The rain let up ever so slightly. Just to our left, a high cliff loomed into view. "That's the point right there," Joe said. "C'mon, Brody. Do something right for once."

The waves were hitting harder now. Not just from one direction either. We were in shallow water. The boat shook. I noticed a kind of A-frame mother of a wave — two waves, I guessed, converging right on the bow. It slammed down on the cabin with a vengeance. Joe held fast to the wheel. I went teetering over. But Ramona grabbed me and pulled me back up.

"Haven't had one of them on me in quite a while," Joe said. "In fact, I haven't been out in weather like this since I was young and stupid."

As we rounded the tip of Fiddler's Point, Joe eased off on the throttle. The waves didn't let up and the sky opened up again full force. "Lot of rocks out here. Stuff you can't see. You guys have good luck with ya? 'Cause I think I've used up most of mine."

It was the first time he'd addressed us together without some kind of curse attached. "Yeah," I said. "Ramona is famous for her luck."

"Absofuckinglutely," she said.

"Hold on to your hats," Joe suddenly said, gunning the engine again. One of those famous rocks had just appeared to our starboard. We lurched past it just as a wave was lifting us and attempting to drop us on the surface of that craggy ledge.

Joe had established that understated cool that I'd seen my father take on. It was an Eastern Shore thing. Fishermen did it. Any time it looked like the sea was about to rattle your bones, or sink your boat, or come up with a clever means to suck the life out of you, you'd pretend it was all a game.

"I always loved this spot," Joe said. "You come out here on a sunny day and sneak in close to these rocks, you find the sweet spot where it's good and deep and drop down a rope and a can of tuna with nail hole punched in it. Ten minutes later you're hauling up a lobster the size of an old Volkswagen bug."

"You'll have to show me some day," I said, not adding, *if we get out of this alive.*

For a minute, it looked like we were dead in the water. The engine was still running, but we weren't moving. Then the squall let up a little.

We peered out through the glass.

"Gotta go in closer," Joe said. "But these damn ledges, they'll sink ya before you ever make it ashore."

"You sure he's near here?" Ramona asked.

"No. It's a hunch. That's all I got at this point."

And a dangerous hunch it was. When each wave sucked out, I saw those rocky ledges now, all parallel to shore, each one as nasty looking as the one before. Joe worked the engine, idling, then revving, weaving in and out, keeping an eagle eye on white water over submerged rocks and trying to make sense of this turbulent sea. Rational thinking probably didn't do much good at a time like this. All you had was your gut.

"There he is," Joe said, just as the next onslaught of rain hit. At first I didn't see a damn thing. Then I saw it.

Kent Webber's shiny new boat was grounded on one of the ledges and head-high waves were pounding it mercilessly.

"I'm gonna have to go in kind of tight. You folks want me to put you ashore somehow or do you wanna stick around for the fun?"

There was no going ashore anywhere there in this maelstrom. I wouldn't have got off the boat, though, even if it was possible. In the last ten minutes I had grown to admire Joe and love the way that he had absorbed the vernacular of generations before him. When the going gets rough, you tough it out. You just do what you have to do.

As we moved closer to the boat, there was no sign of Brody at first. And then we saw him. Someone in a yellow floater jacket was still in the boat trying to hang on to the gunwale as a wave hit and knocked him down. The boat was now tilted far on its side and Brody was up high on the gunwale, waving.

"Gotta get behind that damn ledge," Joe said. "If we come in with the waves, all we'll do is crush the boy."

More engine, more cowboying around behind the rock ledge with the shore only about sixty feet away. "Pray for one of those deep spots," Joe said.

I prayed.

And then we were around it. I could hear the hull grating against the bottom. Brody was down again and we couldn't see him. The waves just kept coming. They'd slam that new boat over and over until there was nothing left but a splintered fibreglass hull. Brody got up again and was now on the down side of the boat, waving frantically.

"Now we have a problem," Joe said, his eyes still on the chaos outside. "Brody's got to get in the water and get his sorry ass over here."

"Is that gonna work?"

"Fuck if I know."

"I got a better plan," I said. "I go in the water, grab him, and haul him here."

"Always wanted to be a hero, didn't ya?"

"No. Never."

Joe slammed his fist into the wheel. He kept looking at Brody, who must have read his mind. He was about to lower himself into the water. "That fucking current will pull him toward the point and out toward the sea and those other rocks. Only way out of this tight little spot is the way we came in."

There was not much of a choice there. Only Joe could keep the boat steady and get us out of there. There was no two ways about it.

I was already out of the cabin before he could say anything else. I found a rope, tied it around my waist. It was a big coil of polypropylene rope. If it didn't do the trick, I was gonna be lunch for one those Volkswagen lobsters who love eating dead anything.

Ramona kissed me once, hard on the lips, wrapped the other end of the rope around her waist, and tied a knot. I was shocked to realize she'd done a perfect bowline, a rescue knot.

As the waves continued to smack away at us, I eased myself over the side just as I saw Brody make the splash into the water. The boat was fully on its side now. Soon it would flip.

Brody was thrashing away, going under with each crashing wave and then popping back up. I was trying to move my arms and legs. I'd like to say I was swimming, but I wasn't. I was wallowing, floundering, moving forward and then being pushed back. I couldn't see a thing. I could hardly breathe as I kept getting smacked in the face by cold seawater. I could hear the engine behind me and just kept moving away from it. That's all I could do. The water was cold, the waves were relentless, and I was terrified.

I think I could hear Ramona screaming something, but couldn't make it out. I just kept going. Dog paddling seemed to work best. First thing I ever learned about swimming. Maybe the last move I'd ever make.

I saw him and then I lost him. How many times, I don't know.

And then we had one of those moments when the torrential rain let up ever so slightly. Still raging wind, still sloppy, bullying waves, but for an instant I could see where Brody was. And I swam like hell.

There were no words between us. I saw fear in his eyes. Desperation. He would have registered the same in mine. Father and son, the thought went through my head again. Nah. More like two desperate souls about to drown.

When I was right on top of him, I locked my arm through the loop on the back of his jacket, but he started trying to work his way around me, grabbing a hold of me in some kind of bear hug. I recognized it as the grip of a drowning man on the person trying to save him. When I'd taken a lifesaving course in high school, they'd told you how to break that grip. Otherwise, the drowning person would just pull you under. Out there, the floater jackets might keep you near the surface, but they wouldn't keep you from drowning.

I wanted Brody to let go of me so I could try to swim us back. But he wouldn't let go. We were dead weight in the water, slopped over again and again by the icy cold waves. I could feel what energy I had draining out of me. All too quickly.

And then I felt a powerful tug on the rope. I felt like it was going to cut through the jacket, cut through my guts. Somehow Joe must have left the wheelhouse and started hauling us in. I felt one long pull, then another. And another.

Brody was coughing, swallowing water over and over. I kept trying to keep my mouth shut and not swallow the ocean, but each smack in the face had me sputtering too.

I wasn't going to get us back to the boat. Brody's dead-man bear hug wouldn't let me move my arms. And I was losing energy fast. The tug was strong and consistent, but the current was pulling us away from the boat. Nothing to do but hang on.

The rain continued blasting down and wave after wave continued to pound us. Eventually, they slammed us up against the hull of Joe's boat. Then I felt the boat smash into something. It had connected with a rock for certain. The engine stalled. But then the engine roared again and Joe was backing us up. I was hanging on to the side of the boat with a struggling Brody hanging on to me, but there was no way I could lift him up and into the boat in this sea.

I saw her arm first, the unlikely slender arm of a woman. I couldn't see her face. She locked a fist onto my jacket loop and then, with her other arm, she reached out blindly and got a grip on Brody's jacket.

"No, let go!" I shouted. I was certain she'd pull herself into the sea with us. But she didn't let go.

The boat moved backward and then slowly forward. Joe was moving the boat ever so slowly but steadily away from the tip of the headland into deeper water. Brody and I kept getting pounded by waves, but Ramona did not let go. She was much stronger than I would have ever believed possible.

Minutes later, with the sea still crazy all around, I saw Joe hovering over us. He leaned over the side and with one massive tug heaved Brody up and over the rail onto the deck. Without missing a beat, he grabbed me by the shoulders and did the same. He didn't even look at me; just dropped me like a big fish from the sea onto the deck and ran back into the wheelhouse. I heard him rev the engine. It was only then I noticed Ramona had tied herself to a cleat mounted on the hull. She looked exhausted and hurt.

I tried to move, but couldn't. Brody was coughing and vomiting. But he was alive.

Once we'd rounded the headland, Joe tucked the boat in behind it on the west side, protecting us from the worst of the waves and wind. As the water began to smooth out a bit, he turned the boat and headed us back to Stewart Harbour. As I untied Ramona, I saw the deep welts in her side that the polypropylene rope had caused.

When he stopped vomiting, Brody wiped his mouth, looked at me, and then crawled to the cabin. Ramona and I sat there on the outside deck of the still-rocking boat, shivering and hugging each other.

"I thought I'd lost you," she said.

"You almost did."

"You can't get away from me that easily," she said and leaned into me.

27

We huddled in the ship's cabin, none of us speaking on the difficult trip back to Stewart Harbour. Cold and wet and exhausted. There was everything to be said. And nothing to be said.

Rolf was waiting for us at the wharf, even though the storm was still pounding the rain down on the weathered boards. He led Ramona and me back to my little shack, where he had a fire going in the woodstove. There was a mickey of Captain Morgan on the bare wood table. "You two need anything else?" he asked.

I shook my head no. Rolf bowed and made his exit.

Ramona and I huddled in front of the fire and began to unbutton our wet clothes. She undid my shirt. I undid her blouse. We slipped out of our clothes slowly, as if it were some kind of ceremony, until we were both naked. Wet, naked, and smelling like the deep blue sea that had tried its best to kill us. But it was a good smell. I put my arm around her and made a tent of the blanket I pulled around us and over our heads.

"What now?" Ramona asked.

"Now we sit here like two naked humans and think about how lucky we are to be alive."

"I can do that," Ramona said within the dark misty confines of our shelter.

We sat like that for what seemed a very long time. Maybe it was only minutes. Maybe a half hour. Breathing. Warmth coming back into our bodies. I don't know who moved first, but we found our way back into the bedroom. And we made love the way people do after a crisis, after a deadly ordeal like this. Desperate in a way. But a celebration at the same time. That's the best I can do to describe it.

The rum bottle sat on the table unopened. The fire went out in the woodstove. We slept.

In a movie, the next morning would be bright and cheerful, with sunlight glinting off every glorious wet surface of the coastal community. But for us, it wasn't like that. It was cold and foggy, and I cobbled together enough paper and kindling to get the fire going again. A dozen eggs were inside the door. I scrambled six of them, cooked them in the old cast iron frying pan and we ate.

Ramona and I found ourselves strangely shy and quiet. Yesterday's events had made us turn some corner in our relationship. I thought it might be one of those you-can't-turn-back-now moments. Or it could be the opposite. *Enough of this. Look, we almost got ourselves killed.*

"Ready to go back to being a city girl?" I asked. I thought maybe I should give her an easy way out if that's what she was thinking.

"And miss all the excitement?"

"That was enough excitement to last me a lifetime. I was certain we were all going to die."

"Me too," Ramona said.

"But you hung on. You didn't give up."

"Did what I had to do. No choice."

"Yeah," I said. "Sometimes you just don't have a choice, do ya?"

She didn't answer. She smiled a Mona Lisa smile. The kind that people could puzzle over for centuries, trying to figure out what it means. That kind of smile.

I took the plates over to the sink and started to scrub them. No dish detergent, so I tried using a nub of an old bar of soap that was probably many decades old. Then I worked at the frying pan.

That's when it clicked. The frying pan. I held it up to my face. There was the small defect in the rim. It was the same one.

I held it up in the air. "Look at this," I said. "What do you see?"

"I see an old cast iron frying pan. The kind that housewives once slammed their husbands with if they misbehaved."

I laughed. "Probably happened more often than you'd think. But it never happened in my home. I can't believe it ended up here."

"It came from your house?"

"Yes. I'm certain of it. I wonder why he kept that and almost nothing else."

"You want to tell me a bit more about what happened to your parents? You've given me fragments, but I don't really have a good picture."

"I haven't really told anyone for a long time."

"Women in bars don't want to hear sad stories about parents?"

"I told you, I gave that scene up a long time ago."

"Could have got you ... what do they call it? Sympathy sex?"

"Really? If only I'd known."

"Okay. So. Tell me about the house. Tell me what happened."

"My mother always said she had her diabetes under control. She was religious with the insulin shots. Checked her blood all the time. She said we should never worry. But something went wrong. My father was out fishing. I don't know where Pete and I were, but we weren't around. Maybe her prescription was filled wrong. Maybe she got the wrong dose. Too high or too low. Nobody every nailed it down.

"My father was at sea having a good day. A really good day. He'd stayed out longer than usual, and it was well into the afternoon by the time he came home. He found her dead in the kitchen. I think he figured if he had come in at the usual time, she'd still be alive. He blamed himself for not being there.

"I can't say my parents were all that affectionate. I'm not sure I even ever understood the relationship. They didn't argue and they always seemed somehow perfectly in synch with each other. But it didn't seem to Pete and me to be romantic love. Their whole way together was more like they were a team. People who would get the job done, whatever the job was. They always seemed so practical."

"Maybe that's another version of love. One we don't see in poems or books or movies."

"Maybe. We couldn't figure it out as kids. They just seemed to be always working at something or doing the things parents were supposed to do. I don't know when they ever had fun."

"Maybe they didn't care about fun. Maybe other things were more important."

"Probably. But when you're a kid you believe that fun is everything. My parents, though, were the poster pair for hard work, clean living — Mr. and Mrs. Responsibility."

"Lucky you," Ramona said.

"Yeah, Lucky me. Except I didn't appreciate it. All I wanted to do was run from there. And did."

"But you're not telling me about the house."

"The house. The house that my mother and father built together when they first got married. Yes. After she was gone, my father kept fishing. But his heart wasn't in it. He'd been the most ambitious man on the wharf in his day. Anxious to get the day's job done. Catch more than the next man if he could. Work hard and then work harder. But after Mom died, he was just going through the motions.

"Pete and I were gone by then. We'd talk to him on the phone once a week, sometimes less. I didn't know what he was up to until I ran into a guy from Stewart Harbour in a pub in Halifax. He told me the whole story. Back home, he said, everyone thought he was maybe losing his mind."

"What was he doing?"

"Dismantling our old home and giving away everything. First it was the furniture, the beds, the pictures on the wall. Then it was the doors and windows. He carefully removed them and sold them for cheap or gave them away if he thought someone needed a break.

"He removed every wooden shake from the walls, every shingle from the roof, made sure someone could use them again — he was that careful. Then, board by board, he took apart the house I had grown up in. He even removed all the nails. He stopped asking money for anything and just gave it away. Young couples building their own homes were mostly the ones who took him up on it. Who wouldn't?

"Electric wires, plumbing, floors, joists, beams — the works. He was living in the fish shack by then. Soon there was nothing but the loose stone foundation and a hole in the ground. People were certain he'd flipped when he took the foundation apart. Stone by stone. There's a pile of rocks there on the edge of the woods. Looks kind of like an ancient Irish cairn where they used to bury the dead.

"Then he used a shovel and filled in the basement one scoop of dirt at a time. By the following summer, wildflowers were growing there. Lupins and daisies and Queen Anne's lace. Pretty much everyone on the Shore there knew the story. Some called him crazy, some kind of admired him for it. I didn't get it."

Ramona grew quiet for a few seconds. "But you didn't go home to check on him?"

It was an accusation and it seemed unlike her, but she had asked the obvious question and I just didn't have an answer that made any real sense. Guilt was written all over me as I avoided looking straight at her. "No. I didn't."

The silence was thick and leaden. I wanted to try to explain why I felt justified in having cut my ties with him and all of Stewart Harbour, but I knew it would sound like bullshit. The worst kind of bullshit.

"Why do you think he did it?" she finally asked, breaking the silence. "Why did he tear down the house and try to erase everything?"

"I don't know. I think part of it was his way of accepting that his life with my mom was over. I guess I never really understood my father."

"I think I would have liked him if I'd known him," Ramona said.

"And I don't think I ever even *gave* myself a chance to get to know him. I fucked up."

"No. You knew his way of life wasn't yours. You did what you had to do."

"But I think he was happy with what he had. I grew up always thinking that just over the horizon or just around the bend there was something more. Something better."

"And there wasn't?"

"No. Not till now. Not till you."

"And look where you are," she said, stretching her arms out to draw my attention to the palatial surroundings of the fish shack.

I suddenly realized I'd been holding on to that old black frying pan all this time I told the story. I looked at it and then ever so gently set it down on the counter with the utmost reverence.

28

The sound of the cellphone ringing seemed so out of place I didn't even know what it was at first. Ramona let it ring until it stopped. She waited a full minute and then checked her messages with the speakerphone on.

"Hi," I heard Beth Ann say. "Ramona? I'd like to talk to Charles — oh, and you too. You put up Brody's bail so you should definitely be included. Anyway, I think we need to all get together and do some serious talking. If you're willing, that is. I think we need to work together on this. Could you come over today at two? I know that sounds crazy. But please. If you will. Call me back." And she hung up.

Ramona looked at me. "What do you think she means by 'all,' and 'work together' on what?"

"I don't know. Beth Ann always had a kind of no-nonsense approach to things."

"I like her. I trust her. I guess we better go."

"I was hoping we would just run off to Paris and visit all the places where Hemingway and Fitzgerald hung out."

"And disappoint your old girlfriend?"

I shrugged. "It's just that I've had so much more practice at running away rather than sticking around. It just seems like the thing to do."

"You got me into this. You played the little-boy-lost routine there in the fog in Halifax. What was I supposed to do?"

"Run. Run far away."

"Well, you didn't warn me."

"I should have. My mistake."

God, the banter always felt good. Like an old married couple. Like an old *happy* married couple who love the wordplay, the roles, the gamesmanship.

Ramona punched a number on her phone. "Hi, Beth Ann. Yes. We'll be there at two. Sure."

When she hung up I said, "We still have time to run. I say Paris."

"I say Stewart Harbour."

"Paris would be more fun."

"Oh, you don't have to convince me of that. But let's do Paris right here. Right now."

"Mais oui, mademoiselle."

And thus we returned to bed, escaped yet again briefly into whatever state that is that takes your mind off problems and puts it entirely on sex. Afterward, we vowed to do something about the bed situation. Creaky old cot, elbows banging each other's chin, arms and legs all twisted around any time one person moved. Having said that, it was still my version of euphoria, but it was time to at least expand the territory.

"I think we need to go shopping for a bed," I said. "No memory foam, though," I insisted. "I hate memory foam."

"No memory foam. Check. King size or queen size?"

"I don't know. We'll have to see what they have at the general store."

She thought I was kidding, but we needed more supplies so I drove us there. The same kid was working the cash register. He recognized us. No. He recognized Ramona. Now I began to understand that look that men gave her. The ones who had seen the sex clip on the internet. And, if Ramona was right, there was a hell of a lot of those horny buggers out there.

We loaded up on food and a couple more pots and spatulas and such. "You guys camping, or what?" the guy asked.

"Something like that," I said. "You wouldn't have any inflatable mattresses by any chance?" I'd seen some Coleman stoves and fishing rods. They seemed to have a whole department store of goods crammed into this place.

"Queen or king size?" he asked, with an all-too-self-conscious wink. I thought he was joking. But he wasn't.

"Queen," I said, realizing king probably wouldn't even fit on the floor of my father's tiny old bedroom.

"Queen it is." He went into the back room and came out a minute later with a big cardboard box. "Electric pump is inside. Keep it away from the woodstove, though."

The kid totalled up our bill and Ramona paid with her credit card.

———————

Two o'clock rolled around all too soon. We pulled into the driveway of Beth Ann's house and I parked by her truck. Brody's truck was there. Beth Ann had probably paid the towing bill to get it out. Joe's truck was there too. It was a family of trucks. Our urban set of wheels looked mightily out of place.

We crunched up the crushed clamshells of the driveway as we walked up to the door. Beth Ann opened it. "Thanks for coming," she said and nodded toward the living room.

Brody and Joe were sitting on wooden kitchen chairs, each holding a can of Keith's. A big case of Keith's was sitting open in the middle of the living room. A case of thirty. I had no idea you could buy a case of beer that big.

There was a young woman there too, sitting beside Brody. She looked shy and embarrassed and just nodded as we came in.

Beth Ann trailed us in and asked us to sit on the sofa. We sat. She motioned toward the young woman. "This is Mackenzie," she said. "Brody's girlfriend. She's gonna have Brody's baby."

Then things went quiet. So quiet that it was solid and thick. Like you could cut it up with butcher's knife, box it, and sell it to people who live in noisy cities. *Here, you want some quiet? Real quiet? Try this. Just open this up and you'll get to know what real quiet is.*

"Hi, Mackenzie," Ramona said. "How far along?"

Mackenzie placed both hands on her stomach. "Four months." She gave Ramona a half-smile.

I wanted to ask the obvious question before we got reeled into something even more complicated than it already was. *Are you sure it's Brody's baby?* But I knew that's just what an asshole would say at a time like this. And I'd left my membership card to that club back in Halifax. Besides, Beth Ann was that no-nonsense person I'd ditched long ago. She hadn't changed. She would have gotten to the truth. So, yes, it was definitely Brody's kid. Poor girl. Poor kid. Now what?

Brody and Joe cracked open another beer. Beth Ann wasn't drinking and neither was Mackenzie.

"How are you feeling?" Ramona asked Mackenzie.

"Okay, I guess," she said sheepishly. "Nothing I can't handle."

I figured she was twenty-one or twenty-two. Quite a bit younger than Brody. But Brody was on the immature side for a guy in his thirties. I had misjudged him early on, thinking he was much younger. I wondered what she saw in him.

"And how are you doing?" I asked Brody.

"Just fucking great," Brody snarled. "I'm so fucking wonderful."

More silence followed, then the screen door opened and someone else walked in. Rolf. His eyes lit up when he saw the thirty-pack of beer in the middle of the room. He didn't speak. Just waltzed in, grabbed a can, and plopped down on the floor in the corner.

"I invited Rolf to come act as referee if need be. He knows why we're all here."

"Couldn't turn down an invite for a front-row seat," Rolf said. He was all smiles.

Beth Ann brought the meeting to order. "Tell me if I'm wrong, but I'd like to think we are all in this together. I don't mean we intended things to be the way they are. But this is what we've been handed. I think we need a plan."

Beth Ann immediately saw the look on my face. "Charles, you can just walk away if you want. I would understand that. And Ramona, one way or the other, we'll get your money back on the bail. So, if you feel it's the thing to do, get up now and go. I would understand."

That was the door I most certainly wanted to take at that moment. But my gut told me one thing and one thing only: if I got up and walked out of there now, I'd lose Ramona for good.

"Guess we're staying," I said. "What's next?"

"Have another beer," Joe said and threw me a second can, even though I'd barely touched my first. I looked at him sitting there beside Brody, both of them looking like they'd been caught stealing candy or something. But they seemed to have made up. Father and son. They had the very same way of slouching down in the chair and they were both in their socks, no shoes, wiggling their toes.

Brody suddenly grew animated. "What's next is you guys helping me figure out how to get the charges dropped." He glared at me now. "You got me into this."

Beth Ann gave him a look that could fry meat. "Brody."

He slumped back. "Sorry," he said to me. "But it was a really shitty thing to do. Why the fuck did you do it?"

Beth Ann was about to say something to him but Ramona jumped in. "My brother died of an overdose of a drug he didn't even know he was taking." She was looking right at Brody. As she spoke, the fire seemed to go right out of him.

"Scooter's out of the hospital," Brody said. "They said it wasn't as bad as it seemed."

"Jesus, Brody," Joe said. "The boy wasn't breathing."

Brody just shrugged. I was convinced he knew what he'd done and felt bad about it even though his mouth was still speaking the lines his former self would have said. Something *had* changed about Brody, although I couldn't quite pin it down. Something about nearly drowning in the ocean would do that to you. Mackenzie leaned forward then and put a hand on Brody's shoulder. She seemed quite tender but also protective. I saw that there was strength in her.

Beth Ann let Joe's words hang there in the air a minute. "Well, we all sort of knew why Charles did what he did. The question is where do we go from here?"

Brody touched Mackenzie's hand on his shoulder. He was looking at the floor when he said, "Don't worry, I'm not going to try running again. Where the hell would I run to anyway? This place is all I know."

No one blinked.

Rolf must have felt the tension needed to break. He cleared his throat. "World's not safe out there, anyway. Why the hell would you want to leave here? No person in his right mind would want to be out there, with terrorists and whatnot. They say they're everywhere and are just waiting to blow off your arms and legs. I seen it on TV. Joe, would ya toss me another of them Keith's like a good fella?" Rolf had always listened to too much news, I recalled, and had a xenophobic streak a mile long.

"Brody goes before the judge next week," Beth Ann jumped in, bringing the discussion back to what needed to be done for Brody. "He needs a lawyer, so I contacted one. He'll be here any minute. We have questions we should ask him. Not too many criminal lawyers around here, but they say he's good. Maybe the best. Alan Romaine."

The name rang a bell. I couldn't keep quiet. "You got to be kidding?" I looked at Joe. "Alan Romaine from school? The kid we called *Lettuce*?"

Joe nodded and threw up his hands. "He became a lawyer. Who would have guessed? Won some big cases. Made some serious money."

"Lettuce?" I repeated. Alan had been one of those kids whose mother had stitched a label on his shirt that read "Victim."

Joe piped up. "They say Alan Romaine could have gotten Hitler off scot-free at the Nuremberg trials. They say he makes Robert Shapiro look like a pussycat."

"Who's Robert Shapiro?" Brody asked.

"He got O.J. Simpson off," Joe answered.

"Knock, knock," someone said through the screen door. And, sure enough, there was Lettuce, right on cue.

I wouldn't have recognized him. Slightly grey, close-cropped hair. Five-hundred-dollar glasses if my reckoning was correct. Black shiny shoes. Expensive suit. Briefcase like you'd expect a successful lawyer to be carrying. He saw the look on our faces when he walked into the room. Here was a man completely out of place.

"Hi everyone. Don't let the monkey suit fool ya. You have to dress for success, they say." Brody lobbed him a beer, but Alan didn't quite understand the gesture of hospitality. He saw the projectile headed his way and held up the briefcase in defence. The unopened beer bounced off it onto the floor. "Oops," Lettuce said. "Wasn't expecting that." He picked up the beer and set it unopened on a small table. "Folks ready to get down to business?"

We were.

Brody started to squirm a bit as Alan Romaine explained the legal situation, summing it up this way: "We're not going to win, but we are going to get the charges reduced. It's that simple. Plead guilty to a lesser offence, save a big court battle and a lot of money on the part of the Crown. Do the time and move on."

"Do the time?" Brody asked.

I think, deep down, he was hoping this whole thing would blow over.

"I don't see any other way," Alan said, pushing his glasses up on his nose. "I say we put it all out in the open. I especially want to know why Charles here turned him in."

I didn't mention Ramona's role in this, but I told Alan the obvious reason. As he studied my face, I could see the kid who had been bullied in the schoolyard by bigger kids, like Joe. But

I could see he'd overcome the victim label and turned it into something else. Something that had made him stronger, more confident.

"No. There's more," Beth Ann insisted.

"Don't go there," Joe said. "That doesn't need to be part of this."

"Yes, it does," Beth Ann replied. "Alan, Charles here is Brody's biological father."

"Fuck," Joe said.

Beth Ann held her ground. "Does it really matter if it comes out?"

"It will come out," Alan confirmed.

"Well, it does matter," Joe insisted. "All these years people believed Brody was my kid. When this comes out, what will they think of me then?"

Beth Ann's voice rose a half octave higher. "Why would you care what anyone has to say about you, Joe? You're still who you are and that's all that matters." It was a kind of backhanded compliment maybe. Or some kind of code between them.

"Fuck it," Joe said, admitting defeat.

"What about you, Brody?" Alan asked. "You okay if this is part of the story?"

"Let 'em talk. No big deal to me. But I'll always think of Joe as my real father." Truth was, Joe wasn't such a hot father, and everyone knew that. But it was a Hallmark card moment and I knew there weren't too many of them around the Harbour these days. Joe shook it off, although I almost thought he was going to blubber.

"Okay then," Alan said. "Now we have a narrative. Caring father — that's you, Charles, in this case — turns in his own son. To save others. But to save his son as well. Tough love. That sort of thing. Charles, you need to get this all down in writing for me to present to the judge, and the wording is of the utmost importance. We need to make sure the judge understands that. Might leak out in the papers, though."

Funny thought. Me in the papers: *Father has his son sent to jail.* I could see the legal proceedings page copy now. Only it wouldn't be in the *Tribune.* "I'll do whatever's needed."

"Then we have something to work with. We have a story. A narrative. And that's gonna reduce the charges."

It was then Beth Ann jumped back into the conversation. "It may come up that Brody was charged with assault before. Twice. What about that?"

"Charged but not convicted," Brody interjected.

"If no conviction, then it shouldn't come up in the case at all. No big deal."

Brody let out a notable sigh of relief.

"Then we're good," Alan said. He looked like he'd already won the case, even though there was no win to be had. As he looked around the room, it seemed that he noticed Mackenzie for the first time. "Sorry, little lady, I was just wondering how you fit into this."

Beth Ann touched Mackenzie's hand and then spoke on her behalf. "She's pregnant with Brody's baby."

"No. Really?" Lettuce asked.

"Really," Beth Ann said.

"I think we just knocked some more time off the sentence. We just improved the narrative." Without missing a beat, he opened up his briefcase. "I took the liberty of doing up a client agreement, with what I think is a fairly accurate estimate of my fees."

He handed the single sheet of paper to Joe. His eyebrows shot heavenward. He handed the paper to Beth Ann. The blood drained out of her face. She leaned forward and handed it to me. I could see what the shock was about. Not too long ago you could buy a house for that price in this part of Nova Scotia. Maybe this was Lettuce's way of getting back at all of us for not treating him better back at school.

Ramona plucked the paper from my grip. She took one look and nodded.

"In for a penny," she said.

"You can't do that," Beth Ann interjected. "This isn't your problem."

"What else are you going to do?" Ramona responded.

No one had to speak. The silence did the talking.

"Settled then," Ramona concluded.

There were some pleasantries after that and then Alan's watch beeped and he was gone. We all heard his tires crunching clamshells as he left.

Rolf was the first to speak. "Bleed you dry, the shysters. Never knew one that I liked or trusted. Mr. Shiny Shoes was pretty full of himself, I'd say. Still, if you want to save this boy's ass, I think he's your man. Fill up his pockets with enough loot and maybe he'll be able to do the job. Joe, toss me another beer, would ya?"

29

After Alan left, Joe, Brody, and Rolf seemed to forget about the big issue of the day. They were well into that case of beer and their talk turned to other topics. Fishing, hockey, beer, assholes and assholery seemed to be the mainstays.

I ended up following Ramona to sit on the sofa with Mackenzie and Beth Ann. Mackenzie seemed a little more relaxed.

"Brody's gonna straighten himself out," she said. "I know it. He just needs someone to give him a break."

"Well, I think he just got one," Beth Ann said. "Still, it seems there's a good chance he's going to be spending some time away. Are you going to be okay, Mackenzie? How do you feel about it all?"

Mackenzie looked sad but then her face brightened a little. "I'm excited about becoming a mother," she said. "I know this wasn't planned or anything, but I feel like it was meant to be. I know it's the right thing."

Naive girl. Nice girl. Tough life ahead, I thought. It looked like Beth Ann and Ramona were trying to avoid rolling their eyes.

"What do your parents have to say about it?" Ramona asked.

"My parents don't really give a shit," Mackenzie replied, with a vehemence that surprised me. "About me or about anything but themselves. I've been staying with my grandmother for the last three years. She thinks I should give the baby up when it's born. But I won't do that."

She was referring to a baby that was technically my grand-child. Good God, I was going to be a grandfather. That is one thing that I never in my life envisioned.

Mackenzie now turned to me. It was like the girl was read-ing my mind. "You can come visit the baby whenever you like. I think that would be just fine. Kind of like family, right?"

"Right. And thank you for being so gracious about it."

She laughed. "Nobody ever called me gracious before."

———

Ramona sat silently on the way back to our little home on the water.

"We got a mattress to blow up," I said. "Gonna be like sleep-ing on air."

"It will be sleeping on air," she reminded me, then added, "Grandpa."

I shook my head.

"Better get used to it," she said.

I cobbled together a not-so-great meal after that. I blew up the mattress and put it on the floor of the bedroom. Ramona lit a smelly candle she'd bought from the general store.

"How do you feel about being a grandfather?" Ramona asked.

"Jeez, I don't know. I didn't exactly do an award-winning job as a father, did I?"

Ramona looked like she didn't know what to say to that. Instead, she said, "You haven't finished telling me what happened to your father after your mom passed on and after the house was all gone."

"Well, he moved out here, as you know. He kept fishing. They say he kept more and more to himself. Folks were worried about him."

"Including you?"

"I'd call him and he'd say everything was fine. Don't worry about him. Said he'd always known he'd end up all alone as an old fisherman, that he'd planned for it all his life. All he wanted to do was keep up the routine: go to sea, fish, watch TV at night, and then get up the next morning and do it all over again."

"But something happened."

"Something. Yeah. He went to sea one fine day — calm seas, clear sky — and he never came back. Rolf went looking for him and found the boat, drifting. No sign of my father. Not a trace. No note, no sign of any problem on board. He'd put out lobster traps that day. Everything looked normal. He was just gone."

"What do you think happened?"

"I don't know. I blamed myself for not coming back to check on him. Truth was, I didn't want to return here for any reason. I should have. And then after he was gone, I had even less reason to come here."

"And you just walked away?"

"I just *stayed* away. Pete was out west. Beth Ann and I were over. I had finally gotten rid of the smell of fish on me — figuratively speaking."

"Was there a will?"

"Yeah. A real basic one. Pete had told everyone he was never coming back here and didn't want any property so it all went to me. Pete got some savings. I would have got the house — if there was a house — but I got the land there on the mainland and I got this little fisherman's palace where we now reside. Only problem with this shack is that I own the building but not the land it's on, since it's technically in the tidal zone. And someday soon, it may just wash away."

"Could we make it float away?"

"What?"

"Like the way they moved those houses when they closed down the Newfoundland outports. Maybe we could float it off somewhere."

"Where?"

"You mentioned Paris."

I laughed. "Well, we'd have to cross the Atlantic first."

"We get a tow. Hitch a ride behind a container ship."

"Maybe. I can just picture us floating down the Seine."

"I can see it too."

We were lying on our backs now on the fully inflated mattress. We were watching the light from the candle dance on the ceiling. Despite the complications and confusion around us, we kept finding moments like this. Moments when the world just went away and left us all on our own.

Grandpa and his girlfriend on a blow-up mattress far down the Eastern Shore, planning to float a little fish shack to the Left Bank where he'd write a great literary novel and she'd tend house. A fantasy world without time or conflict.

30

When you walk away from your everyday life, things are left hanging. Dangling maybe is a better verb. After losing my job and all my saved money, I had isolated myself; there is no denying it. First there was some UI coming in, but that ran out. I had copped a couple of freelance writing jobs producing articles for trade publications, but that never amounted to much. Two hundred dollars here, three hundred there for writing articles about men and their bulldozers or the latest news in the world of firefighters' equipment. I could have made that work, maybe. Hustled like in my early years as a journalist. But my heart wasn't in it.

Maybe everyone hits a wall at some point. Things fall apart and you have to pick up the pieces and somehow put Humpty Dumpty back together again, or you have to start over. I slogged through a depressive state back there and didn't see any future. I started to have much more empathy for people who were down and out. If I could have helped those around me, I would have. But I could barely help myself.

Spent whole days in my rathole apartment where I couldn't tell you a single thing that I did. I think I napped a lot. I did some reading. That helped. Maybe it was the Halifax Regional Library that got me through the worst of it. Autobiographies of Neil

Young, Keith Richards, Bruce Springsteen. They'd all struggled some. They all got through it. I drifted back to Hemingway and Fitzgerald and filled in some books on my bucket list that I'd missed. I read Pat Conroy's book about his father and realized again how lucky I had been to have the parents I had. Why was I so willing to abandon them?

If I ever won the lottery or fell into money, I'd give a stack of it to the Halifax Library for getting me through those days of gloom. On some days, I believed that my unlucky streak would end. But then I lost hope.

And, sometime well after that, Ramona dropped out of the sky. But ...

Things got complicated. And it looked like they were going to get even more complicated.

Right now, though, it was one hell of a life out there at the fish shack.

It was summer.

Ramona and I had the ability to make the world go away when we wanted.

Brody would have his day in court. He would have his narrative. Things would go one way or the other. But all of that was still a long way away. The court date was not until August 25. *A long way away.*

This was summer. The one you want to never end.

We fixed up my father's fish shack. Ramona had taken to calling it a shack as well. We could have called it a cabin or a cottage or something respectable. But shack sounded just right.

"So, is this what you call shacking up with someone?" she asked one morning while we were washing dishes in the old iron-stained sink where my father had once cleaned hundreds of fish.

"Absolutely. You and me shacking up down at the Beach Shack, the Sugar Shack, the Hop in the Sack shack. You remember Conway Twitty?"

"Nope. Must have been before my time."

"He sang 'Rollin' in My Sweet Baby's Arms.' It had the lyric, *Gonna lay around the shack till the mail train comes back, rollin' in my sweet baby's arms.*"

"That's fine with me. Let's do it. When is that mail train expected?"

"Not any time soon."

——————

When I woke up one foggy morning, it must have been the fog that made me think about Halifax. The past that I had left behind. I still had that damned apartment. And I hadn't paid rent for a couple of months.

The landlord said he'd hang on, cut me a break until my luck got better. But how long ago was that? I decided I better give him a call.

Jimmy was a slum landlord, a seventy-year-old man, born in Poland, who had jumped ship in Halifax back in the days of the communist government. He smoked filterless cigarettes down to nothing until they'd burnt his lips. I remember him with two good blisters top and bottom almost all the time. He liked to tell me stories about the women in Poland and the beer. Even in his seventies it was still women and beer for Jimmy. Women of all sizes came and went. Beer flowed freely.

"Hello," he answered, with a smoker's gravel in his voice. Talking to Jimmy was like talking to a cement mixer.

"Jimmy, it's Charles."

"Charlie. I thought you must be dead." I'd corrected Jimmy a hundred times about the name, but it never stuck.

"I'm not."

"Shit."

"You seem disappointed."

"No, Charlie, I'm glad you're alive. It's just that I was sure you weren't coming back."

"I know. My fault. I've been out of town. I got caught up in things."

"Jesus, man. You were four months behind in rent."

"Really? Was it that long?"

"I figured you were either dead or ran out on me without paying."

"Well, I was hoping I could catch up somehow."

"I know. I'm sure you were. But I guess I gave up on you. You know I got bills. I need my tenants to pay. The women, the girls I see, it takes money to keep them around, you know. I don't mean I pay them or any shit like that. It's just that I need to keep them happy. A little gift. A meal out at the casino. You know."

"I should come get my things. And I'm still gonna find a way to pay you what I owe."

There was a pause and then Jimmy coughed long and hard straight into the phone. "Well, here's the thing, Charlie."

I guess I should have seen this coming.

"The thing is, I cleaned out your apartment. I gave up on you. Dead or deadbeat, either way. My father, who used to be a boss in a pickle factory in Warsaw, always said, business is business. *Biznes to biznes.*"

"What do you mean cleaned out?"

"Well, I saw that young man in there one day. He had music blasting. He was hooting it up, and when I confronted him, he showed me the key. Told me to fuck off. Well, I thought that was it. You were gone and you'd given this monkey the key to your place.

"I waited for some word from you. But nothing. I was gonna put your stuff out at the curb, only the city fined me for doing that the last time, the buggers. So I had a kind of open house and gave all your stuff away. You didn't have a whole hell of a lot, buddy."

"You mean it's all gone?"

"Yes, it is. I'm sorry to say. Maybe I made a mistake."

Maybe I should have been upset about this. But I wasn't. I was free of my possessions, once again, free of my past.

"Jimmy, I think you did the right thing."

"Phewy. I like you, Charlie. I didn't intend to do anything mean."

"What did you do with my books?"

"Gave 'em away."

"Good. My computer?"

"Some college kid took it. Don't know his name."

"You didn't happen to see a cardboard box with a stack of papers in it?"

"Your novel you'd been working on?"

"Yeah. That."

"Oh, I kept that. I found it and started reading. I was hooked from the word go."

"You saved it?"

"I saved it. I read it. But it's not finished. You got to tell me how it ends."

"I don't know how it ends."

"I should give it back to you then, so you can finish it."

"I don't know if I'll ever finish it."

"Here's the deal," Jimmy said, punctuated by a staccato of coughing. "I forget about what you owe me and I give the novel back to you if you promise to finish it and let me read the rest."

"Deal," I said.

31

It's hard to say exactly what we did with our days. We lived them. One by one. We went to sea a few times on the calm days. I paid close attention to the marine forecasts. We caught some haddock and some mackerel. Ate a lot of fish. Both agreed it might be time for a bit more turf and a little less surf in our diets.

Ramona hinted that she had some more appointments coming up soon, never quite answering my questions about what for. Alan Romaine came over a couple of times and took down my story about Brody in detail. I could see his mind working all the while about the "narrative" and how he would make it play out. Part of me wished I hadn't got involved and a bigger part of me was dreading that things might not turn out as cheery as Alan made it sound.

But it was summer on the Eastern Shore of Nova Scotia and the nor'easters were on vacation — like half the province. I wanted the warm summer days of life in the Harbour to stretch out forever. But then I woke up one morning to hear Ramona announce that she was going to Halifax. "Appointments," she said. "And I need to visit my mother."

The drive to the city seemed much longer and more difficult for some reason. Worlds colliding again.

"What is the name of that novel you were working on?" she asked. "You never told me."

"I never told anyone."

"Well, Jimmy read it, right? He said he liked it."

"Jimmy isn't exactly a literary critic."

"At least tell me the name."

"*Purgatory Newsletter*," I said. Now that I said it out loud it sounded truly ridiculous.

I think she was trying to suppress a laugh. "Hmm. Purgatory — as in the place between heaven and hell?"

"Well, I didn't mean it literally. Besides, it was just a working title."

Ramona was on her phone now. I kept forgetting that people could use phones to look up things on the internet.

"Here," she said. "I got it. Wikipedia: 'Purgatory is an intermediate state after physical death in which some of those ultimately destined for heaven must first undergo purification, so as to achieve the holiness necessary to enter the joy of heaven…. Only those who die in the state of grace, but have not yet fulfilled the temporal punishment due to their sin can be in purgatory.'"

"Hey, look, I'm not even Catholic. I was probably thinking of Dante and *El Purgatorio*. It was a sophomoric idea, I can see that. It was a book about being stuck in an in-between world. Not heaven, not hell. To be honest I didn't know where it was going. I kept losing the story. Kept changing my mind."

"Was it about you?"

"No. People always make that mistake about fiction writing. It was a story. One I'll never finish."

"I thought you promised your old landlord you'd finish it."

She could tell I was getting miffed about trying to explain it. "I'd like to read it," she said. "Maybe I can help you find an ending. Find a way for your protagonist to move out of purgatory."

"Fine," I said, just to end the discussion. I couldn't figure out why talking about the novel made me so agitated. I guess it was another reminder of what a dismal failure my life had been.

Ramona dropped me off at her apartment, gave me a key, and told me to keep it, said she'd be back by one and we'd go see her mom.

When she returned at 12:15, she seemed distracted and upset. "You okay? What happened?"

"Nothing happened. I'm fine. You coming with me to see Mom or what?"

She seemed angry with me. I didn't understand. This wasn't like Ramona.

"I'm coming. Of course."

My mind was stuck on the purgatory thing. The celestial waiting room. Stuck in limbo. With a way out, but the way out involved punishment. Punishment followed by forgiveness. Is that the way it works? Were the Catholics right? If you made it to purgatory, the good news was you weren't going to hell; you just had to take your licks and then you could go to heaven. But then maybe some people might be stuck in purgatory forever. Forever in between. Forever being tested, punished, but not forgiven.

There was a man sitting in a chair in Brenda Danforth's nursing home room. He had his back to us. He didn't turn around as we walked in. Ramona's mother was looking downright cheerful. She lit up even more when she saw us. It must have been one of her good days.

"Ramona, darling, look who's here."

That's when the man in the suit stood up and turned our way.

"Oh, God," Ramona said. "What are you doing here?"

He was seventyish, maybe older. A man with thinning silver hair in a very expensive-looking suit. A man with a big broad smile on his face. A man who was Ramona's father. I got that at once.

"I came to take your mother out of here. I want her to come home with me."

Ramona looked at father with a look of pure contempt. Then she looked at her mother and realized her reaction was causing her mother distress. She closed her eyes and clenched her fists, but when she opened her eyes, she forced herself to smile.

"Isn't it great to have your father back?" Brenda said.

Ramona's father held out his hands, palms up. I couldn't help but notice the Rolex watch. A very expensive Rolex watch. Old moneybags. I wondered what happened with the woman he'd run off with.

"We should talk over lunch," Ramona's father said. "Your mother and I have been catching up on old times and I think she may need to rest now." He turned to his wife and said, "Isn't that right, dear?"

She nodded a sweet smile. The woman was happy. There was no doubt about it. Her long-lost philandering husband had returned and she was happy to have him back. Maybe we should have stayed, but Brenda had already closed her eyes and nodded forward.

Ramona was positively volcanic, but she held it in until we were out of the room and down the hall and out in the parking lot.

"I'm sorry," Ramona's father said to me once we were outside. "I didn't properly introduce myself. I'm Stanley Danforth. You can call me Stan. And you are?"

"Charles," I said, "but you can call me Charles."

He bloody winked at that. The fucker winked. "Let's go to Da Maurizio, Charles. Ramona and I need to talk. Meet you there in ten minutes?" He was as calm and self-assured as any man I'd met. No hint of a guilt-ridden skirt-chaser who had left his wife in mental decline.

I didn't answer as he got into his blue BMW and eased out of the parking space and drove off.

"That man really your father?" I asked. It was like some strange actor playing a very sophisticated role had shown up in her mother's room.

"Unfortunately, yes. Now, just get in the damn car and drive us to the restaurant."

So I got in the damn car and drove us to the restaurant.

I'm not a big fan of restaurants to be honest. They can be okay, I suppose; however, I have always thought that if you are going to have a family argument, a really big blow-out of some sort, that a restaurant is not the place to do it.

But there we were. Her father acting like a prince among men and Ramona ready to explode with rage at any moment.

Her father had already ordered champagne. "I hope you don't mind that I took the liberty of ordering a little refreshment," he said.

He reminded me a little of the publisher back at the *Tribune*. A man who had been born to money and privilege and oozed it out of every pore of his body. Jock Watson was his name, and he liked to get us all together in the newsroom, grace us with his presence, give a little pep talk, and tell us how much he admired us and how we were all like family. But when things got tight, he pulled the plug on the paper and walked away.

Jock Watson and Stanley not only wore the same Armani suits, but they were cut out of the same cloth. A very expensive fabric with a stain-free, almost Teflon-like coating.

He was looking rather pleased with himself — calm, self-satisfied, adjusting the placement of his fork and knife by his plate. Ramona was studying her own knife, undoubtedly trying to judge if it was sharp enough to do the job she had in mind. The waiter poured champagne for the family reunion.

When the waiter bowed and slipped away, Stanley cleared his throat. "I know I made a mistake, Ramona. A very big mistake. But now I'm back to make amends."

"It's not that easy," Ramona said.

"I know it's not. But I need to do this. For your mother and me."

"You left. You left when she needed you."

"I left your mother in good care. The care she needed."

"Then why are you back? What happened to what's her name?"

"Christina? She was only using me."

"Oh, really?"

"It took me a long while to realize. I can't believe I was so naive."

"I can't believe you are such a shit," Ramona said, raising her voice.

"I deserve every bad thing you have to say about me. I was a poor father and a terrible husband, and it took me all this time to realize it. Now I'd like to make things right."

It was fascinating to see how detached the man was from emotions. He'd made a mistake and now he'd correct it. That was his story. His narrative. A man of wealth and privilege, a man who walks away and feels no qualms about it. Then comes back. Patches things up.

"I love your mother very much. I always did. Then this woman, Christina, came along and cast some kind of spell over me. Looking back, I can't see how that could have happened. But it did."

"But you can't just come home and make everything right that easily."

"I want to take your mother out of that home. They have done a good job there. You can't deny I made sure she has had the most excellent care in my absence."

"You left money. You ran. I don't call that taking care of her."

Stanley folded his hands in front of him as if praying, as if wanting to do penance. "You and your mother were both well provided for. The family trust. It was well endowed. I worked many years to build up that nest egg. And it paid off."

"You never worked hard in your life."

"Money came easily to me, I'll admit. But I was a wise businessman and that was a skill as well."

"Money always came before family."

"Be that as it may, I am here now and I want to bring your mother back with me and provide around-the-clock professional assistance to help with her condition." Then he turned to me.

"Charles, if I may be so bold as to ask your opinion, what would you want if you were to find yourself in Brenda's condition? To remain in an institution or to be living in a real home with a loved one?"

Ramona shot a few daggers at me.

I took a fortifying sip of wine. "Well, Stan, I don't think that is for me to say. But, suffice it to say that Brenda seems to be doing as well as can be expected in the home she is in, and you have proven yourself to be, well, if I may be so bold, unreliable, so maybe she should stay put."

"Unreliable is a polite way of putting it. I do understand."

"Dad," Ramona interrupted. "You are more than unreliable. You have been an asshole your entire life. And I've had to live with it. Now, I think you should just disappear yet again. Do your little vanishing act that you do so well. And leave us all alone."

I guess the waiter wasn't really noticing the domestic squabble that was about to erupt into a verbal firestorm, for he arrived, looking over Stanley's shoulder, and asked if we were ready to order.

Without missing a beat, Ramona's father serenely answered, "I'll start with the Caesar salad, please, followed by the sirloin."

It seemed nearly unthinkable that Stanley could remain so inhumanly calm and aloof as if the current discussion had been over what colour to paint the gazebo or some such thing.

"Fuck this," Ramona said, getting to her feet. "I'm leaving."

I was hoping she meant *we're* leaving. I was right behind her. I didn't look back to see Stan's reaction. My guess is he remained unruffled. I knew that nothing was settled. Not a damn thing.

I followed Ramona out to the car. We got in and it was like a bake oven in there. If we had left a dog in the car it would have been dead by now. I put in the key but couldn't get the windows to go down at first. I fiddled with the key some more until I got it. A puff of air pushed through the interior as I noticed Ramona was crying.

I put my arm around her and she leaned into me until her tears soaked my shirt.

When she pulled herself back together, she sat up and blew her nose. "That appointment I had this morning. It was with Mom's doctor. Well, my doctor too. He confirmed that I've got what she has. Early-onset dementia. I've got the gene. I have some early symptoms. Someday I'll be like her."

"That can't be," I said.

"It's only a matter of time. If you're looking for a way out, I suggest you walk away now."

It seemed we were repeatedly opening doors for the other one to exit from our lives. I thought it odd that, on a day like this, the day that her news came, the day her father arrived, she was thinking of me and not herself. It made me love her even more than I already did. And up until then, I didn't think that was possible.

32

O n the drive back to her place, she dried her tears and pulled herself back together. "Think about what I said. You can walk away from me any time and I won't think any less of you. This thing will catch up with me. Do the research."

Images of Ramona's mother flashed through my head. Was that really why her father had run off? And why in God's name had he returned? No, I didn't think I'd walk away even though I had been so good at just that all my life.

"I haven't seen you do one single thing that indicates you have memory problems of any sort," I said.

"I'm good at covering up. That's one of the first signs."

"Bullshit."

"I've been to three specialists. They all confirm it's true. No one can give me a timeline, but they all swear it is inevitable. They say I need to plan for what's ahead. A five-year plan."

I was angry now. Denial and anger make a fine emotional cocktail. "Fuck the doctors."

Ramona gave one last good blow into her Kleenex. "If I thought it would help, I would," she said and forced a smile. "Now let's forget about it and change the subject."

There was a lot more I wanted to say just then. I wanted to speak philosophically about how we now needed to live each day as if it were our last *good* day before things started to slide downhill. A five-year plan, what the hell was that? So there was a number attached to this. Not tomorrow, not the next day, but within five years. What about medical breakthroughs and all that? But I realized Ramona was way ahead of me on the research there. She read me the riot act because that's what the facts were saying. I doubted there would be an announcement any time soon on the CBC about a wonder drug that cured dementia.

A few years ago, I'd interviewed a doctor at Camp Hill Hospital, a researcher into Alzheimer's and dementia. He said the science had moved ahead by leaps and bounds, but when he took me around the hospital to meet some of his patients, some old and some not so old, I was not impressed.

"The money all goes into cancer," he told me. "That's where the drama is. Old folks and senility is just something that the public accepts. We're not expecting any big breakthroughs in the near future."

Back in Ramona's apartment, we curled up on her sofa and I held her. She fell asleep in my arms and I sat there with her, looking out the big window onto the harbour. I could see the Dartmouth ferry crossing to Halifax and watched a couple of tugboats heading to sea. There was George's Island, stark and unwelcoming, and beyond it, the wide, wide ocean. The one where my father had sailed on his last day on earth.

―――――

When Ramona awoke, she seemed like her old self. She showered and put on fresh clothes. She sat down at the kitchen table and picked up her landline phone. "I'm going to check my messages," she said. "I haven't checked this since, um, since you came along."

I went into the bathroom and took a shower myself. The water felt good. My clogged brain started back in with thoughts about the days ahead. What had I gotten myself into? I knew I was still capable of walking away if I wanted to. Walk away from

Ramona while I still had an open door. Walk away from Brody and Joe and Beth Ann. Alan Romaine already had my deposition. I need never go back to Stewart Harbour. I had no job and no responsibilities. I really could just disappear into thin air. Move out west? Start over? Go crash at Pete's until he kicked me out, maybe.

By the time I turned the water off, I felt physically ill. That's my report from the purgatory shower stall. Only problem is that heaven did not await. I was fairly certain of that.

Ramona was still sitting at the kitchen table with the house phone up to her ear. I sat down across from her. "Listen to this," she said and clicked the speakerphone button. It was a message that had been recorded.

"Ramona. I'm calling as a representative of Christian Women Against Pornography. I'm calling to let you know that you are on our blacklist of those who are responsible for corrupting our boys. We've seen your films on the internet, the ones our sons have easy access to. We want to expose you to the world for the whore that you are." And then the caller had hung up.

"Is that some kind of crude joke?" I asked.

"I don't know," Ramona said. "I told you about that film. And that was a long time ago."

"Things last forever on the internet. But I've never heard of this Christian Women organization."

Ramona was already walking across to her computer. She seemed rattled. After a minute, she found what she was looking for. "There they are. It looks like they're based in the States. Looks like they call themselves C-WAP. They have a hit list of women they've targeted. Looks like I'm the latest."

I looked at the computer screen and there was a photo of Ramona. Beneath it was her address here in Halifax. And her home phone number. "Looks like this just got posted recently."

"Jesus. Why you? Why now?"

"No reason. Maybe one of them saw their teenage boy looking at that damn footage from that damn movie. Tracked me down. It's not like I was hiding."

"I think it's all bluster," I said. "Bunch of redneck fundamentalists with nothing better to do."

"I hope so."

But even as we had finished listening to that first message, a second one had come in. Another one from the C-WAP. It was clear Ramona really was on some kind of hit list.

"This is ridiculous," I said. I looked at the number displayed on the phone. "I'm calling them back. Both of them."

"No," Ramona said. "That will only make things worse." Then she looked at me with a soft sad look of defeat. "Now you have one more reason to walk out the door. Over-the-hill porno star who's about to lose her mind. C'mon, Charles, time to run."

"I say we both get out of Dodge. Every time we come to Halifax, something bad happens. Let's get our sorry asses back to the simple life on the Eastern Shore."

"Every time we show up there something bad happens too," she added.

"Yeah, but at least the air is clean and we have free fish. And if those C-WAP women come looking for you, Rolf will chase them out of town with a pitchfork or something."

"I certainly seem to have made your life more complicated," Ramona said.

"And it all seemed so simple at first. Woman walks up to me out of the fog and offers to buy breakfast. Before I know it, we're all up to our earlobes in deep shit."

"You really should have been a poet."

"I wanted to be one back at Dal. Thought I could be the next Lord Byron."

"For pleasures past I do not grieve, nor perils gathering near; My greatest grief is that I leave nothing that claims a tear."

"How'd you do that?" I asked.

"Do what?"

"Pull that line out of the air."

"Memorization, my dear Watson. Remember, when I wasn't fornicating for the big screen I actually had to memorize lines. *The great art of life is sensation, to feel that we exist, even in pain.*"

The house phone was ringing now. I was about to pick it up and raise bloody hell if it was another of those C-WAP women. Ramona grabbed my hand. The phone stopped after three rings and the answering service kicked in. Ramona waited and then checked the message on speakerphone. It was her father. "Ramona, honey. I'm so sorry you got upset today. We really need to talk. About your mother. About you. About us. I promise. I'm trying to do the right thing."

She clicked off the speakerphone. "When my father says he wants 'the right thing,' he's always talking about what's right for him. Selfish bastard. I won't let him move her out of the home. He's not doing it."

She picked up the phone and called Bedford Manor. She spoke to the manager there and told her the situation, gave her strict orders not to allow her father to even take her mother anywhere off the property. This was the take-charge side of Ramona that I'd only seen a few times. Considering what her day had been like, I was a little surprised she could muster strength to play the role.

"Let's go pick up that manuscript of yours and go."

I tried to persuade her to forget about it, but she was insistent.

As we walked out of the building, we discovered someone had spray-painted graffiti on the side of the building. The graffiti read "Home of Ramona Danforth, the whore of Halifax."

"Looks like the C-WAP folks have a local chapter," Ramona said as we walked to the parking lot.

———

Jimmy was surprised to see me knocking on his door. He was wearing a paint-stained T-shirt and Bermuda shorts. Despite the fact I owed him money for unpaid rent, he seemed happy to see me. "Well, if it isn't Charlie Howard," he said. "Back from the dead."

When I told him I'd come for the novel, he said, "Good," and went to fetch it. When he returned, he looked me in the eye and said, "No story like this should ever go unfinished. If there's anything I've learned in life, it's that once you start a job, you have to finish it. It's no fucking good if you get lazy or give up. It's just no fucking good."

I was about to leave when he said, "Hold on. Don't go yet." He disappeared back into the building as I stood on the steps waiting.

When he returned he had an old black Remington manual typewriter. "You'll need this," he said and set it on top of the box holding my manuscript.

33

We were quiet for a while as I drove us east. The whole C-WAP thing seemed like a bad joke. The return of Ramona's father was definitely a problem. Even more disturbing was the news about what might become of Ramona. I was in denial about that. There was this lively, beautiful, intelligent woman beside me. It simply could not be.

What had become of the broken man on the Halifax pier? Well, he was still a work in progress, a project undergoing repair. And, despite the grenades being lobbed at him by the world, he was doing fairly well, thank you.

I was not ever in my recollected life an optimist. But I had become, against all my better judgment, hopeful. Ours was an unfinished story, just like that three-hundred-page manuscript sitting in the back seat alongside the old typewriter.

I remembered interviewing Farley Mowat a long time back at his home in River Bourgeois in Cape Breton. Farley showed me his own old Remington typewriter. "There," he said gruffly. "That's what I write on. You can't write shit on a computer. It sucks the spirit out of you. If you want to write anything worth your salt, you have to pound on the keys." He put a piece of paper into his old machine, hammered away, and then scrolled the paper out and handed it to me. On it were the words, "Writing should be hard work!"

Not long after that, Farley had been up on a ladder when one of his favourite dogs had knocked the ladder and he'd fallen and gotten injured. But he recovered and I lost track of him after that until I heard of his death in May of 2014.

Farley had been one of the last of that dying breed of writers that I admired. A truth-teller. A masterful bullshitter. A guy who didn't give a rat's ass what anyone thought about him. A man who defended whales and wolves and shot at American military planes flying over his house. I wondered if there was still room for a Farley Mowat in the world we now inhabited.

Ramona had drifted off as we drove. I found myself deep in some kind of reverie. I stopped and bought her an ice cream and we sat by the highway and ate it.

"I was serious about what I said," she said, yet again. "I've complicated your life enough already. If you want out, all you have to do is say it. I would understand. And I would still respect you."

"As in R-E-S-P-E-C-T? Shut up, Aretha, and eat your ice cream." And I kissed her long and hard, our tongues mixing vanilla and chocolate in a most delightful way.

Back in the car, I felt giddy. Despite everything that was being dumped on us, I felt light-headed and optimistic. Don't ask me to explain it.

"I always wanted to have a demented whore for a girlfriend," I suddenly said.

At first Ramona looked stunned. Then she tossed it back. "Well, now your dreams have come true."

"I don't believe the dementia story," I said soberly. "I just don't."

"It's called denial."

"Call it what you want. But even if you could convince me it's true, I have a cure."

"What's your cure, doctor?"

"Live. Live every moment. Every day. Live it till you're dead."

"Or until you lose your mind."

"Whichever comes first."

"Let's not talk about it," Ramona said, ending the conversation.

Before we headed out on the causeway, I drove us to the field where my parents' house once stood. We got out of the car and walked the property, grown thick with daisies, vetch, lupins, wild rose bushes, and tall grasses. I led Ramona to the location where the house had been and pointed to the pile of rocks on the edge of the field. "Stone by stone," I said, still trying to make some sort of sense of it all. Memories swept over me. I'd hidden in what was once a cellar here and smelled the cool damp smell of the packed dirt floor. I'd played outside in the yard. I grew up there and it was there that I had dreamed my dreams of escaping to the great wide world beyond this place.

And now I was back.

"How much money did you say you had?" I asked boldly.

"I never said."

"You have enough to build a house?"

Ramona blinked hard into the sun. "What kind of a house?"

"A nice house," I said.

"You want to use my money to build a house? A nice house? Here on your old family property?"

"Yes."

"Are you sure?"

"Yes, I'm sure. I'd build it myself, but I don't have a cent."

"Same old excuse," she said.

"So? Are you in?"

"Yes, I'm in. When do we start?"

"Soon," I said. "Very soon."

I'd never in my entire life thought about building on that old property. Once my father had torn down the house, I figured the land would just sit there and be like a thousand other properties on the Eastern Shore where homes had burnt down, or been left to rot. The abandoned property would just go back to its natural state.

Ramona had changed everything in my life. Broken man turned into a potentially promising work in progress. A man with an agenda. An unfinished novel, a house to be built, a life to be woven around a woman who might one day in the not-too-distant future lose her memory and maybe even forget who I was. But, goddamn it, she had given me back a reason to live. She had given me a life.

———

Summers are short in Nova Scotia. All too short. The warm days of July rolled by. Ramona and I went to sea on good days in my father's old boat. I started to reread my novel as we drifted with the engine off. It was like something written by a stranger. It was all about loss of innocence and disappointment. Corruption and failure. But there were some fine passages, some eloquent sentences written by a somewhat younger man who had a passion for language. I hadn't yet mustered the courage to start hammering away at what came to be known as the Farley Mowat Memorial Typewriter. It sat in the corner of the fish shack, waiting for me to come pound the keys hard enough to finish a long story that should someday, hopefully, make sense.

By the third week in July, there was a new hole in the ground where the old house once stood. Concrete was poured for a foundation and a contractor was ready to build a two-storey, Cape Cod–style house. A nice house.

The coming of August meant that Brody's appointment with justice was also coming up. There had been several "coaching" sessions with Alan Romaine for the upcoming courtroom date. Brody and I met with him together. At first, Alan had been so confident, but he seemed less so as the court date approached.

The plan was that Brody would plead guilty to the drug dealing charges and Alan would have Brody and me tell our story — the whole father and son narrative and the satisfying conclusion of Brody "turning a corner in his life." We went over the story again and again; it felt like we were being coached to death.

34

Romaine decided that a good way to help enforce the father and son story was for Brody and me to spend some quality time together. "Invite him to the house worksite some evening," Romaine suggested. "Just you and him. Take some beer."

So I did.

We had a full foundation by then. The house was moving along quicker than I would have thought. There wasn't a lot of new construction going on at this end of the Eastern Shore, so it wasn't as hard as I expected to get workers on site. Rolf had turned me onto a guy known simply as Big Carl from Wine Harbour who had a small construction company. Big Carl was salt of the earth, straightforward, and had a team of two young, bearded, tattooed men who looked like killers from a bike gang. But they were ultra-polite, especially around Ramona, and damn good workers. Rolf hung around them quite a bit, offering advice and telling stories.

So there I was one August evening, sitting on the first set of joists anchored into the concrete walls of what would be the basement wall of my new home. Even though it was a little ways along, it was still a pipe dream. The land was mine, but the house, well, it would be the house that Ramona built. I had just cracked open the first bottle of Propeller IPA and was watching the sun glint off the bottle when I had the thought, if a woman builds a house on your property, is that what you call a commitment?

Hell, yes, the sun and the Propeller bottle answered. Bloody hell, yes.

"Hey," Brody said, as he ambled up the driveway.

"Hey. You walked."

"Beth Ann told me to walk. She said you'd have beer and didn't want me to drive."

"When was the last time you listened to your mother?"

He laughed. "Never."

I held out a beer.

"What's this?" he asked.

"IPA. They call it craft beer."

"No Keith's?"

"Nope. Sorry."

Brody took the beer. "That's okay." He held the neck of the bottle up to the top edge of the foundation and hammered it lightly with his fist, making the beer cap fling off into the unfinished basement. Brody sat down on the wall and we stared at each other.

All the piss and vinegar seemed to have evaporated. Father and son sitting together at a house-to-be. The exiled writer in me kept thinking this was a very literary moment.

"Fuck, yeah," Brody said, nodding toward the setting sun. It was relevant to nothing in particular and could have meant most anything. I took it as a kind of acceptance of certain inevitable things to come.

"Same goes for me, I guess." I took another sip of beer. "Were things really that bad for you growing up here?"

"Hey, I don't have a shitload of fond memories, if that's what you mean."

"C'mon, give it a try. Tell me about something — something good from back in the day."

Brody took a swallow and then coughed, nearly spitting the beer on the ground. When he got his breath back he said,

"Somewhere around grade ten I had this teacher, Mrs. Watson. She was like the first teacher I liked. The first one who didn't treat me like trailer trash. I thought she was hot too. So, when she asked me to stay after school, I did."

I sipped my beer and waited. Looked like maybe we were going to swap memories. *All's well so far*, I thought.

"She was from Newfoundland and had one of them funny accents. Told me my school work was pretty terrible, but she saw a spark in me. That's the word she used, a 'spark.' Then she told me about my name. Brody. I'd never even thought about it before. A name is just a name. Something your parents stick you with. Something other kids make fun of. *Brody the Toady. Broody Brody.* But she said it was Scottish. It meant one of two things. Get this. 'Rampart fortification,' was one. She had to explain that to me. But I got the part that it meant 'strength.' Funny, though, the other meaning was 'muddy place' or 'ditch.'

"And then she asked me which one I was going to be. The rampart or the ditch. That kind of pissed me off. Another adult giving me a lecture. I was polite, though. I told her I wanted to be the rampart. The castle wall. Strong."

He polished off his beer in three long gulps. "Guess I called that wrong," he said.

"Brody, you're young. You're gonna have a chance to start a new beginning. It's just around the corner."

Brody shook his head. "Ain't nothing around the corner. I got a bad feeling about what comes next."

"You'll get past it. We go to court. We do what Romaine says we should."

"Fuck, yeah," he said again. But it had a different meaning this time.

"I looked in the mirror the other day," he said, "to see if I could see any of you in me."

"And?"

"Not a damn thing. Maybe ole Beth Ann was a liar. Maybe you weren't my biological father at all."

"We could always do a DNA test."

"No point. It is whatever it is. But I did have this little fantasy. Instead of bloody Joe Myatt trying to raise me, you took my mom off to Halifax once you got her knocked up. You two stayed together and raised me there. And I turned out all different. How come it didn't turn out that way?"

I shrugged. I didn't want to say that would never have happened. I was not ready to raise a kid back then. The world awaited. I wanted it all — everything but a family, that is. "I was young. I didn't want the baggage."

He gave me a dirty look. I'd chosen my words poorly. He flipped the empty beer bottle upside down, holding the neck, then flipped his wrist and threw the bottle against the far wall of the foundation where it shattered and splashed shards of glass all over the new smooth concrete floor.

"Oops," he said unapologetically.

I handed him another beer.

"You'll get through this," I said.

"You think they'll let me off with a fine or something?"

"I don't think so. But I think the judge will see it's your first offence and you are willing to admit that what you've been doing is wrong."

"I've been selling stuff for years. Got away with it all this time because nobody was willing to turn me in."

"I don't think that will come up. You gotta keep your head straight about this. Think positive."

"Mrs. Watson said that. It sounded like bullshit then and it sounds like bullshit now."

I didn't have a comeback line. Jesus, me giving Brody a page out of Norman Vincent Peale. What was the world coming to? "Yeah, it does sound like bullshit," I admitted. "All I know is that we go into that courtroom together. You, me, Beth Ann, Joe, Ramona."

"And Mackenzie," he added. "The judge needs to see I got a baby on the way. Gonna make sure he sees her sitting there with the big belly."

"Okay. So what about Mackenzie? What about the baby? Do you love her?"

Brody was peeling the label off the beer bottle now. That familiar gesture of men when confronted with tough questions.

"I don't know."

"She seems like a fine young woman."

"Fine? Not too smart if she let me into her life."

"But she did."

"I told her when we found out about the pregnancy to have an abortion. But she didn't. Then I said she should give it up for adoption. But she doesn't want to do that."

"What about her parents?"

"No. She can't raise the kid around those assholes. The kid would turn out worse than me."

"Then what?"

Brody looked frustrated. "I don't know. I can't think about anything until I get past this court thing."

The sun was dipping below the trees. The wind had dropped and the mosquitoes were looking for dinner.

"I'm gonna make you a promise," I said. "We get through this legal stuff and then we come up with some kind of plan."

"What kind of plan?"

"You, Mackenzie, the baby. Ramona and me will help you get started on a life."

"Hey, I had a life. Until you came along and wrecked it."

"You wanted to be a drug dealer for the rest of your life?"

Defiance had returned to the fortified ramparts. "Yeah, maybe I did."

"Please don't say that in court."

"I'm not that stupid." And then he shook it off, looked around at the worksite.

"What kind of house is this gonna be?"

"A nice house. Nothing fancy. But a nice house."

"This was where you grew up, wasn't it?"

"Yep."

"And your father tore the old house apart board by board?"

"Nail by nail."

"And gave it all away, right?"

"He did."

"He was fucking nuts. Everyone said so."

"He probably was."

"Parents, shit. Maybe we'd all be better off if we didn't have parents."

The logic of that statement eluded me, but the sentiment stuck. Despite his age, I knew that emotionally Brody was still a little kid.

Brody hopped down off the foundation and swatted at his neck. "These mosquitoes are killing me. I'm gonna go." He paused. "But, hey, thanks for the beer." And Brody made his way down the driveway toward home.

I looked around at the property — the tall spruce and fir trees that had been saplings when Pete and I had run around here as kids. I thought about my mother and father then. Brody was wrong, of course. We all needed parents to be there for us. I was lucky. Mine were.

Too bad that I had decided to abandon them once I was ready for my freedom. I remembered once reading a biography of Hemingway back in my young and oh so literary days at Dalhousie. The book was titled *Hemingway: A Life Without Consequences*. No consequences? Wouldn't that be nice.

As the mosquitoes came in for the kill and the beer buzzed my brain, I realized there was no such thing as a life without consequences. Every little thing — or big thing — you do in life sends out ripples in the pond that keep getting wider and wider.

35

As the court date drew ever closer, Ramona and Rolf teamed up to take charge of the progress on the house. While they were on the worksite, I found myself sitting in the fish shack at the old Remington typewriter staring at a blank sheet of paper. I hadn't written anything on a typewriter since university and even that had been an IBM Selectric.

I'd reread my novel-in-progress a couple of times and deluded myself into thinking it was better than I remembered. Not great. Just better. But my mind was still in complete rebellion against finishing it. And that damn piece of paper kept staring back at me. Here's what went through my head as I stared at it.

First off, we were well into the twenty-first century so why was I wasting my time with an ancient typewriter? A real writer needed a computer, a MacBook perhaps. Something sleek and silver and ultra-thin so I could take the sucker right out on the boat if I wanted and work. Is that Hemingwayesque enough for you? *The Old Man and the MacBook*. Hah.

But of course I could take the typewriter out to sea if I wanted. I was just making excuses.

One day, I came to the conclusion that if writing a novel was like building a house (as a number of writers have claimed) then I had a house with four walls and a roof, but no foundation. Maybe that was the problem.

And what if I actually finished my novel and nobody would bloody publish it? Well, I could counter that one with the belief that the writing itself was much more important than the result. The process not the product.

Still the page remained blank.

My protagonist was a man unlike me. Even though the novel was filled with angst and despair, doubts and misgivings, I had created a man of action. He was confident, worldly, and involved in the affairs of movers and shakers. I was convinced that he did not like me, the author, and that he looked down on me. Why didn't I write about a protagonist more like myself? He confronted adversity with courage, grace under pressure. I confronted adversity with what?

I'd allow myself no more than an hour sitting at the typewriter. Sometimes I'd end up writing a poem for Ramona. Yes, a gushy love poem. Then I'd walk it over to her at the worksite. She'd read it and drive me home and we'd end up in the sack. Now that seemed much more like real literature. Literature that served a purpose.

Of greater importance was the real story of those around me. Ramona. Brody. There would not be a real trial. It wouldn't be like that. Alan had continued to coach us on the matter. "You go before the court," he explained. "Brody pleads guilty. He tells his story as to why he did it. We all stick to the narrative. We bring in the girl. Brody shows remorse. Lots of remorse. Remorse to the nth power. It will be a light sentencing. Who knows? Community service maybe. I can't promise."

I tried my best to believe the outcome would be okay. I tried to convince myself I was not the instrument of my son's potential destruction.

And yet, in the midst of my own fears and worries, there was a summer like no other in my life. Ramona and I waking each morning in each other's arms. Warm weather. We saw dolphins at sea and even a sea turtle once when we took the boat far from shore and made love on waters as calm as a lake at sunrise.

The house finally had walls and a roof. It was a long way from complete, but you could walk up the front steps on 2 x 6s temporarily nailed to the risers and walk into it. No door yet. No windows. Just holes in the walls. Plywood subfloors. Everything had the smell of freshly sawed wood. Intoxicating.

Brody would drop by from time to time, admiring the progress. "This is what I'm gonna do," he announced on one occasion, running his hand along a beam. "I'm gonna build houses. I'm gonna build the best goddamn houses anybody ever imagined."

And why not? Never too late to take up a trade. Go to community college, study carpentry. Make a go of it.

Brody asked me once on the sly if there was anything he could do to help out with the project. I said I didn't know but that worksites always needed continual cleaning up. If he wanted to drop by anytime and keep things orderly, he was welcome.

And he did. Ramona and I would arrive in the morning and find scraps of wood piled up outside. Inside the house, he'd have swept up sawdust and thrown bent nails into a bucket. He didn't like it if I said anything to him about it or thanked him. So I just didn't mention it.

Beth Ann told Ramona that Brody was hanging out at the house sometimes in the evenings, occasionally with Mackenzie, who was having more trouble at home. She asked if we minded and we said no, not at all.

And so, it was the summer we built the house.

Twice, Ramona went back to the city to see her doctor. She insisted I let her go alone, that I was to stay there and keep an eye on the construction. But there really wasn't much for me to do except try and stay out of the way.

More than ever, I was refusing to believe there was anything wrong with the woman I loved. It became more of a joke than ever. I'd wake up in the morning and watch her still sleeping. God, I loved the way that woman breathed. Then, it was like, even though she was sleeping, she could sense I was watching her. And she'd open her eyes.

"Lose your mind yet?" I'd ask.

"I lost it a long time ago when I met you," would be one of her stock responses.

"Why me?" I'd ask in one form or another. I never ever got it. Why did she pick me, pluck me out of the fog and give me a life?

She never had a real answer. "Divine intervention," was one of her many responses. "God told me to do it."

"I didn't know you believe in God."

"God is the sum total of all things."

"Then how does the sum total of all things tell you to take me out to breakfast?"

"A voice in my head. A voice that said, *Look at that lonely man who is in desperate need of eggs and bacon.*"

"Really, the sum total of all things told you I should eat bacon?"

"Yes."

And that would be the beginning of our day. Summer. Building a house. Building a life. I even began to get some writing done. The page stopped staring back and finally spoke to me. It said, write a story within the story and see if that triggers something. It was a short story all on its own really, entitled, get this, "The Third or Fourth Happiest Man in Nova Scotia."

And it wasn't bad. I even imagined it was publishable.

Imagine. Me writing a story about being happy.

And then this.

I drove with Ramona to the house late one afternoon. We were checking in to see how the work had gone that day. The white Tyvek house wrap was up on the walls, windows were in place, and a door was on the house. But there was Brody up on a ladder, ripping away at the Tyvek, tearing it off sheet by sheet. Not before we could see what had been spray-painted in large red letters across the front of the house, though: *This is the House of Ramona the Whore.*

The goddamned obsessed and tenacious Christian women had found us all the way down here in Stewart Harbour. We seemed pretty far off the beaten track, but I guess if you wanted to, you could track down anybody anywhere these days.

"Brody, stop," I yelled to him.

He climbed down the ladder. He was seething with anger.

"The bitches. I caught them at this. Who the hell are they?"

Ramona just shook her head, kept staring at the words that were left on the walls of our house.

"I caught them," Brody repeated. "There were four of them. They'd already done it. But I scared the shit out of them. They won't come back."

I was afraid to ask Brody what he said or did. Whatever it was, I was sure it wasn't pretty.

Ramona kept staring at the wall and what was written there. I went looking for a second ladder. Together, Brody and I ripped the rest of the Tyvek off the front of the house. The workmen could replace it easily. We crumpled it up on the ground, added some wood scraps and branches, and burned it.

The chemical smell of the smoke made my nose burn and my eyes water. Who the hell were these women anyway? And how dare they desecrate our house and our lives.

The next morning, as Ramona and I watched the workers putting up new Tyvek, a car pulled up. Ramona's father stepped out. Someone else was in the car. It was Ramona's mother.

"My, would you look at this," he said, all smiles. "I'm very impressed."

Ramona saw her mother and ran toward the car. She opened the door. "Mom, are you all right?"

Her mother looked a bit confused but fine otherwise. She tried to stand up and Ramona helped her out of the car.

"So, we meet again," Stanley said, holding out his hand. I shook it and looked him in the eyes. Still trying to figure him out. "I had no idea you were building a house," he said. And then he turned from me and watched as his wife and daughter approached.

Ramona's mother was smiling now, her face alight. "Is this heaven?" she asked me. "I think maybe it is. Those trees are so beautiful. The sky is so blue." But when she looked directly at the house, the confusion returned to her face.

She looked at Ramona. "Your father said he was taking me to someplace really remarkable. And here you are. But if you're here, this can't be heaven. Since you're still alive."

Stanley walked toward her and put his arm around her. "I picked her up at the home this morning. She's just out for the day. With me. I thought I would bring her here. To see you. At the store back down the road, they told me how to find you. They told me about the house you are building."

"What a lovely spot for a house," Brenda said. "Are you sure this isn't heaven?"

"Yes, Mom. I'm sure. But we like it almost as much."

"Will you show us around?" Stanley asked.

The front steps had only recently been finished. We carefully guided Brenda up them and into the house. Inside, we sat down on some boxes of hardwood flooring that had yet to be installed. The smell of sawdust still hung like lumber perfume in the air. Ramona was trying to contain herself.

"I don't think it is a good idea bringing her all the way here."

Stanley just smiled and patted his wife's hand. "She's just fine. Aren't you, dear?"

Brenda smiled and put her hand on top of his. "Yes, I am just fine. And it is a fine day. Even if this is not heaven."

Stanley turned back toward Ramona. "We've got your mother on a new medication."

"You should not have done that without my permission," Ramona snapped.

Stanley remained cool despite her wrath. "I consulted with the doctor. The new medication allows for longer periods of clarity. They're not even sure how it works, but it steadies the mind somehow and we've tried it several times. I've taken her around town before and we've had a wonderful time. Haven't we, dear?"

"Yes, Stanley, we have."

"She knows your name?"

"Yes. For a while."

"And this must be Charles," Brenda said, turning to me.

Ramona was wide-eyed.

"I was a bit astonished at first," Stanley said. "Just remember, it's temporary. I got a bit overly excited when she first took the medicine. I thought it was like a miracle. And in some ways it is. We've found that it works well for an hour or two. Not perfectly. But well. And then, when it starts to wear off and the confusion sets in, she will simply fall asleep."

Right now, Brenda looked bright-eyed.

"What a lovely smell," she said, inhaling deeply. "I remember going to an old sawmill once with my father when I was just nine. And it smelled just like this."

Stanley splayed out his fingers. "She's had moments like this. Many of them. I write things down. I record her memories." He took a small notebook out of his suit jacket and jotted a note. "Lakes, trees, birds, traffic, now this. All triggers to her memory. The doctor says that the memory is not truly gone. It's just that you can lose the mechanism to retrieve it."

Ramona looked at her father in a way that I had not seen before. The hostility was gone. "She is still not well enough to leave the home," she insisted.

"No, she is not. Not permanently. I now agree with you. The best care for her is there. I am not moving her out."

"Thank God," Ramona said.

"But I did not lie to you before. I regret, deeply regret, abandoning your mother before. I can't explain it. I should not be forgiven for it. But I do want to be part of Brenda's life again. And I want to be part of your life."

Ramona said nothing.

Stanley looked around him. "And here you are building a home. How wonderful."

"Yes," Ramona said. "Charles and I are building a home together."

Stanley looked me over again. An assessment perhaps.

"I assume he is a good man," he said, even though I was right there.

"The best," Ramona said.

"Then I approve."

"I do not need your approval."

"Of course not. I was just stating a fact."

Small talk ensued. The workmen were returning from their lunch break. It was time for us to get out of the way. Stanley offered to take us out to lunch, but I told him that there was not a single restaurant within easy driving distance.

He looked puzzled at that, as if such a thing could not be. "So we've come to the ends of the earth," he said with a half-smile. Then, turning to his wife, said, "Well, then, my dear, it's time we should go."

As they drove away, Ramona turned to me. "Back when he left us, he never even said goodbye. To me or to her. Instead, he left instructions with a lawyer. That's how we both heard. Phone call from a lawyer to tell me my father had abandoned us to start a new life and he had left a sizable sum to take care of both of us."

"Then it's your father's money that's building this house."

"Guilt money."

"Do you think it was guilt that brought him back?"

"I don't know," Ramona said. "Partly. But it's more than that. He's changed. Before, I could always tell when he was bullshitting or manipulating my mother or me or anyone else. But there's something different about him."

"People change," I offered.

"I didn't ever think so. But maybe it's possible."

And with that the small work crew — Big Carl and his two carpenters, Wade and Bernie — with Rolf in tow, walked in the front door.

"Honey, I'm home," Rolf shouted jovially.

36

We never had a face-to-face encounter with the C-WAP women. Hard to say how they found their way to Stewart Harbour or how they knew about the house we were building. But then, with the internet anyone can pretty well find out whatever they are looking for. Anyway, they found us out. My hope was that they weren't local folks, and I reckoned they weren't. Here, people who didn't approve of you were more likely to say it to your face and maybe stir up some gossip or, worst case scenario, spit in your face. But graffiti was a bit too urban and just wasn't that popular down there on the Shore.

———

The twenty-fifth of August was the court date. Alan said this was the easy part. We'd be in and out of there. Brody was pleading guilty. That was all there was to it. Sentencing would come at a later date, after the judge had studied what Alan and the Crown attorney provided him with.

Ramona and I had both read the information Alan had given us about how sentencing worked. I was familiar with much of it from my work as a reporter. Brody would be charged under the federal Controlled Drugs and Substances Act. Sentencing would depend on whether Brody accepted responsibility for doing what he did, if he showed remorse, if it was his first offence (strangely it was), his family situation, his character references, his mental health, and other factors.

I had already explained my relationship and why I had turned him in and Alan had provided a record of that statement to the judge. Beth Ann, Joe, and Mackenzie had all done the same. All of that would help reduce the sentencing, and it looked like Brody was grudgingly going to go along with whatever happened.

Of course, the Crown attorney might be looking for a harsher conviction. Undoubtedly, he'd know Brody had been dealing one drug or another for many years. He'd probably know that Brody had been able to get away with it because no one wanted to turn anyone in to the Mounties in Stewart Harbour. Mounties and fishery officers were not liked, not trusted and considered to be the enemies of the people. But with the near-death of Scooter, his father, Brian, had made sure that Brody's past was now out in the open.

Tom, the arresting officer, had already filed his report. That would not look good since Brody had put up a fight. We didn't know who else might give incriminating statements to the Crown attorney. He'd no doubt go after Scooter and Scooter's father might jump in and have his say. But we hoped that was all.

Despite all the possible sources for problems, when the twenty-fifth rolled around Alan exuded his signature confidence. He had the clothes, the briefcase, the manner of a polished professional. He insisted Brody say nothing. The judge, as it turned out, was a woman. The Honourable Delia Green.

Joe, Beth Ann, and Brody sat with Alan. Ramona and I sat across the room and watched as drunk drivers lost their licences, tavern brawlers got stiff warnings, a bootlegger was fined for selling beer to teenagers at three o'clock in the morning, and reckless drivers were fined for texting, speeding, not stopping for school buses, and running stop signs.

And then Brody's case was up. The judge read the charges in a monotone voice, noted the Criminal Code, and asked, "How does the defendant plead?"

I almost thought Brody was going to stand up and say something. He had an antsy look about him and I knew he was a wild card. Maybe he'd throw it all in the trash. His hands were on his chair and Alan gave him a look that said, *Don't do it*. Alan himself hesitated as he watched Brody. Then the judge peered up over her glasses. "Well?"

Alan stood tall, cleared his throat and said, "My client, Your Honour, pleads guilty as charged."

"Then it's guilty as charged. Crown and defence, make sure I get documents. Sentencing will be held on September twentieth."

And that was that. Brody's day in court.

Because it all seemed so routine, so matter of fact, I think we all felt relieved. Brody was still out on bail. He didn't have to wait in jail. We could all get on with our lives.

There was still a chance that Brody would run. Just say to hell with it and leave. But, as the days passed, he kept showing up at the worksite. He seemed to be fascinated by the building process and the workmen seemed to like having him around. Big Carl, who owned the construction company, even went so far as to hire Brody part-time as a gofer. Brody seemed to like his new role just fine. He liked joking with the workmen and learning about carpentry. It could not have gone much better.

But before you start thinking that it was an idyllic month down on the Eastern Shore, it wasn't all sweetness and light.

Ramona deleted her Facebook and email accounts. She was getting C-WAP hate mail from an alarmingly large number of people. Scooter's father, Brian Deacon, was always trying to pick a fight with me or Joe down at the wharf. There were also some problems with the engine on my father's boat and it took me a while to find someone willing and able to tune it up. Rolf had gone on a bender — drinking through the days and staying up late at night howling at the moon. Tropical storms were brewing in the Atlantic, but so far they'd all passed us by, the ocean water being cold enough at this time of year to tame the storms as they blew north.

The relationship between Ramona and me had deepened. It still seemed like a miracle to me. We both laughed at how quickly we'd become like an old married couple, but that wasn't really the case. The passion was there. Every day.

Ramona would awake sometimes in the night, especially if it was a full moon. Especially if Rolf was next door howling like a wolf. Sometimes she'd be disoriented. Sometimes she'd say something that didn't make sense. But it was no big deal. I'd awakened plenty of times in my life in a strange location and bumped into walls trying to figure out where I was. Her "condition" continued to seem mythical to me. There was no one more fully alive and alert than Ramona.

———

The boat engine was repaired by a one-armed boat engine mechanic from Port Bickerton. Ramona and I returned to sea on calm days. That was where the magic was most in our relationship. On one particularly idyllic afternoon at sea, Ramona looked at me and asked, "How did we do this?"

"Do what?" I asked.

"Us. How did we make this happen?"

"I'd been wondering that myself. I'm pretty certain it was all your doing. You took the initiative and I ... well, how could I reject such an offer?"

"No," she said, "it wasn't like that. We came together at a time and place in our lives when we desperately needed something, someone to commit to."

"Okay, I can buy that. But how did we get *here*?"

"On the boat?"

"On a boat that was my father's, on an ocean I knew so well as a boy, with a girl like you who is both beautiful and intelligent."

She liked the flattery. "So you don't think I'm just an over-the-hill porn star?"

I laughed and grabbed her around the waist. We kissed.

"I'm going to take you to an island," I said. "I want to show you something."

"How mysterious. Let's go."

So I hauled up the anchor and started the engine. Ever since it got tuned up, it was running beautifully. I circled out around Prosper Point, remembering that terrifying day when we'd chased after Brody, thinking about how close we'd all come to our deaths. It was hard to imagine on a day as warm, sunny, and benign as today.

I pulled the boat in as close to Gammon Island as I dared, and then cut the motor and dropped the anchor. "We'll have to swim ashore from here," I said. It wasn't far.

Ramona didn't say yes, no, or maybe. She dove overboard and looked back at me with a smile. I joined her and felt the sting of the cold, felt it biting into me in the most invigorating way.

We'd both been wearing only shorts and T-shirts, so we weren't bogged down by heavy clothes. I nodded toward the shore and we both swam slowly forward. The barnacles on the stones were sharp and painful as we stumbled across them onto the thin white beach.

"Welcome to Elvis Island," I said.

"Why Elvis?" she asked.

"I'll show you."

I led her down the beach until we came to an overgrown path and we followed it into a straggly forest of half-dead spruce and shoulder-high ferns. It was tough going in bare feet, but we soon found what I was looking for.

The cabin was in much worse shape than the last time I had seen it many years ago. The door was off, but the windows and roof were still surprisingly intact. Unfortunately, the inside had been inhabited by more than one generation of porcupines, who must have been living in the rafters. There was a knee-high pile of porcupine poop on the floor.

"You brought me here to see this?" Ramona asked, holding her nose and easing back out the door.

I reached for her and pulled her back in. "Damn city girl," I chided and waited for our eyes to adjust to the dim light. Oddly enough, the old magazine photos, some of them in glass frames, were still on the walls. There were at least a hundred pictures of Elvis Presley.

"My theory was that Elvis didn't die. He just got tired of all the attention and came out here to live his final days."

"That was your theory, was it?"

"Yes. Look over there." I pointed to the old cookstove and the sink. "That was Elvis's frying pan and the pot he boiled grits in." Atop the mouldy mattress and rusted bedsprings sat a pile of old, half-eaten hardback books. "Porcupines sure do like good literature," I added.

Ramona carefully took a few steps farther in and picked up something from the rotting boards on the floor. "And this would be Elvis's fork, I presume."

"Damn straight," I said.

"Why did he come here?"

"My guess was that he just got tired of people and that he liked wild creatures more. So he faked his death in Memphis and came up here. Didn't tell anyone. Got himself a couple of raccoons and porcupines for pets and tacked up those pictures of himself to remind him of what he'd left behind."

"And then what?"

"I think he died here and the creatures took over."

"Anyone ever find a body?"

"Nope. But then I don't think anyone knew Elvis was here but me."

"Only you?"

"Me and Beth Ann."

"So I'm not the first girl you brought out here?"

"That was a long, long time ago."

"I know," she said. "But I'm still jealous."

I gingerly walked over to a small table that had a single drawer. With difficulty I opened it and inside was an American quarter, a small framed picture of Jesus, a broken wristwatch with a picture of Elvis on the faceplate, and a tiny notebook, not unlike the kind that I used to take notes as a reporter. When I flipped it open, there was only writing on one page. It read: *Truth is like the sun. You can shut it out for a time, but it ain't goin' away. Elvis Aaron Presley.*

I showed it to Ramona.

"That proves it, then," she said. "Elvis was here."

I carefully put the watch, the quarter, and the notebook back in the drawer and closed it.

As we walked back to the beach, I had the feeling that the island itself was watching us. Nothing spooky, nothing overly weird, just this notion that this island knew we were here. When we got to the beach, we sat down in the warm white sand and Ramona lay on her back and closed her eyes.

"What do you really think the story behind that cabin is?" she asked.

I shrugged. "Could have just been a place that someone from the mainland came to once in a while to hunt ducks or go fishing. Or it could have been a place where someone came to live out their days to escape from the world. I doubt if anyone ever comes ashore here now. There's hundreds of islands like this along the Eastern Shore."

"Life would be lonely. I'm certain loneliness is the hardest thing for many people."

"You afraid of being alone?"

"Yes."

"Really. Someone like you would never be alone. There'd always be a man who'd want to be with you."

"That could change in a heartbeat."

And I knew she wasn't lying. And I also knew that the fear of loneliness may have been what drew her to me. If so, then that was okay with me as well.

"You're not afraid of being alone, dying alone?"

Truth was it wasn't one of my big fears. "I'm afraid of boring social situations, drowning, or maybe getting eaten by a shark.

But loneliness isn't up there. I thrived on being a loner for as long as I can remember."

"Wanted to be a hermit like whoever had lived in that cabin?"

"Thought about it once or twice. But I decided that I preferred the urban wilderness to this. Much easier to be alone in the city. At least you can buy good coffee and you have all that noise to keep you from thinking too much. Out here on a calm day, the quiet would kill you. Nothing but you and your thoughts."

"So, see, you are afraid of being alone."

I nodded. "I guess we all are. Maybe that's why my father disappeared. Couldn't handle facing life without my mom. Trouble is, no one knows for sure."

"They never found his body?"

"Just the boat. Perfectly intact. No note. No nothing. Truth is, he could have gone to an island just like this one and kept on living. Could have let his boat just drift back out to sea. Maybe he just didn't want to make small talk with the boys on the wharf anymore."

"Do you think that's likely?"

"My father seemed to have a set of rules in his head. He was a stubborn man and he stuck to them. *Work hard. Take care of your family, but don't overdo the emotional part. Never cheat anyone. Lie only when you have to and only to fisheries officers. Drink only beer. Never hard stuff. Don't ever go wishing you had it better than what you have. Cut your losses when you have to, but stick to it. Never walk away.*"

"But isn't that what he did? Walk away. Sail away. After your mother died."

"I don't know. Pete wasn't here. I wasn't around. He didn't really walk away on anyone or anything. Even our old dog had died, so it was just him, all alone. I should have come back here to him."

"Yeah, you should have at least stayed in touch."

"He was a hard man to talk to on the phone."

"Then you should have come to visit."

"He was an even harder man to talk to in person as he got older. He and my mother often sat through entire meals not saying anything to one another. They didn't even look like they cared if anyone else was at the table. But I think they were okay with that. They just didn't talk unless they had something important to say."

Having said that, we both grew rather quiet until we knew it was time to swim back to the boat. The tide had risen and the distance to the boat was greater. The water seemed much colder now and as we boarded the *Sheer Delight* we were shivering.

37

A funny thing happened after that day. It was like we had invoked the spirit of my father somehow, because people started bringing things back to us at the house. They brought back items that he had given away. An old wicker chair for starters. Then a maple table and a bookshelf. A woman named Elsie Blanchard brought a teapot and a set of dainty English teacups that she said had belonged to my mother.

Rolf had decided to ease up on the booze and spent more time at the worksite offering up advice — some of it good, some not so good. I think he loved the idea of people returning things that had once been in the old house and he had started making phone calls. Bud Lasky showed up one day with the old back door, finely refinished with Varathane. Dell Grigg brought a couple of windows he'd kept all these years in his barn.

I asked the workers to make sure these things could be incorporated somehow into the new house and they did. Brody thought it quite amazing that so much stuff from the old house was being dropped off. He offered up some ideas as to what should go where and I usually went along with him. It made me feel like something of my parents' life together would be with us there.

Finally, the day of sentencing arrived. September 20. The court-room was mostly empty and it looked like Brody's case was the main order of the day. I noted a young reporter there from the *Herald*, the court recorder, the Crown attorney, two police offi-cers, and four women clustered together in the back who I did not recognize. Brian sat sullenly alone. Scooter wasn't with him. This time, Ramona and I sat in the second row behind Joe, Beth Ann, Mackenzie, Brody, and Alan. I tapped Brody on the shoul-der. He turned to say hi. I couldn't read his state of mind. But I did detect that Alan Romaine looked uncharacteristically ner-vous and fidgety. That threw me. I felt a cold wave of something come over me. Something was not right.

Judge Delia Green made some opening remarks and read the charges aloud, referencing again the Criminal Code of Canada and the Controlled Drugs and Substances Act. She stated that the defendant had pleaded guilty as charged and reminded us that this was a sentencing hearing.

I had been told that the Crown, the judge, and Alan would have met ahead of time, before the proceedings, and that all information regarding the case had been put before the judge. At this point, things were mostly a formality. No courtroom the-atrics like in the movies. Just the judge stating what comes next for Brody.

In fact, it all seemed so dull and matter of fact at first that it seemed unreal.

The judge cleared her throat and began to speak. "The court recognizes that this is Brody Myatt's first offence, but the Crown has shown reasonable evidence that Mr. Myatt has been selling various illegal substances for a long time. It would seem he has made a career out of it.

"It was noted that he put up a struggle during the time of arrest, but since then has been co-operative, has admitted his guilt, and appears to be sorry for what he has done. But the court has also noted that he has sold a very dangerous drug, fentanyl, to an unsuspecting person, resulting in that person overdosing and going to hospital. We are all pleased that the victim is well now and back to work.

"I am not convinced that Mr. Myatt has knowingly sold drugs to persons under eighteen years of age but have not ruled it out. Nonetheless, I have not factored that in to his sentencing since I had no hard evidence, only hearsay.

"The court has made note of a difficult family situation from which Mr. Myatt arose but also registers that he is a grown man, not a boy, and fully responsible for his actions. I have also noted that he is soon to be a father and I am not a person who wishes fathers to be in prisons instead of being home to raise their children.

"The Crown wishes me to make an example of this man who has sold potentially life-threatening substances to unsuspecting individuals and the Crown has good reason to make that argument.

"But what troubles me most at this point are the statements of four women who recently had an encounter with Mr. Myatt at a building site in Stewart Harbour. I have sworn testimony from them that Mr. Myatt threatened them and came after them wielding a hammer before they could get in their car and drive away. This prompted me to look further into his record. I found that Mr. Myatt has been charged with other acts of violence, although there were no convictions.

"In light of this new information, my decision is based on the fact that Mr. Myatt has a clear potential to do more harm to the public, either from selling dangerous substances or using threats and violence against others. So I sentence him to two years in federal prison, sentence starting today."

The women in the back of the room were clapping. The judge silenced them. Brody was on his feet now, his fists clenched. Alan was standing beside him and began to speak, "Your Honour, I would like to approach the bench."

Joe was trying to get Brody to sit back down, but he would have none of it. "The bitches," he shouted. "They were vandals and I caught them." Alan turned to him and put up his hands.

"Sit down, Mr. Myatt," Judge Green said sternly. But Brody would not sit.

"I change my plea," he shouted. "I'm *not* guilty!"

"You can't do that," the judge said.

"This is not fair. I don't deserve this." He was full-on yelling now, his face red with fury and exertion.

"I'm sorry, Mr. Myatt, but your actions have determined your fate here. You are the one responsible."

"I demand a retrial!" He was leaning forward and looked like he was ready to explode.

"But this is not a trial," the judge said calmly. "You have already pleaded guilty and now the sentence has been determined." She turned to the uniformed men. "Gentleman, please have Mr. Myatt removed from the courtroom."

38

I tried to speak to Brody as he was being led away, but he just glared at me. I'd betrayed my own son. I'd come back into his life decades after he'd been born only to have him handcuffed and sent away to Springhill.

As he was led out of the courtroom, the C-WAP women were smiling and clapping a silent applause. Brody looked defiant. It was a look that I surmised he would hang on to for a long, long time.

"We'll appeal," Alan told us. "We can change this decision." But his words were hollow. They were just words.

Beth Ann looked at him desperately. "Then he can come home, right? Until the appeal is over."

Alan shook his head. "No, it doesn't work that way. He has to go into custody. That's the way the law works."

"The fucking law," Joe said. "The goddamn fucking law. You tricked us, you little asshole. You told us this was going to work out okay."

"There were unforeseen circumstances," Alan offered. But as he said it, I could see that Alan Romaine still had a weakness about him when he let his guard down. He was still the wimpy kid in the school hallway picked on by the likes of Brian Deacon and Joe Myatt.

Beth Ann hung her head and sobbed. I'd been nothing but bad news for that girl since high school. I had no way to make up for the blunders I'd made. What to do now? Create a problem and then walk away — that was my style. I just didn't know if I could do it again.

Mackenzie looked like she was in shock. She sat silently and kept twisting a Kleenex in her hand.

Ramona just looked stunned. She sat silently looking straight ahead.

Joe slammed his fist into the chair in front of him.

The judge left. The courtroom cleared.

Alan looked at me and started to speak but stopped himself. Then he snapped his fancy briefcase shut and simply walked out of the courtroom.

Joe gathered up Beth Ann and Mackenzie and ushered them out of the room.

It was just Ramona and me.

"I'm sorry," she said. "I convinced you to do it. I made a mistake."

I felt her moving away from me. We had done this thing together and, yes, she had persuaded me. I would not have done such a thing on my own. Damn. Brody was beginning to change. I had seen it in him. He'd stopped dealing. He liked the work on the house. He was changing for the better, I was convinced of it.

And now this.

"I don't know if I can live with what I made you do," Ramona said. "I don't know what I was thinking. This idea of building a house in your hometown was a mistake. People will know what we did. We sent one of their own to prison."

I could feel her slipping away from me with each new word. "Not everyone will think we did the wrong thing."

"But what about Beth Ann, Joe, and all their relatives? They'll hate us."

"Beth Ann approved of what I did. She told me it had to be done."

"But she'll see it differently now."

"If Brody plays his cards right, he'll be out well before two years. And maybe the appeal will work. There are possibilities here." But I knew these to be empty words as well. I felt a great weight on me. I sensed an awful inevitability. I'd seen it in Brody from the very first time we met. He struck me as someone who would make one bad decision after the next. And that trait would follow him to prison, I was certain.

Ramona and I said very little on the drive back to Stewart Harbour. There was really nothing to be said.

The next morning, she told me she needed to go back to the city. To see her mother. To visit her doctor. To meet with her father and his accountant about the family trust. She didn't say anything about me coming along.

"Don't go," I said. I was convinced I was losing her. That once she left, she'd likely never come back.

"I have to," she said. And she packed a bag with what little possessions she had brought out there and left.

As soon as her car was out of sight, I felt a panic creeping up my spine. It was like a living but icy thing was about to devour me. I hadn't felt it for a long time. It was fear. Fear of abandonment. Fear of being alone. But it was more intense. It was a kind of mental paralysis that was unlike anything I'd known. I'd been depressed before. I'd felt anxiety. I'd felt an absence of emotion that became common to me — a person alive but not living.

But this was different. Cold hard panic, fear, and hopelessness.

I looked around to see if Ramona had left me her second cellphone. I could call her, reel her back in. Tell her I loved her now as much as ever. But she had taken the phone.

I walked out of my father's fish shack, down to the water, and then onto the wharf. It was empty. The men were at sea in their boats. Just me and the herring gulls and the smell of fish guts.

Broken man on another pier. Isn't that where the story began? The only real difference now was that I had hate in my heart. I hated myself for what I'd done; hated myself for having been optimistic about Ramona, about a life together, about getting to know my son.

Pure delusion. Pure fiction. Just like my unfinished novel. Because of Ramona and because of the summer we had shared, I had returned to work on the novel. It moved from the depths of existential despair to a kind of reluctant but hopeful vision of the world. My protagonist had the air of Hemingway tragedy, but had begun to move on to something transcendent.

Thinking about my novel and the way it reflected various threads in my own life, I walked back to my little cabin and reread what I'd banged out on the old typewriter over the summer. The parts of it I'd read out loud to Ramona had met with her approval. I think I was blindly hoping that there would be something there in the fiction, some thought, some idea that would allow me to make sense of my own life as it was now. Some small but essential sequence of words that would give me a clue as to what I could do next to make peace with the world, to move forward into whatever empty life was ahead of me, some glimpse of some possible salvation.

I sat at the old wooden table and read.

But there was nothing. It was the work of an amateur and it was much more trite than I had realized. Words on a page. Empty words. Cardboard characters, sophomoric notions. I was like a million other wannabe novelists. The only difference was that they probably had a life, a real life to go back to, once the fiction was over. I didn't.

I opened a drawer and found the stick matches. I gathered up the pages of my manuscript spread out on the table in front of me, carried them to the water's edge, crumpled some pages to light, and then proceeded to burn the manuscript.

That's when Rolf walked out his door and saw what I was doing. He slowly came my way, looking rough around the edges, unshaven and stooped. He leaned over and put his hands up to the flames as if warming them on a winter day. "Chisel, this isn't what I think it is," he said. "Is it?"

"Yes. It is."

"And so you're burning your book?"

"It wasn't much of a book."

"It's okay. You can write another."

"I doubt it."

"I heard what happened at the trial," Rolf said.

"I made a mistake."

"Not necessarily. A lot of people around here are still saying you did the right thing. Someone had to stop him."

"I just wish it wasn't me."

"I haven't had a drink in three days," Rolf suddenly said.

"Why not?"

"Fuck knows. I had this feeling you'd need me sober after that legal business was over. I never trusted the law. Now look how it turned out."

"Do you think he deserved it? Brody, going to prison for two years."

Rolf shrugged. "Don't know. I don't know who decides what's fair and what's not fair. Your father used to say, the whole damn world operates under a fixed set of rules. We just never really know what those rules are until we break them."

"He really said that?"

"Oh yeah. Your old man was quite the philosopher."

"I guess I never thought of him that way."

"I did. He had that kind of quiet wisdom. Your mother was a saint and your father was wise as Solomon, that's my view."

"Well then, how did I turn out so fucked up?"

"That is a bit of a mystery, I guess. You can't blame genetics. Might be that you got all caught up in what gets hyped as free will. My view is there's no such thing."

"You don't believe in free will."

"Nope. And neither did your father."

"I don't understand."

"I can tell you don't. It's the old way of seeing things. You go to sea and you have a good catch or a bloody storm comes up and flips your boat ass over teakettle and you die. You can try to save yourself, but it's already written down somewhere — metaphorically speaking — whether you live or die. Like what happened with Brody out there that day of the storm. You worked bloody hard to save his sorry ass, but it could have gone one way or the other. It turned out good, so you think you had something to do with it. But it wasn't that way at all."

"Thanks, Rolf, for your own philosophical insight. But I'm not sure it's helping."

"Why do you think that a lot of these fishermen believe like their granddaddies that there's no point learning to swim if it's only gonna draw out the pain of drowning? Listen, Chisel. Brody lived that day so he got another shot at making some kind of life for himself."

"Except now he's in prison."

"It's called a setback. And, yes, that too was set in stone somewhere. Don't beat yourself up. That's where your belief in free will can get you. Blaming yourself for something that's not your fault."

"Fuck," I said. "Fuck it all."

"Now you're talking."

"But it's not just Brody," I said. "It's Ramona. She's gone."

Now Rolf looked shocked. "Jesus, boy, no?"

"Yeah. This morning. She's gone."

He pursed his lips together, then took a deep breath and looked me in the eyes. "Now *that* you gotta fix."

39

Joe showed up that night at my door, drunk and threatening to kill me. It was not an unexpected visit. He was much bigger than me and I was fairly certain he could do it if he was so motivated.

"I should have taken care of you that first day you came back. Right there on your father's boat. Could have taken you out and dumped you in the sea where you could visit with your crazy dead father. That would have avoided all this trouble."

"I agree," I said. "It would have saved all of us a lot of trouble."

Joe kept clenching and unclenching his fists and he looked like he was about to explode. The fact I didn't say anything in my own defence seemed to make him even angrier. But Rolf, my patron saint of protection, waltzed in the door just then.

"What are you two boys jawing about?" he asked matter-of-factly.

"No big deal, you old turd. I just thought I'd drop by and kill a rat."

"Only rats I've seen lately are those big Norwegian suckers skittering around the wharf. What we need around here are some cats worthy of their heritage to root 'em out and clean the place up."

"What the fuck are you blathering about, old man?" Joe said.

"Joe, you and me go a long ways back," Rolf said. "And you know I've never tried to steer you the wrong way. So now I'm saying you got to let this go."

"He sent my son to prison."

"Because your son was selling drugs that could have killed a horse."

"I would have straightened him out if I'd known what he was up to. It didn't have to come to this."

"Joe, you couldn't straighten Brody out. No one could. He got himself into it and he nearly killed dumb-ass Scooter."

And just then all the steam seemed to slip out of Joe. His shoulders slumped and he deposited himself into the old wooden chair at the table. "I need a drink," he said.

All I had was one of Ramona's bottles of wine. So I set it on the table and went looking for a corkscrew.

"What's this?" Joe asked, like he'd never seen a bottle of wine before.

"Apothic Red. 2014."

"I don't drink wine."

"It's all I got. Sorry."

"Well, then open the sucker. Let's give it a taste."

What little wisdom I had left in my brain suggested that getting an angry drunken man drunker was not necessarily a good plan. And then too, Rolf was in attendance and apparently trying to stay sober for an extended period of time.

Nonetheless, I located the corkscrew, popped the cork, and set the bottle down on the table. I turned to look for a glass, but Joe already had the bottle to his lips and took a big slug. A really big slug.

"This tastes like shit," he said and he plunked the bottle down on the table.

"You're supposed to let it breathe," Rolf offered.

"What the fuck is that supposed to mean?"

Rolf decided not to answer the question. Nor did I. We watched as Joe took another slug and then handed the bottle to Rolf. Rolf did a funny little salute to the bottle and then waved it away. Joe shoved it out at arm's length in my direction. I accepted the toast and took a healthy swig.

"I say we break Brody out of prison," Joe said. He wasn't serious, but it seemed like the appropriate thing for a loving stepdad to say when he was drunk.

"I think it's harder than it sounds," Rolf said.

"You got any better ideas?" He glared at Rolf and then at me.

"I say we meet with Alan," I said, "and push him hard to get the appeal going."

"The little weasel. What did we used to call him in school?"

"Lettuce," I said. "Like Romaine lettuce."

"Like fucking wilted lettuce," Joe added. But no one was laughing.

Joe kept at that Apothic with a fairly steady rhythm and then, after several successful attempts at setting the bottle down on the table, he finally missed. The bottle fell to the floor and rolled toward Rolf's feet. Rolf picked it up and sniffed the top of it. "Jesus, that smells some good."

Just as Rolf said this, Joe pitched forward — with perfect aim for the table this time. And he was out for the night.

"Think you boys can stay out of trouble if I slink on home for the night?"

"I think we'll be okay," I said.

Rolf left, I decided to let sleeping drunks sleep and I went to bed.

In the morning, Beth Ann was knocking at my door. Joe was still hunched over at the kitchen table.

"I just came to see if anyone got killed last night," she said.

"No," I said. "We just had a little talk."

Beth Ann let out a big sigh. "Joe's a good man, at heart. He just lets his emotions get the best of him. I'll get him out of your hair."

"I thought you two broke up a long time ago."

"We did. We try to have as little to do with each other as we possibly can, but that's not easy around here." She was tapping him on the shoulder now. "C'mon, Joe, wake up."

Then Beth Ann turned to me. "Just because we hate each other's guts, it doesn't mean we don't look out for each other." Joe popped his head up but was having a hard time figuring out what was going on.

"He threaten you?" she asked.

"Sort of," I said.

"He's all bluster, the goof." Beth Ann was lifting him now. Joe let her get him on his feet. "Guess we'll be going," she said.

Once she had him propped up along the door frame, she turned back to me. "Don't blame yourself, Charles. You did what you had to do. If there's anyone to blame, it's me for not setting Brody straight a long time ago. No mother of the year award for me, I guess."

And they were gone. Beth Ann loaded Joe into her pickup and they drove off.

———

On the morning of September 25, there was no wind at all. The air was heavy, humid, sticky. And as warm as it ever gets along the Shore here. It hadn't rained for a while and, as I sat on the stones by the water, the land looked parched. Shore plants had died. Summer had killed them. I remembered what it was like to wake up on a September morning like this and get ready to go to school, my brain unwilling to accept that the joys of summer were all gone, memories of it quickly fading.

I didn't hate school, but I always felt out of place there, like I was playing some kind of game whose rules I did not understand. Even now, I still woke up on a September morning like this with a kind of dread that somehow the freedom of summer was over and the prison term of school had begun.

Yes, it was a kind of metaphorical prison sentence. But not like the real thing as it was for Brody. I wondered if he made the connection. September. Going to school. September. Going to prison.

I looked at the spot where I had burned my novel. The rocks were still black, even though the ash had all blown away. Words in the wind. Meaningless, charred words blown away on the sea breeze. And that asinine title: *Purgatory Newsletter*.

This was my purgatory. Some kind of in-between state. A static, pointless waiting room between what was and what will be. Only, I didn't really see any kind of future. Construction had ceased on the house. Ramona was gone. I had not heard from her. I had not tried to contact her or find her. I didn't seem to have much of a will to do anything in particular. If you asked me outright, I would have told you I didn't really much care what happened to me next. I had no opinions about living or dying. A man just taking up space in a meaningless universe, wasting good oxygen in his lungs. I didn't really even feel sorry for myself. I didn't have that much gumption.

And it was on that day, September 25, that I heard the news when I went down to the wharf to check on the boat. I heard it first from Brian Deacon. He was talking to one of the Henderson brothers, Mickey. Brody was dead, Brian said. Drug overdose or something. Found in his cell and it was too late to do anything about it.

40

I went and sat down on the boat. I just sat there for a really long time. The gas tank was full. I could go far from there. Maybe not far enough. But far. I could do like father like son. But I didn't have that kind of courage. There was a gun still hidden on the boat as well. There was always that. Go far out to sea, put a bullet in my head. One little squeeze of the trigger. No wonder cowards did it that way. I could join the club.

But I didn't have the strength, the will, or even a whiff of courage to end my life. Easier to just go home and lie there in my bed, wait for Joe to get drunk or get sober or whatever he needed and come to do the deed he so wanted to do before.

———

Ramona returned that afternoon.

"I heard about it on the radio," she said. "I decided to come back."

I stood silently, not knowing what to say.

"Actually, it was my father who urged me to come back. I thought I'd already brought you enough grief. But he convinced me."

Ramona put her arms around me and I leaned into her. I was no longer alone. That's all I could think of.

We held each other silently for a long time.

And then she made coffee. Black. Strong. Good.

"What did they say on the news?" I asked.

"They said there was a known drug problem in the prison. Something even stronger than fentanyl was being smuggled in. Even the tiniest amount could get someone high or even killed. They suspect it was being smuggled in under inmates' fingernails."

"What else? I mean was it intentional or an accident?"

"They don't know. Brody was alone at the time. His heart just stopped. It was too late to inject Naloxone when they found him. There'll be an investigation."

"We should probably leave here," I said. "Go back to the city."

"No," Ramona said. "I think we should stay."

"I'm not sure it's safe."

"I don't care. When I left here I felt the same way as when I left you after the deer. I felt lost, like I'd given up on something important. Both times I abandoned you."

"For good reason."

"Both times I felt empty and hopeless."

"I know the feeling. But here you are with the guy who can't do anything but bring hurt into the world."

"I don't see it that way. I see someone trying to do the right thing."

But those words didn't ring true for me. "And what's the right thing for me to do now?"

"Stay. Do something good for people here. Even the ones who might hate you."

"What could I do that would have any meaning to Joe or Beth Ann after this?"

"I don't know. Just don't run away. If you stay, I'll stay with you."

"I can't ask you to do that."

"You're not asking. I'm saying. I'm not leaving."

The young guy at the general store just glared at us this time when we showed up to buy food and supplies. My guess is he'd bought goods from Brody. He might even have been Brody's friend. The look he gave me said it all. Some people around there really did hate me now.

Joe didn't show up with a temper or a weapon. I saw him a couple of days after Brody's death sitting on a fish crate at the wharf, crying in front of his fellow fishermen, who stood around looking embarrassed.

I didn't walk over to try and console him. I watched another broken man trying to make sense of a senseless existence. And I watched as he stood up, those men still staring at him. He looked old and defeated as he stumbled away.

As the days passed by, Ramona and I became more like brother and sister than a pair of lovers. We had been changed by the events and I wondered if we would ever recover what we had lost.

There was a small memorial service at the old United Church on the mainland. I hadn't been in there since I was a kid. Back then we only went to church on Christmas and Easter. I didn't think it was a good idea to go, but Ramona insisted. We sat in the back and listened to a eulogy by a minister who had probably never had any personal contact with Brody. He made Brody out to be a saint. He was portrayed as someone who had made mistakes and was ready to make amends. But he wasn't given a chance.

Beth Ann and Joe sat up front. Neither one got up to speak during the service. Mackenzie was sitting by herself farther back in the church. She was crying. The minister was the sole person to speak at the service. There was no coffin. Brody had been cremated. There were a few photos of him as a boy on a display. A couple of him in his twenties but nothing more. I remembered my first impression of Brody. He had been like a big kid who had never grown up. And that would be how he was remembered.

The service was short. There were hymns sung, but I didn't join the small congregation who seemed to know the words by heart. I remember the last song of the service was "Abide with Me," an old Christian standard. The words came back from childhood:

> *Abide with me; fast falls the eventide;*
> *The darkness deepens; Lord, with me abide.*
> *When other helpers fail and comforts flee,*
> *Help of the helpless, oh, abide with me.*

> *Swift to its close ebbs out life's little day;*
> *Earth's joys grow dim, its glories pass away;*
> *Change and decay in all around I see;*
> *O Thou who changest not, abide with me.*

No, I didn't suddenly get religion, find Jesus, repent of my sins, or ask God for forgiveness. But I did need saving and I knew the only person who could save me was sitting right beside me. *Change and decay in all around I see. Ramona ... please.*

Thank God there was no social function after. We were the first to leave the church. We drove back to the shack without speaking.

That evening, Beth Ann's truck pulled up in front. I opened the door. "You know," Beth Ann said, "that house you were building. That was the first decent thing Brody got excited about in a long time. I was beginning to have some hope." Then she held out a small wooden box, not much bigger than a box for stick matches. "Believe it or not, this was Joe's idea. We kept most of the ashes. But this is your share."

It was the strangest thing to say. Why would Joe want me to have some of Brody's ashes? My share? "Thank you," I said. "Why?"

"Because, Charles," she said, now sounding downright angry, "we're all in this together. Whatever the fuck *this* is." She started to walk away and then she turned back. "And whatever you do, don't dump his ashes in the ocean. Leave that to Joe and me."

And then she looked past me toward Ramona. "And Ramona, you and Charles here better finish that damn house. I don't care what you do after that. But finish the bloody house. Do that for Brody."

And she left.

41

By mid-October the house was mostly weathertight. The inside had not been finished — the floor had been installed downstairs but there were still no finished walls. Nonetheless, the house had been wired and connected to the grid. On the outside, there were shingles on the roof, vinyl siding over the Tyvek. Big Carl and his two workers were quieter than before, shaken by the fate of Brody perhaps. A couple of windows and interior doors from my parents' old house had been incorporated into the structure, and there were a few chairs, a kitchen table, and a sofa that my father had once given away, which had now found their way back to here. But there was a sadness about the place that I feared might never go away.

No C-WAP women returned to write nasty things on the walls. Perhaps they were satisfied when Brody got sent to prison. I wondered what they thought when they heard about his death on the news.

Ramona and I were living in the unfinished house now. We rather liked it that way. It always smelled of freshly cut wood, and when the outside was finished, we asked the work crew to take a break for a week or so. The head guy said he had some work to finish on the rafters in the attic, but that could wait if we wanted. I said yes. I think we wanted privacy more than anything right then, and we just wanted to enjoy the experience of living inside the rough shell of a house, before the insulation and wallboard went in. Like I say, it was just like indoor camping. And that felt just right.

Ramona had wanted a fireplace. I had argued against it, saying it was too inefficient, but I gave in, of course. A fireplace was romantic, after all. We spent our evenings with the blow-up mattress on the floor in front of a blazing fire of wood scraps, even though the month was uncommonly warm.

The death of Brody had so shaken us that I must admit our actual romance seemed permanently on hold. I'd written about tragedies many times as a reporter, but I'd always been able to keep my journalistic distance. It had always happened to them and not me. I'd felt the sting of the death of my own parents, of course, but, not having returned to Stewart Harbour, I kept that too, somehow at a safe distance from me. Looking back on it all, I realized that I had cultivated a powerful ability to shut off my emotions. A handy trick, I suppose, but I wondered now at what cost.

There was a mantel over the fireplace made from a thick beam from the old house. On top of the mantel was the small wooden box of Brody's ashes. Ramona placed it there one day. And it just stayed.

"I don't think I want them to finish the inside of the house. Ever," Ramona said one evening in front of the fire.

"Gonna get damn cold without insulation," I said, but I understood what she was saying. Something about living inside an unfinished house felt incredibly right.

"But once it's done, it's done."

"I know what you mean. Unfinished house, unfinished lives."

"Well, I didn't really mean that. But, yes, we'll only live through this house-building phase once. And it's something special."

"Oh, I don't know," I said. "If you've got enough money, maybe we can build some more houses in other parts of the world and live in them too."

"I don't want that," Ramona said, suddenly sounding serious. "I want one house. One life. Back when I was acting, I thought I wanted to live in a number of places. The dream was to have a place in L.A., get some film work maybe in France or Australia. Do the jet set thing."

"Bet you never dreamed you'd end up in Stewart Harbour, shacked up with an unemployed writer."

"Wasn't exactly on the agenda, no. But here we are. And here we stay. Speaking of unemployed writer, when are you going to get back to that novel?"

I hadn't told her. Shit. "Never," I admitted. "While you were gone, I got frustrated and I burned it."

"The whole thing?"

"All ninety thousand words. So long *Purgatory Newsletter.*"

"Jesus. Why?"

"Because," I answered, just like a little kid would.

My answer seemed to suffice. She didn't say another word about it.

"I want you to start a new one," she said after a long silence as I put another piece of wood into the fire.

We had a few lights so that we could read at night. Ramona and I each had a pile of books from the library and we spent many quiet hours reading. We'd given up on the cramped quarters of the fish shack for our haven of plywood floors, unfinished rooms, and wall-to-wall sunlight and moonlight. We had a big stove and a giant refrigerator that made its own ice and enough cooking utensils fit for a five-star restaurant. And Ramona was right. We really didn't want to see the house finished. We liked it just the way it was.

But winter was around the corner. Back in July, it seemed like summer would never end. How could it? We'd become accustomed to our idyllic days at sea and our nights back in the fisherman's shack making love. Now we were on the mainland and headed toward something resembling respectability.

And maybe that scared us both.

The money side of things had started to bug me. I was still the guy without a quarter to his name. But Ramona had all we needed. The word *gigolo* had cropped up in my mind more than once. Part of me still felt guilty about not carrying my weight. Probably my father speaking inside my head. A man thing. *Men are supposed to work.* If he could see me now, he'd wonder how he could ever have produced a son so totally reliant on a woman.

"I'm thinking of starting a community newspaper," I told Ramona at breakfast one day, out of the blue.

"Great," she said. "But I thought newspapers were on their last legs. The end of an era and all that."

"Not small local papers. People still want local news, local gossip. Articles about church dinners and fish stories. They still love fish stories."

"Then do it."

"As soon as the house is finished, I'll suss out the possibilities. A weekly. Full of folksy stories about men with beer can collections and women who have noontime socials wearing funny hats. And fishing news of course. 'Fred Osborne finds hundred-year-old boot in mackerel net.' That sort of thing."

"I love it. Just don't forget about the novel."

"The trouble with novels is that they're so ambitious. Big stories with the intention of coming to grips with the meaning of life. Or the meaninglessness of life, as so many express it these days. I think the real truth about living is in the minutiae. The little things. The everyday things."

"I agree. Your newspaper will be filled with stories about the ordinary events of people's lives."

"I'll get Rolf to write editorials. Rants on whatever he wants."

"And I'll do the gossip column."

"Now you're talking.

We had plenty of warning about the approaching storm. Days in advance, Environment Canada was issuing statements that Hurricane Greta was arcing north from the Caribbean after being spawned off the coast of Africa. But then it stalled just past Bermuda and we all thought it was like so many other tropical storms, just going to spin itself into nothing in the colder northern waters.

Nova Scotia hadn't seen a real hurricane since Juan back in 2003, when massive winds had knocked out the power for weeks and whole forests were levelled in its wake. The memory of that hadn't faded exactly, but we had all begun to feel that we were safe from any repeat of a big storm.

Ramona's father showed up with Brenda in tow again. She looked healthier than I'd seen her before and Stanley was cheerful and pleasant. Ramona had slowly accepted that he was back and was trying to get adjusted to the new man that he seemed to be. Stanley was genuinely interested in our new home and asked me endless questions about how we were going to finish it.

Despite the new drug that the doctors had found for her, Ramona's mother still had bad days, days when she seemed able to remember only a little. On those days she would forget my name, referring to me as "that boy." From her tone of voice, however, it was clear that she thought of me in a good way. She seemed to have accepted her day-to-day confusion but grew frustrated when she couldn't remember something. Yet, occasionally, she would recount stories from her past with perfect clarity. But, of course, the drug didn't always work and overall there was a steady decline.

"Ramona, I remember when you were a little girl and you sneaked into the bathroom with my good scissors and cut off all your hair."

"I had decided that I wanted to be a boy," Ramona added.

"You never told me this," I said, pretending to be shocked.

"It was just a phase," Ramona said.

"She got over it," Brenda added, "when she discovered that men had penises. She found them disgusting."

"I was only a child," Ramona said. "I let my hair grow back after that." She paused and then, smiling at me, said, "I got over my disgust. Eventually."

By midafternoon, the sky began to look dark. My father's old barometer on the wall, the one returned by Ernie Pike, showed that the air pressure was dropping rapidly.

"Stanley, I think you might want to head back to Halifax," I told him. But he looked over at his wife who had suddenly fallen asleep on the old sofa. She looked so peaceful.

"Just like an angel," he said. "I think I'll let her have her nap first."

Old fishermen speak frequently of being able to predict storms with bad toes or back injuries, headaches, or congestion. It all probably has something to do with air pressure. But other things are deeper seated. A kind of ancient and reliable instinct in the primitive part of the brain that lets someone know there is danger coming.

I walked outside and saw a wave of gulls and cormorants fly over. I could feel the weight of an approaching storm. I turned on the car radio and heard the news. Greta had started moving. Winds at sea were already at gale level. There was a chance the hurricane would make landfall by night somewhere east of Halifax.

I went back inside and told Ramona. "I think your parents should get on the road now," I told her. But just then a powerful gust of sea air hit us.

"I think they should stay," she said. "My father is a crazy driver. Even if we just get rain before they get to Halifax, I'd rather he wasn't driving. I don't trust him."

"Could be a long night," I said.

"You okay if they stay?"

"Sure."

I drove out to the harbour then to see that the shack was closed up and to check the lines on the boat. Other fishermen were battening down their boats and looking more than a little worried. I saw Joe's boat; it looked like he'd already added more lines to keep it in place and he'd stowed his gear.

We all knew, though, that if a real hurricane hits, there isn't much you can do to ensure your boat doesn't get battered or sunk. Some fishermen, fearing for their boats getting smashed against the docks, take them out to sea to ride out a storm. But that is a deadly gambler's game and not one anyone around there would be willing to play.

I think I talked to *Sheer Delight* the way people speak to their dog or their car. "You're gonna be all right," I said. "Just hang in there and you'll be fine." I had a fleeting image of my father just then, bringing us back to the harbour in the middle of a November squall on his last day of the year at sea. And I realized those were his words I was speaking, not mine.

"Keep an eye on her," I said to my dead father. "Help her get through this."

You bet I will, he seemed to say. As I stood there on the deck of his old fishing boat, I looked out to sea at the darkness on the horizon. All at once, I felt a powerful surge of emotion — an overwhelming feeling of loss. I missed my parents. I deeply longed to be able to see them again. I can't say why it hit me just then. But it did. This feeling that I had denied myself for decades hit me hard like a powerful punch to my gut. Suddenly, I was on my knees, crying in that way children do, in great, heaving gasps.

That was when the first few drops of rain fell. If anyone had been looking, it probably looked like I was praying, and maybe that's as close to prayer as I ever came. I felt the cool drops of rain on my head and on my back and, as I stood back up, I felt the sea beneath the boat drop and then rise in slow motion. Waves coming from a storm probably still a hundred miles away. But heading this way.

But so far it was only droplets of rain. I put two hands on the gunwale and promised *Sheer Delight* I'd be back when the storm was over.

I went to Rolf's shack and banged on the door. No answer. So I opened the door and walked in. Rolf was sitting at his wooden table staring at a full bottle of rum.

"What the hell?" I said.

"If I can stare at it long enough, I can win," he said. "It's me or the bottle. Always good to keep your enemy close at hand."

"Rolf, you idiot, there's a storm coming. A big one. Come stay at my new house overnight."

"Oh, Jesus, Chisel. It's just a little weather. If you listen to those sissies on the CBC, you'd think it's something out of the Old Testament. Get the animals on the ark, Noah. Before it's too late."

"Really, Rolf. I checked the boat and I'm going to the mainland. Come with me. Bring your friend there if you like."

"No, no, no. I'm staying put. This ole shack has been through many a storm. This one ain't gonna be no worse. Besides, I like a little bad weather. Good for the soul."

"I insist. Come on, you old coot."

But Rolf would have none of it. He was staying put.

42

O n the short drive back to our new house, my brain began to chart the hours ahead. Rain, wind, trees with smashed limbs. No doubt we'd lose electricity. We'd have to ride through the storm in that shell of a house. Big Carl had expressed worries about the house being unfinished, but he had assured me the place was watertight, or "weathertight" as he called it. But this was a hurricane coming our way, the real thing.

Like most folks there in Stewart Harbour, I believed the media hype about the approaching storm to be just that. Hype. City people would be worried, crowding themselves into super-markets, buying up canned goods and bottled water like it was the end of the world. Hunkering down in their homes, frantic when they lost electricity. Funny how any storm that was tropical in origin would get so much attention. As a kid, I'd seen winter storms with waves towering at thirty feet and winds that could suck your skin off, but you'd never hear a word about those on the news.

A little wind. A little rain. By morning it would be all over and everyone would wonder what the fuss was about. On the car radio, they spoke of the path of the storm and it sounded like we were going to be right on the "eye wall" and could experience some serious winds. There was talk of a tidal surge as well. High tide would be the middle of the night. No time to be anywhere near the wharf.

As I drove over the causeway, the water on both sides looked choppy but normal. Still, time to get myself back inside, ride it out with Ramona and her parents. Could be a mighty strange evening.

As soon as I pulled in the driveway, it started to come down in buckets. Not much wind, just an avalanche of water pouring down from the sky. I got soaked running to the house. Ramona was relieved to see me and gave me a big hug. She had made some coffee and was trying to figure out what to feed us for dinner.

Despite the rain, part of me still thought the whole storm news thing was fear-mongering. But suddenly the sound of the rain on the roof was deafening. With no insulation, no gyprock on the ceilings or walls, and just a big empty shell of a wooden house, the pounding of the rain was amplified out of all proportion.

Ramona's mother and father were sitting on the old sofa that had come from my childhood home. Brenda looked frightened and Stanley was soothing her. She closed her eyes and leaned into him.

The rain let up ever so slightly, but we could still hear some kind of drumming. Someone was knocking at our door. Ramona rushed to open it. There was Mackenzie, soaked to the skin.

Ramona ushered her into the house and grabbed a blanket to throw around her. She was crying and hyperventilating. Ramona sat her down on the floor as I closed the door. When she could speak, she said, "My grandmother kicked me out of the house. I was headed toward Beth Ann's house, but then the rain started. I got scared. I didn't know where else to go."

"You're here now," Ramona consoled her. "You're gonna stay here until this thing is over."

Mackenzie tented herself under the blanket and sobbed some more. I watched Brenda studying the girl with the utmost concern. When Mackenzie poked her head back out from under,

Brenda suddenly reached out her arms into the air, but the pregnant girl pulled herself away and coiled the blanket around herself. Ramona's mother looked a little hurt, but then turned to her daughter and said, "Ramona, see if you can find something dry for her, please, honey."

I decided to make an inspection of the house to see if there were any leaks or anything else to worry about. The wind hadn't hit yet. Just rain. But plenty of it. I could see some leaks around a few of the windows but nothing really to worry about. The concrete floor on the basement was dry, but I did see some water dribbling down from the top of the foundation. When I went up to the second storey, I could see water coming in around the eaves. I also noticed a big pile of metal rafter hangers on the floor. The house was still a work in progress, so no surprise there. The roof looked solid, though. No big worries. Just the pounding, drum-like sound of big drops of rain again. Lots of rain.

The downpour let up around five o'clock that evening. Ramona had been able to cook spaghetti. The power had not gone out but then we still hadn't been hit with the wind. I turned on the old radio, the beat-up ancient thing I'd brought over from the fish shack. Our only entertainment. The cellphone wasn't working, so this was our only way of knowing what the outside world had to offer us.

After dinner on paper plates, Stanley said, "Just like having a picnic."

Mackenzie had settled down and was dressed in some of Ramona's dry clothes. She lay down on the mattress I had hauled into the bare living room, and I watched as Brenda covered her with a dry blanket. Then the rain stopped. Just like someone had turned off the faucet. It grew quiet. Strangely quiet. But also peaceful.

I instinctively knew all the rain was just that — rain. Something advancing ahead of Greta, drenching us good, but just a warm-up act to the main event. It wouldn't be over until it was over. And it hadn't really begun yet.

And then I heard this on the CBC. "Environment Canada has just announced that it expects to see a storm surge of one to two metres along the Eastern Shore as the storm approaches, coinciding with a rising tide and significant wave height. They have issued a warning to anyone living in low-lying coastal areas to move inland, away from the coast."

Ramona looked at me. "What do we do?"

"We're okay here. I'm certain. It's why my father had built the old house here on the mainland. He said it was here instead of closer to the water because of what he called the once-in-a-hundred-year storm. My father liked to be prepared just in case."

"What about the boat?"

I shrugged. "Whatever will be will be." I figured we'd be lucky if we could even find the boat by tomorrow.

"The fish shack?"

"Who knows?" And then it hit me. "Rolf."

"I thought you said he'd be okay."

"I did. But I didn't know about the storm surge. Shit. I gotta go get him." I reached for the car keys on the table but Ramona grabbed my hand. "No. Call someone."

I held up the cellphone. "Not working, remember? Tower got knocked out by the rain somehow."

"Don't go. Please." Ramona pulled me to her, a frantic look in her eyes.

"I gotta."

And I did.

Everything was soaked outside. There was only a light drizzle now and a whiff of a sea breeze. The proverbial calm before the storm. How many times had my father used that phrase? His presence seemed to be with me again. That would be just like him. Looking over my shoulder, advising me what to do next like I was still a little kid. What would my father do in this situation? He'd go haul Rolf's ass away from the harbour whether he wanted to co-operate or not. And that's exactly what I was about to do.

There were no other cars on the road. I could see that the causeway was already flooded; waves were lapping up on both sides and spilling over onto the road. I slowed the Lexus and proceeded with caution. Halfway across, however, I realized the water was seeping in under the door. Shit. Then I heard a loud, double-barrelled *whump* as a wave on each side of the causeway slammed into the protecting rocks, vaulted spray up into the air, and slammed it down hard onto the hood and roof.

The engine sputtered and stalled. I got the engine to turn over several times, but then I got nothing but a click. And then, nothing at all. The water had shorted out the battery. *Should have seen that coming*, my dead father seemed to say. *Now get your ass moving.*

I got out. The water was knee deep. It was warm. Gulf Stream warm. I started slogging toward the wharf. A couple more waves hit the rocks and I was pummelled with seawater. But I kept moving, all the while thinking about the way back.

I was almost back on land, that narrow peninsula jutting to sea that was home to the fishing village and the wharf. The sky off to the south looked pitch black. Ominous. When I looked back toward the mainland, I saw an old truck racing across the causeway at speed, sending up a rooster tail of water on either side.

It was Joe. I kept walking until I was past the causeway and up on dry land. He pulled up out of the water and stopped.

"What the fuck are you doing here?" It was a familiar line.

"I'm worried about Rolf. He said he wasn't leaving."

"That stupid piece of shit. C'mon. Get in."

I got in. "What are *you* doing out here?" I asked.

"I needed to check on my boat one more time."

"Tide's rising," I said. "Better make it quick."

"I lose that boat, I lose everything."

"You heard about the storm surge?"

"I heard. Anything else you want to lecture me about?"

"Nope," I said. Joe sped to the wharf, skidded to a stop on the loose stones. He ran off down the wharf. No one else was around.

I could see all the boats bobbing eerily up and down. The water was up to the top of the decking already. Soon the wharf would be awash.

I ran to Rolf's shack, knocked on the door. No answer. I opened it and there was Rolf. Passed out at the kitchen table where I'd left him with his full bottle of rum. Except now it was empty. The bottle had won. Captain Morgan had spoken.

"Rolf, wake up!" I yelled at him.

"Take me now, Jesus," he said without raising his head.

"I never knew you to be religious before."

"Is the storm over?"

"No. It hasn't really started yet. I came to get you."

Rolf lifted his head up now, reached for the bottle, and seemed appalled that the liquor was all gone. "Me and the captain here were just having a little *tête-à-tête*. I must have dozed off."

"I'm sure the conversation was most stimulating, but I got to get you out of here. We have to leave and we have to leave now."

"Why now?"

"Fuck off," I said as I lifted him into a standing position. I was shocked at how frail he actually was — this man who had once been strong and healthy and robust like my own father.

"I should stay here and ride out the storm," he insisted, trying to pull away.

"You're not gonna ride this one out, ole buddy. This whole place is going to be underwater in a few hours and you're not gonna be around to watch."

That ominous darkness I'd seen out to sea seemed much closer now. The wind was on the rise. I poured Rolf into the cab of the truck and yelled for Joe, but I couldn't see him. There was no one else around. Even the other men worried about their boats had fled to the mainland. Nothing left to do but come back after the storm and see what's left.

There was still no Joe.

I ran out on the wharf and found him standing on the deck of his boat. "I got Rolf," I said.

"I think I need to stay here, ride it out with the boat. If we break free, maybe I can steer up the bay and beach 'er into the marsh. Take the truck."

"Don't be a fool, Joe. This storm, this Greta, is a monster. You heard the latest forecast. Storm surge of a metre, maybe two."

"At this point, who cares? I'm gonna stay. I'd rather have it this way. Save what's left of my pitiful existence or go out trying."

Damn.

I wanted to say something. Anything. Something about Brody and that he wouldn't want to see Joe die in a hurricane. Something. What?

"What about Beth Ann? What's she gonna do if she loses you too?" I knew they'd been apart for years, but Brody had been their son. I'd seen them together in the courtroom. There was something there. Something real.

"What's she got to do with it, you son of a bitch?"

I didn't answer. The rain started up heavy again. Right on cue. Just like in the movies.

"Damn it, Joe."

He looked up at the rain, then down at the deck of his boat. "Fuck it," he said, and leaped onto the wharf. "Get in the fucking truck and let's get the hell out of here."

43

Joe floored it as we approached the flooded causeway. "Ford 150, Ford 150, Ford 150," he repeated as a kind mantra as his tires hit the water. The engine roared and the salt water seeped in through the floorboards. "I may not believe in much, but I believe in this truck," he grunted out as he gripped the wheel with an iron fist, downshifted, and bulled the truck through the deepening water over what we all hoped was once the road that tethered the peninsula to the mainland. The windshield wipers were beating frantically, fending off rain and waves both. As we sped past the swamped Lexus, Joe felt obliged to comment, "Foreign cars aren't worth shit."

Rolf looked on with dull wonder, but let out a loud whoop when Joe's Tiger's Paw tires found purchase on some real gravel. Within minutes we were back in the driveway of my new house.

"Come in and stay with us," I said, as I lifted Rolf out of the truck, the rain now streaming down on us.

"Hell, no," Joe said. "I'm gonna go see if Beth Ann is gonna be okay. I think I better do that." All the bluster had gone out of him. But I understood.

"Thanks for the ride, Joe," I said.

"Yeah, sure," he answered in his usual brief fashion but without the usual hostility. "Anytime." And left.

I guided a wobbly Rolf into the house.

As I bolted the door behind us, Rolf blinked, looked at the unfinished walls of the house, then turned to Ramona, who was standing there. "You folks wouldn't have anything to drink by any chance?"

"Coffee," Ramona said. "That's all you get."

Rolf wiped some water off his face and looked up. Here in the living room was a vaulted ceiling that went all the way up between the roof boards. "It's like being in church," he said, smiling.

"How would you know?" I asked and punched him gently on the arm. Ramona held out a towel to me and then kissed me. "I was worried. Really worried. It's getting bad out there. They say on the radio it's gonna get much worse."

"Where's your mother and Mackenzie?" I asked.

Ramona took my hand and led me to what would one day be our own bedroom. There on the mattress on the floor lay Brenda with her arms wrapped around Mackenzie. Both were fast asleep.

"What was it like out there past the causeway?"

"Hellish. Your car didn't make it. Sorry."

Ramona looked shocked for only an instant. "How'd you get back?"

"Joe," I answered.

Just then it sounded like something solid hit the side of the house. Like a truck had just crashed into it. This was the kind of wind you rarely felt in Nova Scotia. Wind that could uproot trees, wind that could do real damage.

"Flashlights, candles, what do we have?" I asked.

"Not much. Six candles. Two flashlights. Do you think we're going to need them?" she asked.

"Very likely. This looks like it's shaping up to be a pretty bad blow. Juan was about the worst I've seen. I went out into the wind, thinking it would be fun. Got hit in the head with a flying shingle. Could have lost my eye. You could lean into the wind at a forty-five-degree angle and still not fall. Nothing quite like it."

"Well, stay inside. No one gets to go out and play. Including you."

I found some dry clothes and shone the flashlight around the inside of the house. "Guess we get to see how good the workmanship is. Hope those boys knew their stuff."

At around nine o'clock, we lost power. It came back on briefly once, then twice, then a third time, and that was it for the duration, I expected. The wind roared. Boards groaned. Ramona lit a single candle. Rolf and Stanley seemed to be having a chatty conversation about God knows what.

I looked at my watch. It was going to be a long night. No one was going anywhere. Trees would be down on roads by now, many of those would be flooded. I expected that out by the wharf, Rolf's shack and mine already had knee-deep water sloshing around. Nothing for it now but to wait.

The candle produced a gentle but eerie glow. I suddenly realized there was enough scrap wood lying around that I could make a fire in the fireplace. I found some matches and old newspapers and made a little campfire there. Mackenzie and Brenda slept on through the madness of the storm. Stanley hovered nearby, chatting with Rolf, looking in on them every few minutes to make sure they were asleep. Best thing to be doing on a night like this, maybe. Sound asleep.

Me? I knew this was a storm bigger than Juan. The sea had finally begun to warm a bit through September; nothing now to ward off a tropical low pressure system. This one had somehow refuelled in strength as it moved north on the Gulf Stream. It had teamed up with another low pressure system. Not exactly a "perfect storm," whatever that was, but something that may not have happened in Nova Scotia for well over one hundred years.

Ramona and I sat on lawn furniture cushions by the fire. Light and heat. I felt the chill of rain start to fade from my body. I felt the warmth of a woman tuck into me. Somewhere around eleven, I heard shingles lifting from the roof. They had only recently been nailed down, and the tar had not felt enough really sunny days to melt them together for good. You'd hear a kind of rip and then snap. I soon heard the first bit of vinyl siding pull loose, slap several times along the outer wall until that too ripped and sailed off to parts unknown.

———

I kept watch on my father's old barometer. Pressure still dropping. Ramona thought I was crazy when I went to the back of the house and opened two windows. "Air pressure," I tried to explain. "I don't know if it's true, but I think it has something to do with balancing the inner and outer air pressure to keep windows from imploding."

But, as if on cue, a big tree branch crashed into the glass of one of the living room windows on the front of the house. Glass blew in and sprayed across the room. The wind roared into the building.

Ramona was on her feet first. She walked to the pile of unused plywood, found a half sheet and tried to hold it up to the window, but the invasive wind pushed her back. I grabbed one end of it and we wrestled it across the room and set it on the floor while we scrambled around for a hammer and some nails.

When it came time to try to hold it up there against the onslaught of rain and malevolent wind, Rolf and Stanley both braced it with their backs while Ramona and I hammered away like maniacs. We were all breathing hard by the time the sucker was nailed down, me realizing we should have done this from the outside before the storm. Too late now.

Without a word to each other, we nailed plywood on the two other windows facing south. My hands were bleeding from the shattered glass, and when we settled by the fire, Ramona gently picked out some shards and wiped my hands until the bleeding stopped.

"I gotta go upstairs and see if I can do anything about those windows." She reluctantly let go of my hand and I cautiously took the unfinished stairs to the second storey. It was an other-worldly view up there, looking down on the living room with the vaulted ceiling. There was, of course, no way I could get to those front windows high up above the living room, but so far they were holding. I took the flashlight and shone it up toward the roof. Rainwater was being driven up under the eaves. That was to be expected. But there was something else.

The flashlight beam glinted off the metal brackets — the joist hangers — holding the rafters to the ceiling joists. Weren't they also called hurricane hangers? Probably for good reason. Problem was, although they were all in place in the back half of the roof, many were missing from the front rafters. That bit of unfinished work Big Carl had mentioned. All the rafters were nailed in with angled nails, but this was an unfinished house. A house in progress. Not quite ready to take on a storm like this.

Shit.

The wind was constant. It roared. It had a voice of its own — dark, malevolent, insistent. Like something in a horror movie. A monster. It would let up ever so slightly and then roar back. As I stood there on the second floor with my flashlight aimed at the roof, I felt the next assault of air — a blast that first shook the walls, then made the floorboards beneath me shudder. Then I heard the creaking boards of the roof and the nails fighting back. Good carpenters, I told myself. Good roof. But it may not be enough.

I went back downstairs and found Rolf, Stanley, and Ramona feeding triangles of scrap pine to the fire.

"We have to wake your mother and Mackenzie and get us all into the basement," I said.

Ramona nodded. Her father went into the bedroom. We had no electricity, no battery-powered radio. No cellphone service. We didn't know if the storm was about to blow itself out or hammer away all night. Was it going to ease up or was this only the beginning? All I knew was that it had been hyped up as massive, based on the early reports. Too bad that I, like many around there, hadn't taken it all that seriously.

The doorway to the basement had been one of the first of the returned items. Opening it, I had the strangest flashbacks of days as a kid, going into the old cellar by myself. Not a scary place, but an alone place. A place where I could hide out from the daytime world among old Mason jars and my father's workbench and tools. A place to daydream and plot a life of adventure. God, I loved that old cellar as a kid.

This was different. I was opening that old door to take us to what I hoped would be a place of safety and refuge from the monster storm. We were well up away from the water, away from those ever-rising tides. It was a new basement, sealed from the outside. If we were lucky, we'd be dry at least, and safe if more windows shattered or if the outside doors blew off.

People, candles, matches, flashlights, mattress, blankets. All were carefully but quickly carried down the temporary, two-by-ten stair steps into a basement that still smelled of fresh concrete.

Mackenzie seemed to well understand the gravity of the situation, but Stanley had to comfort his wife and assure her things were okay. She looked frightened and confused, but he seemed to have the magic touch. His facial expression and voice told her all was well. Nothing to fear. The daughter had gotten her acting skills from her father, I could see.

The voice of my father was in my head again. *Do what you have to do. When push comes to shove, you will know what you have to do. And you need to keep your wits about you. You have no choice. It's your duty.* Those platitudes probably saved his ass a hundred times at sea. Far from land, you're on your own most of the time. No one is going to come save you. He'd never used the word once in his life but his religion was self-reliance. His bible was that set of bromides, probably handed down to him by his father.

The comfort of the fireplace flames gone, we now huddled together around a single candle set on the concrete floor and watched its flame. That night, we returned to the world of our most ancient ancestors, circling a small, hopeful flame in a hostile, dark wilderness, with nothing to keep us alive but our collective ability to comfort and care for each other.

Ramona must have thought me crazy when I suddenly, without explanation, ran back up the stairs, ripped open the cellar door and then, after a mere second or two, came back through, and ran back down.

In my bleeding hands were Brody's ashes. Mackenzie was looking at me now. She knew what I had gone upstairs for. I handed her the little box and she tucked it with two hands beneath her chin.

Silence can be good or bad. The wind was doing all the talking. The storm carried the narrative — big and brutish. Even in the basement, it was hard to hear each other when we spoke, so we were mostly mute. We heard things hitting the house and more shingles being ripped from the roof. There was howling of wind and a ripping sound as it shifted direction. And other ungodly sounds we couldn't even begin to identify.

The candle flickered. I studied the walls, the piles of goods people had returned. The things my father had given away. And he had given away everything. There were some end tables, a lamp, a box of mouldy records, three of the worn wooden chairs that my mother had once stripped and repainted. And an old heavy tool box that had once so fascinated me in my reveries in the basement as a kid. Inside were tools that had belonged to my grandfather. A carpenter's compass, small saws, screwdrivers, and items I didn't have names for.

I sidled away from Ramona and undid the clasp on the lid, wondering if there might be something in there of value to us in this time of crisis. I opened it and shone the light inside. The smell hit me first. Old tools, old tools that had been oiled and kept usable over maybe a hundred years. I couldn't even remember who had returned the box. So many folks had just shown up, even when I wasn't there, and returned things. Things they thought a son might want from his father.

But it wasn't just tools inside. There was a package of something there. It was a small canvas bag, the kind of sack a sailor might take to sea for a shaving or medical kit. As I tried to open it, the string holding it closed disintegrated. Inside was something wrapped in three layers of clear plastic freezer bags like my mother would have used to freeze summer vegetables. Beneath the flashlight beam, I could see that these were letters.

The battery died on my flashlight right then and the candle flickered. What kind of letters? Certainly my mother and my father were not the sort of people who wrote letters to people. I couldn't even conjure up who would be writing to them or who they would write to. In what dim light there was, I left the freezer bags unopened. I put them back into the canvas bag and locked it back into the tool box.

A quick draft swooped down from above, the candle went out and I thought the worst.

But then the wind suddenly stopped. All was quiet. Ramona tried to light another candle but the match broke.

Rolf was the first one to speak. "Holy Mother of God. Do you hear that?"

What he meant was the quiet. It was deafening. Brenda had fallen back asleep, held fast in her husband's arms. Mackenzie, however, was wide awake. She was rubbing her round belly. I had forgotten that there were more than the six of us. The storm had made us into an extended family, a tribe. We represented generations past and generations to come. And we were in the middle of one of the most horrific storms ever to hit this coast.

No one had to say it out loud. The storm was not over. You didn't have to know much about hurricanes to know that this hiatus was the so-called eye.

"Everyone stay put," I said, even though I don't think it needed to be said.

Ramona leaned into me and, with her voice shaking, said, "I don't know what's going on." Her grasp on my arm was tight, almost painful. There was something different about her voice, almost like she was acting. The fear had not been there all night. I refused to register what might be happening.

She fumbled a couple of times with matches again, trying to relight the candle in the dark until I took them from her and succeeded in bringing a small pool of light back into the immensity of the dark. I saw the fear in her eyes and said, "It's going to be all right. I promise you."

No one else spoke. The term *eye wall* echoed in my head again. That's the term Environment Canada had used. Somewhere on the Eastern Shore of Nova Scotia would experience the eye wall of the hurricane with winds more powerful than the storm itself.

And we were most certainly in the eye. The rain had even stopped.

But then it started again. Rain without wind at first. And then wind. A freight train this time instead of a truck. A wall of raging air. Ferocious. A fist of wind. It hit once hard enough for the house to shudder yet again. With the second fist, I heard glass breaking — the upper windows, no doubt.

The third punch made the very concrete shake and I heard boards groaning. The next blow was much the same, but the fifth hit created an ominous, unearthly crack, an explosion of some sort. A splintering and banging, and I knew that at least half of the roof had been torn from the house and lifted away. I was pretty sure I could hear it slam into the trees behind the house.

I think we all bent over then into a kind of huddle. I was leaning over Ramona, Stanley had tucked himself over Brenda, and Rolf was on his hands and knees over top of Mackenzie. We had pushed ourselves together like a single living organism. A living thing trying to survive.

We heard more glass breaking, boards jetting about above and crashing into walls. As the cellar door was ripped from its hinges, wind poured into the basement and we were once again in total darkness. Rainwater began to stream down on us, penetrating the floorboards above.

It seemed to last forever. Wind. Rain. Darkness. All of us now wet and cold on a concrete floor, wondering how long this could possibly last. I wondered if the floor above us might come crashing down at this point. Was there more I should do? No, there wasn't. There was nowhere to go. I'd been wise to get us down there, but this was it. We would either live through it or all die together.

But my father was with me again. *Stay put. Keep your wits. Tough it out.*

Eventually, the wind began to subside. The rain continued beyond the wind. It seemed like it would never end. I left the huddle to find an old tarp to put over us, but we were all soaked and cold.

And then it was over. At the top of the stairs I could see a dim, grey light. When I tried to stand up, every bone in my body ached, every muscle was cramped. But as I straightened myself, I lifted Ramona to her feet. We all groaned as we tried to find strength in our limbs again.

I checked the stairs to be sure they were safe, then Ramona and I guided her parents, Rolf, and Mackenzie up to the first floor. Mackenzie was still clinging to the box of Brody's ashes I had given her.

As we ascended back into the world of light, I kept thinking that all of us who had just endured this had discovered we were much stronger than we realized. Self-reliant. Resilient. What would my father's expression be? *Stubborn and strong. That's all you need to be to survive in this world.*

44

The sun was still rising to the east and the sky above was perfectly clear. Gulls flew overhead. You could see all this looking up from inside the first floor of the house. The entire roof was gone. Not fully secured, the wind had pushed up under the eaves on the south side and literally ripped it off. None of us said a word. It was the strangest sensation, standing there in the shell of what was left of the house looking up at the most benign sky I could imagine.

Plywood and other pieces of lumber were scattered around on the floor. A couple of windows were broken. The roof was in the field and most of the vinyl siding had been ripped from the house. Everything was soaked by rain. Stanley kept his arm firmly around his wife. She was looking up at the sky above smiling. Then she laughed. Stanley tried to shush her, fearing perhaps that it was not a moment for laughter. But Ramona walked over to them, hugged them both, and laughed as well.

Mackenzie didn't seem to share the joke. Still holding Brody's ashes, she sat down on the wet plywood subfloor and began to cry. I sat down beside her and put my arm around her. "Rough night," I offered, not really knowing what to say.

"I have nowhere to go," she said.

"Stay with us," I said. "We'll figure something out."

"Here?" she asked, still sobbing, looking around at the wreckage of what once was a half-built house.

"Yes," I said. "It will be like camping."

"I don't like camping," she said, sounding like an unhappy little kid.

"We'll make it work," I told her.

Ramona was watching us and she knew what we were talking about. She nodded her approval.

Stanley was the first go outside, leading his wife through the open doorway. Rolf, Ramona, and I followed. Mackenzie was not far behind, wobbling over the debris.

Everything had changed. Trees had been uprooted and were lying jumbled in crazy patterns around the perimeter of the yard. Power lines were down along the road. The road itself looked like it had been a river during the storm. It was covered with wet earth and stones, and in places the water had carved gullies out of the pavement.

Stanley's car was still intact, although a large branch had fallen and dented his trunk.

Despite the carnage, the world appeared bright and shiny, if somewhat wet. It had a feeling of renewal and rebirth. Maybe it was just because we were so happy to be alive.

Rolf's jaw had dropped from the second he had reached the top of the stairs. He'd followed us outside and took in the sight of disaster. I could tell from the look on his face that the once-familiar landscape must have been unrecognizable to him. "It's over, Rolf," I said. "We made it."

"Wasn't much of a storm, was it?" he said.

"Bit of wind. Rain. What's the big deal?"

"Guess the party's over. I should get going."

"Not yet," I said, nodding toward the causeway that was still underwater. I could just barely make out Ramona's black car, which had been washed off the road and was nose down in the harbour. "Give it an hour and the tide will drop." Rolf nodded and walked off behind the house to have a pee.

I was thinking about what it must have been like out at the fish shacks and the wharf last night. I hoped that every one of the fishermen had had enough sense to stay away.

Ramona came to me and I put my arm around her. I pointed to the Lexus in the distance. "Sorry about your car," I said.

"I have insurance," she said. "Don't worry about that."

I looked back at the shambles of what once had been a beautiful house under construction. "I'm also sorry about your house."

"*Our* house," she corrected me. "Besides, I took out insurance on that too."

I was shocked. She'd never told me. "You rich people like insurance, don't you?"

"Yeah, we do. It's all about protecting your assets."

"I love you, babe. You protect my assets and I'll protect you, how about that?" I gave her a big squeeze.

"Deal," she said.

I went in the house and brought out some bottled water. Big Carl and his guys had left a case of it on the worksite and it had come in handy over the night. I handed everyone a bottle as we stood in a little circle. "Cheers," I said. "Here's to one hell of a party."

Stanley said he wanted to get Brenda back to the city, but I told him to hang back for a couple of hours until the roads would be cleaned up and safer. He seemed to appreciate my advice.

I had this crazy desire to make love to Ramona just then and wondered what that was about. "I'm horny," I told her.

"Me too," she said. "Disasters always make me horny."

"Guess we'll have to wait," I said.

"No problem," she said. "We have the rest of our lives."

A few cars were driving by on the road now. Drivers stopped and gawked at us and the roofless house. "Everybody all right?" one man asked.

I yelled back that we were all okay and he drove on.

Soon, I saw the first pickup truck cross the causeway. The water had receded some, but the road was still underwater.

Then Joe arrived, gingerly driving up our washed-out drive-way. Beth Ann was in the cab with him. When they got out, she went over to Mackenzie and spoke to her. Joe approached Ramona and me, looked up at the roof that wasn't there. "How bad was it?" he asked.

"Bad," I said. "Real bad. But we're all okay. Might need a new roof."

"Sorry for your loss," he said, the classic line usually reserved for consolation when someone dies. Joe studied the carnage for a few seconds. "Beth Ann's place took a real beating — flooded basement and water damage in through the roof. My old shithole didn't do much better. I'm gonna go out and see what's left at the wharf. Wanna come?"

"Sure. Rolf's itching to go home too. Looks like the boys'll be back in town."

"Somethin' like that."

Beth Ann stayed with Mackenzie. Ramona told me to be careful and hurry back as Rolf and I got into Joe's cab and he backed down out of the driveway.

I recalled the hellish drive to the mainland last night as we had made the crossing on the narrow ribbon of land. On the peninsula, the water was still ankle deep. What few trees had been standing yesterday were knocked down and piled atop each other in odd angles. Several of the fish shacks had been battered by the waves; they looked like bulldozers had smashed into them. I noticed at once that my father's beloved fish shack was simply gone. Nothing but rock and rubble beneath a skim of seawater where it once stood.

Miraculously, Rolf's shack was still standing. The door was mostly knocked off its hinges and the glass in the window was out, but it looked perfectly okay, aside from the fact that it probably still had a foot and half of water inside.

"See," Rolf said. "I told you. You didn't need to worry about me. Could have kept my feet up and just rode the storm out as usual."

"Fuck you, old man," Joe said, but there was no venom in his voice. Joe was looking toward the wharf, wondering what he would find.

We left Rolf to inspect his waterlogged home and walked toward the battered wharf. There were about eight other fishermen there. They all looked stunned and pale. As we approached, we could see a dozen boats that had sunk to the bottom, including Beth Ann's. Some were completely below the waterline on their sides, hulls smashed by the killer waves that had driven them into the wharf. Joe's boat lay on its side up on the rocky shoreline. The cabin had been crushed and there was a gaping hole in its hull like it had been blasted by terrorist's bomb. Like a lot of the others out here, I knew he didn't have insurance. Just too damn expensive.

We left the wharf and walked over to Joe's boat. It was even worse than it had appeared at first. "Guess that's that," he said. "Now what?" It wasn't really a question.

Sheer Delight wasn't anywhere to be seen.

Gus Barton walked over to us just then. He looked at Joe's boat. "Motherfucking storm," he said. "The goddamn motherfucking storm."

"You find your boat?" Joe asked.

"Found what's left of it," Gus said. "No better than yours."

There was a flat, lifeless tone to the way he spoke. Same as Joe's. Men in defeat. Hurricane Greta had just sucked the life out of this little fishing community.

Gus turned to me. "Charles, somebody said they saw your old man's boat way up the harbour. Guess you didn't have her tied proper."

"Guess not," I said. "Where'd they say it was?"

"Up near Kendell's Marsh. Storm drove her right ashore. Doubt if there's much left of her. We're all fucked. That's the way she goes." And he walked off.

Joe just stood there looking at his wrecked boat, his ruined livelihood. "Nothing to do but walk away from it. That'll be the end of fishing for me. Have to find a real job."

But I knew there was very little in the way of "real jobs" on this part of the Eastern Shore. What he meant was he'd have to move in to Halifax or go out west. A lot of the men who had lost boats the night before were probably already thinking they'd have to go somewhere else if they wanted to make a living. On this day, I knew many a dark thought was passing through the skulls of the fishermen of Stewart Harbour.

Joe was in a sullen mood as he drove me back across the causeway. The water had receded some more, but the road-way was littered with rocks, sand, kelp, and driftwood. As we approached the mainland, Joe suddenly pulled off the road and got out of the truck. He was looking up harbour toward the uninhabited marshes where Kendell Creek drained itself into the harbour.

"What do you see?" I asked.

"Not sure. You up for a little walk?"

"I should get back," I said.

"I think I see your ole man's boat," Joe said.

"I'll go check it tomorrow. I'm sure it's like all the rest." I could not envision that anything that had been floating at the wharf could have survived the storm.

"Take the truck, then. I'll catch up with you later," he said, tossing me his keys and heading out into the marsh.

When I returned to the house, Big Carl's crew was already there. They had a generator going and I could see that Ramona had some kind of hotplate plugged into it and was boiling water in the coffee pot. Beth Ann and Mackenzie were sitting on a couple of plastic milk crates chatting. When I walked toward them, Beth Ann looked up at me. "You don't have to say it. I knew it last night. I lost the boat. Joe's too, right?"

"Yes. I'm sorry."

"Like I say, it's old news."

Wade and Bernie were picking up boards that had been tossed around and trying to create some order at the worksite in the wake of the storm's destruction.

Big Carl walked up to me as I got out of the truck. "My fault, Charles. Ran out of those hangers and let it go, thinking it was no big deal. Meant to finish it later. Now this. When the winds started, I tried to call but the lines were already down and the cellphones weren't working. Hit me if you want to."

"I'm not gonna hit you."

"You should. I deserve it. In fact, I'd feel a little better if you did."

I shook my head.

"What was it like when she let go?"

"Like the world was coming to an end."

"I lay awake last night thinking about that roof. I even thought of coming over, try to jury-rig something, but the wife told me she'd ask for a divorce if I did."

"Didn't know anyone went in for divorce along the Shore here."

"Not that popular, it's true. Still, I stayed put and look what happened."

"They call it an act of God. Something like that."

"Gonna sue me?"

"Fuck, no."

"Wouldn't get much anyway."

"Waste of money on lawyers," I told him.

"Tell me about it."

"What you gonna do? Tear it down and start over?"

We both stared at the sad-looking remnant of a house. Though the vinyl siding was ripped mostly off, some of it was still attached and dangling in places, making it look like the house had skinny, useless arms and legs.

Big Carl scratched his jaw. "Here's the thing," he said. "Here's the good news."

"I could use some good news."

"Foundation and basement are perfectly good, right?"

"Kept us alive down there."

"Well, I say, we rip off all the siding, strip the Tyvek off and let her dry. There was no insulation, no gyprock, no plumbing that's in. Let the whole shebang dry and see what we got." And then he paused and looked up at the sky. "Think of it as a baptism." He gave me a wink and a sly smile.

"Blessed by a hurricane. Gift from Greta."

"Now, you're talkin'," he said. And he let go the loudest whistle I'd ever heard from a human being. "Wade, Bernie, get your scrawny asses over here and listen to this plan Charles has."

Of course, it wasn't my plan at all. But Big Carl was right. Houses under construction could take weather, lots of it, as long as the wood could dry before closing them up.

45

Big Carl and his two-man crew also seemed to have found religion. Maybe the place *had* been baptized. Or maybe it had been crucified and now was about to be resurrected. Wade plugged an old boom box into the generator and began blasting some old tunes by Rush. Bernie let out a whoop, tossed his hammer high into the air, spun around once, and then caught it behind his back. He and Wade started ripping off the vinyl siding like they were having the time of their lives.

Ramona made more coffee for everyone, and Big Carl passed around a pile of sandwiches. "The wife thought you all might have needed some nourishment. She said it was all she could do now that we weren't getting a divorce."

By noon, Ramona's parents had left, but not before everyone hugged. It was hard to believe Stanley was the man she had hated so fervently just months before.

Mackenzie had curled up for a nap in Joe's truck, snuggled beside Beth Ann, who sat behind the steering wheel reading a book.

"Let's go for a walk," Ramona said.

I told her what Big Carl had explained about salvaging the house.

"I would have been okay if we'd lost the whole thing. As long as I had you."

"We've been through a lot in a short time," I said.

"That's what I was thinking. Your life always this … chaotic?"

"Not till you came along."

"Then this is all my fault?" Ramona asked.

"Well, I wouldn't put it that way. But things were pretty dull before you came along."

"But we made it this far. You think that's some kind of commitment?"

"It would appear so to the casual observer," I concurred.

"The casual observer. How third person."

"It would appear so to me too," I said.

"That's pretty wimpy, but it sounds like a commitment of some sort."

"Of some sort."

A Nova Scotia Power truck went by then. We were walking toward the causeway and the truck stopped by three power poles that had snapped in half. Two men got out and studied them. We nodded as we walked on by.

The water on both sides of the causeway was still brown and turgid. It would take a while before it settled back and grew clear again. We noticed some dead seagulls and ducks along the shoreline. And there was Ramona's car, half buried in mud and seaweed and flooded with water.

"Must have been terrible for anything with wings in that storm." Ramona looked sad now. I remembered back to the deer on the highway. Her compassion for the animal and how my actions had offended her and sent her packing. It had all almost ended right then.

Up ahead I saw someone walking our way. As he got closer, I could see it was Joe. When he saw us, he waved. And he started to jog.

When he reached us he was out of breath. "Found her," he said. "Beached in the marsh just like Gus said." He struggled to regain his breath. "Mostly in one piece," he added. "Nice soft bit of marsh to come ashore. Bit of water inside but nothing busted. That ole boat of your father's has more lives than a cat."

"How do we get it out of there?"

"Salvage boat can do it. Get some lines on it and tow it back to deep water at high tide. I know a guy down in Port Dufferin. He's probably gonna be busier than a one-armed man at a chainsaw throwing competition, but he owes me big time. I'll get you a good price."

"Call him," I said. "I'll pay him to tow it out and it's yours."

Joe gave me a dirty look. "You can't do that. It was your father's boat. I can't just take it."

"Why not?"

"That boat survived that mess last night for a reason."

Coast talk again. It so often came down to this. Things happened for a reason. We'd probably never know that reason, but supposedly there was some kind of cosmic plan. What used to be called destiny. Something I knew must all be bullshit. Leftovers from religion and superstition and days when people felt they had no real control over their lives.

"Yeah," I said. "And the reason was so you'd have a goddamn boat to keep fishing."

Joe looked at me and I saw a look that reminded me of Brody. A defiance. A stubbornness. A strength.

"Here's the deal. You arrange to tow the boat, make it seaworthy, and get it back out to sea. Do some fishing. When you start to make some profit, maybe you can pay me some kind of rent on the boat."

"Deal."

"Just one more thing, though. You gotta take Rolf on as a hand. He's gonna waste away if he doesn't get back out to sea."

"That old bastard's bad luck."

"Then how'd he end up with the only building left standing out there after a hurricane ripped everything else apart?"

Joe swallowed a grunted laugh. "Not everything."

"What do you mean?"

"I mean I found your father's fish shack too. Floated off and came ashore near the brook. Bumped up against a tree and when the water dropped, there she was. A bit beat-up but in one piece. Looks like a little cabin some trout fishermen built for himself. On government land, I think. But then it always was on government-owned land, so maybe this was just nature's way of relocating it." Joe looked off to the mainland. "Gotta go. I need to tell Beth Ann we found your boat intact. You're okay if she takes on to work as partner with me? Me and Rolf, that is."

"Of course," I said. "But I thought you two hated each other."

"We did. But that's old news. We figured that after all those years apart, we've gotten over old grudges. I asked her if she'd take me back. And she said she'd think about it."

"Well, that's a start," Ramona said.

"That's what we all need — a new start. Look, I gotta go." And the big guy awkwardly began to jog back toward the mainland.

When he was gone, Ramona looked up into the sun and took a deep breath. "Someone should write about all this."

"Yeah, someone probably should. But not me. I'm living it. I don't want to record it. Besides, I'm no longer a writer, remember?"

"Once a writer, always a writer. You can't fall out of love with words."

"Don't forget, I come from a couple of parents who never trusted words. *Too much empty language,* my father used to say at the dinner table. *Speak only when you have something worth investing your breath in.* They weren't much for self-expression, my parents, either one of them."

But then I remembered. The tool box. The freezer bag with the letters.

"Oh, my God," I said out loud. "The letters."

46

By afternoon, a tow truck had fished the Lexus out of the bay and towed it off to a garage to see if it could be salvaged. I didn't think it could.

Beth Ann had taken Mackenzie home with her and the workers had done all they could until the shell of the house could dry out in the sun. All the vinyl siding and the Tyvek moisture barrier had been removed. New materials had been ordered and work would resume in the days ahead.

"Just a minor setback," Big Carl said before he drove off. "Now the house has a story. Every house needs a story. Nothing worse than a house that has no history."

Now it was just Ramona and me, alone with our storied house, ready to camp out on the first floor, under the stars. We had food and water, and, despite what we'd just gone through, we were feeling like we were on track to our new beginning.

Just the fact that we'd survived the night, all of us together, huddled like an ancient clan facing the worst of the elements, should have made me feel euphoric. But I kept thinking about Brody — the poor bugger's life snuffed out before he even had a chance to figure out what to do with it. The pain and loss that would linger on for Beth Ann and Joe. And Mackenzie, all on her own to give birth and raise a kid.

The guilt swept over me again. And I knew it would never really go away. What do you call it when a father kills a son? Filicide? Not a word you hear very often.

I tried to put Brody out of my head as I walked the creaky stairs down into the basement and found the canvas bag. How it had found its way into a tool box, and then been left forgotten all those years, only to find its way back to me on the property where my parents once lived remained a mystery. And why now at this turning point in my life?

I carried the bag upstairs and Ramona watched me sit down in one of the plastic lawn chairs we had been using for furniture, one that had miraculously survived the storm. She left me alone, pretending to fuss with what was left of our kitchen.

I opened the canvas bag, set it aside, and carefully opened the sealed freezer bag. There were two stacks of envelopes, one tied up with a blue ribbon, the other one with a pink one. Each had an empty envelope on top with a label: Desmond to Elsie, Elsie to Desmond.

Every envelope had a carefully folded letter inside; each one had been opened with a letter opener or a sharp knife. At first this seemed like some cosmic joke. *My parents writing letters to each other.* When, how, and why?

I opened one addressed to my mother first. It was postmarked Lunenburg, NS.

> Dear Elsie,
>
> Well, here I am. We ship out tomorrow for the Grand Banks. I got a job right away with a Captain Groening. All he did was look at my hands and ask me where I grew up. Then he signed me on. Good pay, he says, if we make a good catch. He asked me how I liked bad weather at sea. I told him I loved it.
>
> If this all goes as planned, I will have that nest egg I promised. I love you enough to be away

from you so I can guarantee our life together. I believe this will all work out. I'll be home once each month to see you and it will be hell to leave again. But we've talked about it. We can do this. You must stay with your parents for two years and then we will marry.

We've been planning this all through high school. We've watched the others who dive right into things and struggle. I won't do that to you. I love you too much.

At the end of two years, I'll have enough saved to buy a boat. Then it will be you and me and nothing else will matter.

Love,

Desmond

It was inconceivable that the father I knew, the man of so very few words, could have written this. His handwriting was elegant. The words were straight from his heart. I knew some of the story of him going to sea as a young man, but he had never wanted to talk about it. He never mentioned anything about his "plan" to save money, buy a boat, get married. It was as straightforward as that, but it meant them not being together for the better part of two years. How could anyone do that if they were really in love?

Those were very different times. I thought of Ramona and I being apart. Two years would be an eternity.

I opened the top letter in the second pile.

Dear Desmond,

You must be at sea now and far from shore as I am writing this. I want most for you to be safe and to be careful. If anything were to happen to you I could not go on. I think I love you even more now that you are away than when we were spending time together. What was that quote we read in school? "Absence makes the heart grow fonder." 'Tis true, I now can see.

My mother is still treating me like a little girl and bullying me around the house. My father I hardly see. I so look forward to the day when I am free of them and we can shape our own lives.

That property you had your eye on. I spoke with Mr. Robichaud when I saw him at the store. He said you had spoken to him and that he liked you very much, said you were a lad with "character," as he put it. He said he wanted us to have it and if you had a down payment by January, it would be yours. He said you can pay in monthly installments for however long it takes.

I walk there in the day when I can and I stand in the field and imagine the house. Our house.

I know you don't like me to talk about it, but I am glad we didn't listen to what others say we should and shouldn't do when we are together. I am glad that my first time was with you and that we let nothing hold us back when you and I are alone. I love you and will wait for you.

Love always,
Elsie

When I looked up from the letter, it was like the world had turned itself upside down. These could not be my parents. As I remembered them, they were two adults who always did what they were supposed to do. They felt duty and responsibility, were never frivolous with words, expressed little emotion, and had hardly ever shown outward signs of real affection for each other. And now this.

And what did that last paragraph have to do with? Clearly they'd been having sex as teenagers. High-school sweethearts stealing away to some safe and hidden place to make love, despite the uptight morals of the day.

Was I invading their privacy by reading the letters? Or had they been preserved so I would one day find them? I would never know.

I opened the next one from my father. It was postmarked November 20.

Dear Elsie,

We are back ashore now but will return to sea in just a few days, so it will not be until December when I can see you. I miss you more than ever.

The sea is cold and it is a hard life on a big vessel where the men are rough and no one seems to have a good word for each other. It is a different life. But I am adjusting.

That's wonderful news about the Robichaud property and assure Mr. Robichaud I will have the down payment promised.

I am learning the awful ways of the world and will be happy when I can leave this all behind and return to Stewart Harbour. Just writing these words breaks my heart to think that I am not with you but so far away. Rest assured that once I return, I will never go away again.

I miss your warmth and your smile and our time together when we pushed everything, absolutely everything away from us so it was just you and me. And we will return to that soon, I promise.

You are everything to me. Remain just as you are and believe in me, please.

Always believe in me.

Love,

Desmond

I carefully placed the letter back into its envelope and did not read another. Not then. This was enough to digest in one day.

I walked over to Ramona and put my arms around her. "Do you think all of us are wrong about our parents? Is it possible that children never understand them?"

"I think it's very possible. What did you discover that so shocks you?"

"That my parents were in love."

47

In the days that followed, I read a few more letters and then I stopped. I soon hit a point where I felt like an interloper, a spy. Even though they were long gone, I felt my parents deserved some privacy. But now, finally, after so many years of having shut them out of my life, I knew who they really were.

And I understood well my father's final trip to sea. I think he fully understood what he was doing and I respected him for that. And the fact that those letters ended up in the tool box told me that it was my father who had kept them all those years. Or maybe he collected them from my mother after she was gone. But then why would he have given away the tool box with the letters in them? Could have been that he did that on purpose. Maybe he wanted someone to find them, to save them. But, then again, that too didn't seem at all like my father. I'd never know the full story. I just knew they had somehow found their way to me. I was the one who had abandoned my family as my brother had done. But Ramona had brought me back.

⸻

After the storm, life went on. The storm had done its best to hurt us. The damage was done. Some things could be repaired, some boats could be refloated, some weren't worth the effort or the money. Ramona said she didn't want another new car, not another fancy car. So she wrote off the Lexus and we drove to Antigonish to buy a truck. Nothing fancy. Just a used Ford 150 pickup truck, a little newer than Joe's but a truck that fit right in here.

"In California," Ramona said, as we drove home from Antigonish, "if a psychic told me that one day I'd own a pickup truck, I would have demanded my money back."

The warm days ended one morning in November when the ground was covered in frost. We didn't have a lawn yet, just raw dirt and rock around the house. The field with the tall wild grasses wilted to brown. In Nova Scotia in September you believe that the heat of summer will never end. When those cold November mornings roll around, you find it hard to believe summer ever happened.

I thought of my father heading out of Lunenburg on a big steel fish trawler on an icy day, working the sea, turning raw and painful through the day. A man with a vision of the future. *Work hard. Don't complain. Sacrifice. And you will be rewarded.* Old times. Old rules. Old dreams.

Big Carl had promised to have the house fully finished "by the time the snow flies," and he kept his word.

Ramona had started on some preventative medication by then, even though I saw no sign of deterioration. We were both settling. Both changing. Putting parts of our lives far behind but building something new and solid at the same time. Hanging on. Making things better. Not worse. Learning about our neighbours, watching out for them, them watching out for us. Becoming part of the community. Not just outsiders.

I went to sea once or twice a week with Joe and Beth Ann when Rolf wanted a break. Lifting lobster traps or handlining for haddock, I'd get flashbacks of my father fishing, my mother cooking fish. But the work at sea really wasn't for me.

Ramona was getting a bit of cabin fever by the end of December (*shack wacky*, people around there would call it), so I booked us a room at the Marriott on the Halifax waterfront for

New Year's Eve and we drove the truck to Halifax in a snow-storm. We had no intention of taking part in festivities; instead, we drank some pinot noir and, toward midnight, put on our winter coats and walked along the harbour until we came to the pier where we'd first met. It was closed off by a chain-link fence now and was under reconstruction. The sign read: *No Trespassing. Under Repair.* Fortunately for us, some vandal had busted the lock on the gate with bolt cutters, so we walked out on the pier into the darkness as the snow swirled.

"Under Repair," I said. "Forget the No Trespassing. But I like the repair part."

"Who repaired what?" Ramona asked.

"I don't think I need to answer that," I said.

We heard the dark water lapping beneath us. Same ocean as Stewart Harbour but a different world.

After that, we went back to our room at the hotel. We stayed up all night talking. But I can't remember what we talked about.

On the second day of the new year, Mackenzie had a baby. I had a grandson and his name was Dylan. She settled in with Joe and Beth Ann, who were indeed back together. You'd never know they'd split up, or hated each other's guts for thirty years. People change. They grow apart but sometimes they grow back together. Is it strange or is it normal? Who cares?

I never did start that community newspaper but it could happen yet.

I started to write again, although there were many false starts. I started to think about what words were important to me and which ones weren't. I started to think long and hard about what was worth writing about and why anyone would want to read it. Which was most important? The process or the product?

We visited with the new baby and mother and made the usual fuss. Mackenzie looked like she was up for the job. She was doing just fine living where she was but knew she could move in with us if need be.

After our visit with her, we decided that the trip to Halifax had been a waste of time. The Marriott was so the opposite of who we were now. So we decided to spend one winter night in the old fish shack for old times' sake. Joe's friend who had towed the *Sheer Delight* out of the marsh had floated my father's fish shack and towed it up the inlet as well, and with the aid of a bulldozer skidded it back to where it once stood before the storm. "No big deal," he said and didn't charge me any money. He said he was from Newfoundland and it brought back old memories, seeing a house afloat.

We must have burned a half cord of wood that night trying to stay warm, but it beat the hell out of the Marriott. And in the morning, there was a skim of ice up and down the edges of the inlet as the sun shone brilliantly upon the sea ghosts swirling up out of the water.

"Otherworldly," Ramona said.

"Ourworldly," I retorted as I watched our breath collide in an amazing manner in the clear, frigid air.

Epilogue

W e've been in the house for five years now. Already the place holds many memories. It's become my responsibility to remember everything. Ramona says that's my job. I must hold onto everything. Every detail. And so I write it down. Nothing is lost. Nothing.

She has been slipping of late. Slipping but not lost. Sometimes she can't recall what we did the day before. She's stopped pretending when her memory slips. "Tell me about yesterday," she'll say. And I get out my journal and read to her.

I've given up on fiction. Real life is more important. Call it creative nonfiction if you like — a fancy term, a vague term. But it means I can tell the story the way I want to tell the story. Isn't that what every writer wants to do? My story. My way.

But of course, it's our story. Our world.

It may surprise you to know that we got married. We had both pronounced that we were "not the marrying type." But that changed.

It was a simple ceremony, performed in the house three years ago. Attending were the usual suspects: Rolf, Joe, Beth Ann, Mackenzie, Stanley, Brenda, and little Dylan. Dylan is now five, nearly as old as the house. He's smart and cute. What else can a grandfather say about his grandson? He has three grandfathers — Joe, me, and Mackenzie's father, who shows up from time to time claiming his title to a grandson.

We have a dog. I guess it comes with marriage. The dog — a black Lab mutt — was dropped off in the woods by the house, abandoned. We blame it on someone from the city. He arrived the day after we were married. Showed up at the back door. We fed him. He never left.

We have a house, a marriage, a dog, a life. Broken man, fully repaired.

Is it that simple, that easy? No, of course not.

I am Ramona's memory. And I remind myself of that every morning. She continues to lose pieces of her past. But she does not seem to lose her beautiful self.

Yesterday, when we woke, as I was getting my focus on the room around me, she leaned up on her elbow and said this: "I'm sorry, I can't remember your name." Then she paused, leaned forward to kiss me and added, "But I remember that I love you."

And so. Maybe that is enough.

Folks around here still find it curious that I do not work. I know that the fishermen, all men who think much like my father, believe me to be less of a man because I am not employed. I've discussed this with Stanley. I've asked his advice. It's his money really that has allowed us this life.

"Work's not all it's cracked up to be," he said. "I worked my ass off and used work as an excuse to wreck my life. The smartest thing I ever did was to bail out of what I was doing. The dumbest thing I ever did was walk away from Brenda. If my money can allow you and Ramona to live your life, then that's one good thing that came out of my so-called career. So let 'em talk."

Stanley knows I take good care of Ramona. What he may not know is that Ramona takes care of me. I am her memory but she is my anchor. The medication seems to prevent the sort of fear and anxiety that comes with memory loss, and so Ramona remains calm and, too often, quiet. She sleeps more often in the days now. She slips in and out of time on occasion. Sometimes she recites scenes she once memorized from plays and films she acted in. Sometimes I can't fully tell if she knows she is acting or if she believes those scenes, those lines, were once part of her real life.

When this happens, I roll with it. I tell her I've forgotten my lines.

And then she returns to me. "Once upon a time, there was a man alone on a Halifax pier."

"And then there was a woman," I add, "a beautiful actress."

"No, a princess," she says and smiles. Her eyes tell me she, the true Ramona, is still there.

"A princess of spirit, a healer of wounded knights," I say.

"Oh, now this is getting good," she says.

"Not getting good. Is good."

"What did you say your name was?"

That's her favourite line. She uses it at the strangest times. The other day, midafternoon, she grabbed me and pulled me into the bedroom. After we made love, she rolled over and looked at me. "What did you say your name was?"

And we both laughed.

I keep my parents' letters in a safe place, my father's old tool box, under our bed. I keep a copy of our story, my unfinished work of creative nonfiction, in the box as well. I take it out from time to time to read in sequence to Ramona when she asks. Sometimes I get several chapters into it and she says, "Stop. Go back to the beginning."

And I do. I go back to the beginning. I am Ramona's memory. And I have promised to be faithful and diligent in recording the details of our extraordinary life together.

Acknowledgements

I would like to acknowledge the use of lyrics from the Stan Rogers songs "Barrett's Privateers" and "The Northwest Passage." I would also like to express my gratitude to Julia Swan for her initial editing of the manuscript and to Dominic Farrell for his diligence in the final edit. The writing of the novel took place at Lawrencetown Beach on the Eastern Shore of Nova Scotia with the support of my loving wife, Linda.